ARt ONLINE

PROGRESSIVE

004

REKI KAWAHARA
ILLUSTRATION BY abec
DESIGN BY bee-pee

SWORD ARt ONLINE

"Yep. The limited-supply buff dish."

Kirito

A swordsman aiming to beat the top floor of Aincrad. He adventures as a solo player but temporarily teams up with Asuna.

"...It looks just like a normal blueberry tart. Is this the...?"

Asuna

A player trapped inside *Sword Art Online*. Without a care for her life, she throws herself into battle against monsters.

"*Yaaaaaah!!* Make it go away! Drive it off right now!!"

"W-well, we have to move the quest onward for that..."

"All right!"

"You betcha!"

Argo
Aincrad's information broker, who shows up here and there.

Liten
A member of the Aincrad Liberation Squad (ALS), a major guild. Plays as a heavily armored tank.

"Dammit, not again!"

"..."

Shivata
A member of the Dragon Knights Brigade (DKB), a major guild. Fights with a longsword.

"Affirmative! We'll try attacking next!"

"We will, too!"

Agil
Leader of the Bro Squad. Wields a two-handed battle ax.

Hafner
A member of the Dragon Knights Brigade. Fights with a two-handed sword.

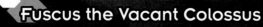

"I'm going to trigger a
line on purpose—get ready
to use sword skills!"

Fuscus the Vacant Colossus
The boss of the fifth floor of Aincrad.

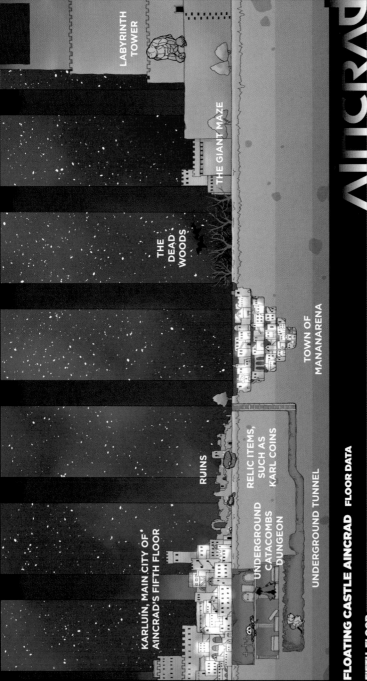

FLOATING CASTLE AINCRAD FLOOR DATA

FIFTH FLOOR

Just as it was during the beta, the design theme of the fifth floor is "ruins." Only 30 percent of the six-mile-diameter floor is natural terrain; the rest is all mazelike ruins. It's also known for being the first floor to have more vertical elements than just the flat features of earlier floors. There are underground catacombs, dungeon ruins that stretch down belowground, and a town excavated out of the earth, all of which have little light—making them fertile PK areas during the beta.

The main city, Karluin, rests in the middle of a massive swath of ruins on the southern end of the floor. Though the buildings of bluish stone blocks are falling apart here and there, the center of town is full of leather and canvas tents, which give it a chaotic liveliness. In the ruined temples and plazas near Karluin, gems and accessories known as "relics" can be found.

The boss of the fifth floor is Fuscus the Vacant Colossus. If all is the same as in the beta test, it should be a golem that runs on magic power...

LABYRINTH TOWER

THE GIANT MAZE

THE DEAD WOODS

TOWN OF MANANARENA

RUINS

RELIC ITEMS, SUCH AS KARL COINS

UNDERGROUND CATACOMBS DUNGEON

UNDERGROUND TUNNEL

KARLUIN, MAIN CITY OF AINCRAD'S FIFTH FLOOR

SWORD ART ONLINE PROGRESSIVE

VOLUME 4

Reki Kawahara

abec

bee-pee

YEN
ON

NEW YORK

SWORD ART ONLINE PROGRESSIVE Volume 4
© REKI KAWAHARA

Translation by Stephen Paul
Cover art by abec

SWORD ART ONLINE
© REKI KAWAHARA 2015
All rights reserved.
Edited by ASCII MEDIA WORKS
First published in Japan in 2015 by KADOKAWA CORPORATION, Tokyo.
English translation rights arranged with KADOKAWA CORPORATION, Tokyo,
through Tuttle-Mori Agency, Inc., Tokyo.

English translation © 2016 by Yen Press, LLC

Yen On
1290 Avenue of the Americas
New York, NY 10104

Visit us at yenpress.com
facebook.com/yenpress
twitter.com/yenpress
yenpress.tumblr.com
instagram.com/yenpress

First Yen On Edition: October 2016

Yen On is an imprint of Yen Press, LLC.
The Yen On name and logo are trademarks of Yen Press, LLC.

The publisher is not responsible for websites (or their content) that are not owned by
the publisher.

Library of Congress Cataloging-in-Publication Data

Names: Kawahara, Reki, author. | Paul, Stephen (Translator), translator.
Title: Sword art online progressive / Reki Kawahara ; translation by Stephen Paul.
Description: First Yen On edition. | New York, NY : Yen On, 2016–
Identifiers: LCCN 2016029472 | ISBN 9780316259361 (v. 1 : pbk) | ISBN
    9780316342179 (v. 2 : pbk) | ISBN 9780316348836 (v. 3 : pbk) | ISBN
    9780316545426 (v. 4 : pbk)
Subjects: | CYAC: Virtual reality—Fiction. | Science fiction.
Classification: LCC PZ7.K1755 Swr 2016 | DDC [Fic]—dc23 LC record available at
    https://lccn.loc.gov/2016029472

ISBN: 978-0-316-54542-6

10 9 8 7 6 5 4

LSC-C

Printed in the United States of America

"THIS MIGHT BE A GAME, BUT IT'S NOT SOMETHING YOU PLAY."

—Akihiko Kayaba, *Sword Art Online* programmer

SWORD ART ONLINE
PROGRESSIVE

SCHERZO OF DEEP NIGHT

FIFTH FLOOR OF AINCRAD, DECEMBER 2022

1

I NEVER EXPECTED THIS DAY TO COME, THOUGHT Asuna, the level-16 fencer, as she held up her Chivalric Rapier +5 in a mid-level stance.

Sixteen feet ahead, a swordsman with black hair and a black coat was doing the same with his sword. His stance looked lazy and relaxed, but the sharp point of the blade stayed utterly still, gleaming coldly as it absorbed Asuna's gaze.

They were facing each other within a square surrounded by mossy, ancient ruins. The area was silent, with no hint of player or monster alike. The light coming through the outer aperture of the floating castle was weak, closing toward the dark purple of twilight moment by moment.

Today was the fifty-second day since the official start of *Sword Art Online*, the game of death in which the loss of a player's avatar ended the life of the player. In the real world, it was December 28, 2022. In four more days, a new year would arrive—assuming they lived to see it.

I'll survive until next year.

When she first ventured out into the wilderness, she'd never even considered that possibility. She had taken store-bought rapiers, not bothered to do maintenance on them—hadn't even realized that was possible, in fact—and used them up as she fought relentlessly against countless monsters, resigned to eventually run out of strength and die...A part of her had even hoped it would happen, looked forward to that oblivion.

But at some point, that Todestrieb—that death drive—had disappeared. It wasn't that Asuna had a clear hope for the future now. There was no certainty that they would one day defeat this macabre arena and be free to return to the real world. But she did want to live to see another day...to fight her way through this floor and see the next. That emotion was palpable within her.

And the reason for that change was undoubtedly the black-haired boy before her, holding up his longsword. He had taught her a great deal about the game and how it worked. He had saved her from many perils. And not just that...Despite the soul-crushing danger that surrounded them all, he kept a breezy attitude, never forgot to smile and enjoy himself, and even lightened her heavy heart with the occasional silly mistake. As her constant partner in clearing the game, he gave her hope for tomorrow.

But now, the only thing in the black eyes of Kirito, level-17 swordsman, was sharp, unsentimental concentration. There was no kindness or frivolity there. His sword and mind were one, ready to react to Asuna's every movement without pause or delay.

Yesterday—December 27—as they'd climbed the circular staircase from the fourth floor to the fifth, Asuna had turned to him and asked, "How long are you planning to work with me?"

She wasn't expecting to get a concrete answer. Perhaps she'd been led to that sentiment only after parting with the dark elves from the third and fourth floors. Kizmel and Viscount Yofilis were NPCs, but in a certain way, they were closer to her than any player had been.

Kirito stared back into Asuna's eyes, shrugged, and in his usual aloof manner, said, "Until you're strong enough to not need me."

It was a practical response, devoid of emotion in his typical style, but Asuna still couldn't move that suffocating weight from her heart. On the fifth floor, and likely the next after that, he'd continue to stand beside her as her partner, fighting at her back. She didn't want to admit it, but the thought made her happy.

And yet…

"…If you're not going to come at me, I'll take the first move," Kirito said suddenly, cutting through her wavering thoughts with a measured voice. The longsword in his right hand began to swing. The vanishing evening sun slid along its edge like a drop of red blood.

Kirito's Anneal Blade +8, which had served him all the way from the first floor, had broken at last in battle against a forest elf knight on the fourth floor, so now he was using the Elven Stout Sword that his opponent had dropped. The handle and hilt had fittingly delicate decorations for a weapon of elven make, but it was not a particularly elegant weapon. The polished blade gleamed coldly in the dusk.

As a matter of fact, the base specs of the weapon were nearly as good as the Anneal at +8 level. In other words, if Asuna did not block or evade this attack, her HP—the numerical representation of her life—would suffer huge damage.

But the same could be said of Kirito.

The Chivalric Rapier in Asuna's right hand was an excellent weapon augmented by the NPC blacksmith of the dark elf camp on the third floor. According to Kirito, its stats were abnormally high, which made its single attack strength higher than most longswords—a deadly quality for rapiers, which were meant to have frequent but weak attacks. It was hard to guess how much of Kirito's HP would be taken if Asuna hit him cleanly with her best skill, the three-part combo Triangular.

Each combatant's vision narrowed, focusing solely on the moment either sword hit home on its target. Their breaths shortened. The normally unavoidable sound of boots scuffing against the hard stone ground grew distant.

They had fought countless monsters up to this point, and not just nonhuman animals and insects. They'd fought a pitched battle at Yofel Castle on the fourth floor against forest elf soldiers who looked just like any player. Even that experience had not been as frightening as this.

How can fighting another player be so different from that? Is it because...I'm fighting against Kirito?

The tip of the Chivalric Rapier she held wavered. Kirito didn't miss his chance, lunging forward on his left leg.

The elvish sword was no longer held lazily, but dead still at eye level. He would either unleash a propulsive normal attack...or a leaping sword skill. She had to guess which one and react ahead of time. But her rapier wouldn't stop trembling.

"...No."

Another rasping groan escaped her quavering lips before she realized it.

"...No. I don't want to do this."

She held down her misbehaving right hand with her left, pushing it toward the ground. Her eyes left Kirito's face and settled on the stone below, indigo in the darkness.

She knew it was a childish reaction, and there was no guarantee that Kirito would stop. But Asuna kept her face stubbornly pointed down.

With time came the sound of boots scraping on stone. Next, the sound of a blade slicing air. The light *ting* of metal.

When she looked up again, Kirito had returned his longsword to the sheath on his back and was throwing up his hands in exasperation.

"So now you've changed your mind..." he said with a wry smile, checking the duel timer in the upper half of his vision. "You were the one who asked for a PvP lesson, Asuna."

Five minutes later, Kirito had started up a little campfire in the corner of the ruins that had been their dueling arena. He pulled an iron kettle out of his inventory and set some water to boil.

To her surprise, he even had the branches to burn for the fire. "When did you pick up those?" she asked.

"Hmm? Oh, here and there on the third and fourth floors," he replied, smug for some reason. He pulled one of the lit sticks out of the fire. "See how the color of the flame is a bit different from your average fire?"

Now that he mentioned it, the flame glowing on the tip of the branch looked a bit greenish.

"This is a harvesting item called a Fossilwood Branch. They burn a lot longer than typical dead branches. I spotted them while walking around on the lower floors, so I picked some up just in case. After all…"

He paused, and gestured with the branch at the stone ruins around them.

"The fifth floor is a floor of ruins. There are very few trees here, so it won't be easy to come across these supplies."

"Ohh…If you'd told me, I would have picked up a few of those, too, you know," Asuna said, which earned her a skeptical smile from Kirito.

"I dunno about that. You can only find Fossilwood half buried in damp soil. I have a hard time imagining fastidious Asuna placing such a muddy item in her storage."

"I-I wouldn't mind that. It's just a digital storage place, so it's not like the other items would get mud on them."

"Also, when you pull them out of the ground, they sometimes have gross bugs on them, sooo…"

"…"

Asuna widened the distance between herself and the flaming stick in Kirito's hand. The swordsman returned it to the campfire with a hearty laugh. By that time, white steam was issuing from the kettle, so Kirito poured the boiling water into the already-packed teapot, waited fifteen seconds, then poured the liquid into two cups.

"Here."

She took the cup, thanked him, then breathed in its scent. She'd bought those leaves in Rovia, the main city of the fourth floor; they smelled somewhat like a fruit-flavored rooibos tea.

With her arm around her knees, she took a sip of the hot liquid and sighed contentedly.

The last bit of sunlight was gone now, and the area was covered in blue darkness. On the lower floors, the moonlight shining in through the outer aperture of Aincrad provided a little illumination to go by, but here on the fifth floor, there was hardly any light at all. If it weren't for the campfire, Kirito would just be a black silhouette beside her.

Yesterday they'd gone from the exit of the spiral staircase straight to the main town, and by the time night had fallen, they were resting at an inn. All day today, they were busy fulfilling quests, so she hadn't realized the night was so dark here outside town. As a solo player by trade, Kirito had the Search skill, so he would warn her if a monster or some other danger was approaching, but she couldn't stop her mind from imagining *something* lurking out there in the darkness, beyond the stone walls that surrounded the ruined square.

Asuna unconsciously slid her rear an inch and three quarters closer to Kirito, then mumbled, "I'm sorry about earlier."

"Huh? For what?"

She was expecting that response and immediately continued, "For quitting the duel that I asked you for in the first place."

"Oh…Well, look, I don't mind at all…"

Kirito took a huge swig of tea, then grimaced at the heat. He glanced over at her.

"…It just seems a bit rare for you to give up on something you started."

"Mm…"

She nodded and rested her chin on her knees as she hugged them with her left arm.

"It just…wasn't quite what I imagined. This duel…but it's not really a duel because it was in the—what did you call it—first-strike mode? So since the first clean hit wins and it's basically safe, I thought it would be more like…a match. A sports competition. But…"

Asuna's mouth worked soundlessly as she tried to come up with the words to describe the fear that snuck into her heart when blade matched blade. But before she succeeded, Kirito muttered, "There's at least one major difference...between *SAO* duels and real-life sporting matches."

She glanced at the swordsman in the black coat sitting cross-legged on the stone. His eyes, blacker than the darkness, were looking into the fire. They were slightly narrowed, staring back into distant memories.

"I think it's the motive for fighting. In sports—even in competitive fighting—it's victory you're hoping to gain, right? The desire to win becomes a huge source of energy. On the surface, duels in this game are a lot like sports. When players of about the same level and gear fight on first-strike-finish mode, there's absolutely no fear of HP dropping to a dangerous amount. But..."

As Kirito trailed off, the piece of Fossilwood popped and burst. A shower of red sparks shot up, melting into the dark.

Asuna traced the hilt of the Chivalric Rapier equipped on her left hip and picked up where Kirito had left off.

"...But we're not using bats or rackets or even bamboo *shinai* swords...They're real steel. Sure, they're digital lines of code, but if they touch your opponent, they take away real life..."

"Exactly. The more seriously you take the duel, the less it becomes about seizing simple victory. Those who have no fear of slashing their opponents with steel weapons and taking their HP—those who most purely follow the purpose of 'killing' their foe—will get closest to victory. At its core, dueling is not a sport here. It's just bloodshed for the sake of survival. Winning has nothing to do with it."

As those last words left his lips, Asuna felt a shiver run through her body. She recognized it as the very sensation that had foiled her hand earlier, in that attempt at a duel.

"...I don't want to have a fight to the death with you, Kirito," she blurted out, then hastily clamped her mouth shut. He didn't tease her, though.

"Yeah. Me too. I don't want to do that with you, either…Even if it's just a first-strike-finish duel."

She looked over in mild surprise and saw that Kirito was looking at her, too. His black eyes reflecting the orange light of the campfire, her temporary partner continued, "But…I still think you ought to have some experience with dueling…with PvP, before we start tackling this floor in earnest."

"…"

She stared back at him, unsure how to respond.

Their aborted attempt at a duel was Asuna's idea. But that idea had come from something Kirito had said the previous evening, as they climbed the spiral staircase to this floor.

After they'd defeated Wythege the Hippocampus, boss of the fourth floor, with the help of Kizmel the dark elf knight and Viscount Yofilis, Asuna and Kirito had left the members of the other guilds back in the chamber and continued up the spiral staircase to the fifth floor.

The wall of the staircase hall was carved, as was customary, with reliefs that symbolized the landscape and sights of the new floor, but most striking and memorable was always the one on the large door at the top of every staircase.

The relief was of a large, ancient castle. It was not an elegant manor like Yofel Castle standing in the middle of a lake, but a heavy, imposing fortress. As he'd looked up at the carving, Kirito sighed and said, "Looks like the basic terrain is the same as it was in the beta test…"

Asuna had asked him what kind of terrain that was, and he'd shrugged and explained, "Ruins. Maybe thirty percent of the map is natural ground, and the rest is all mazelike ruins. Meaning the entire six-miles-across terrain is one huge dungeon, in a way…And it's really dark…There was a lot of PK-ing going on there in the beta…"

PK-ing: player-killing. And one who player-killed was a PKer.

She was familiar with that as a gaming term. Kirito had once said he wanted to buy the same hooded cape she wore, to hide his face in town. When she'd pointed out that he could just as easily wear a burlap sack over his head, he had replied that he would be mistaken for a PKer if he did that.

At the time, it was a lighthearted, silly conversation, so Asuna had essentially ignored and then forgotten the term. After all, there would never be PK-ing in Aincrad in its current state. Every player's wish was to escape the virtual world, and attacking or, God forbid, actually *killing* another player could only set the progress through the game back. That was how Asuna always saw things, and she assumed she shared that opinion with Kirito.

But when he'd mentioned the term *PK* in front of the door to the fifth floor, there was a firmness to his expression she'd never seen before. It had looked as if he was certain that the fifth floor and its ruins would be home to rampant PK-ing in the new, deadly *SAO*, just as it had been in the beta.

The more she saw that look on his face, the more Asuna was convinced that after they activated the town portal and restocked their items, she should ask for a lesson on the basics of PvP combat.

Their first attempt at a duel had reached a premature, pathetic end, and Asuna wasn't in the mood to try again very soon. So as she sipped the sweet-smelling tea, she asked, "Kirito…do you really think…there will be PKers on this floor?"

"Hmmm," he replied, swirling the tea in his cup. He stopped abruptly and looked at her. "Do you remember the player I dueled on the third floor…near the forest elf camp?"

"Yes…His name was Morte, right? The one who was plotting something because he was secretly part of both Lind's Dragon Knights Brigade and Kibaou's Aincrad Liberation Squad…"

Kirito had told her about him just before the battle against the boss of the third floor. It was a very intriguing and troubling story, and Asuna had briefly spotted the man himself in the spider queen's cave, so she'd been on the lookout for him on the fourth floor. That signature metal coif had never appeared, though.

Her partner nodded and returned his gaze to the fire. There was an unusual tension to his features.

"Morte challenged me to a half-finish duel, whittled my HP down to just above half, and tried to hit me with his ax for massive damage. If he'd been successful, he would have wiped out all my HP and killed me…and having won a duel fair and square, he wouldn't have become an orange player. That would make it just as legal a PK method as a monster PK…A duel PK, I guess. I'm amazed he thought of that."

"Don't start being impressed with him," Asuna snapped. The swordsman wore a strained smile and agreed.

His expression serious again, Kirito murmured, "The problem is *why* Morte would do such a thing. Based on the way he showed up, I don't think he's a pleasure PKer doing it for fun. The reason he challenged me to that duel was because he wanted to prevent me from completing the quest at the forest elf camp. And while I was held up, the DKB and ALS were closing in on the same camp for different questlines. He wanted them to have a showdown… to fight."

"Yeah…" Asuna murmured, recalling the event. "When Kizmel and I raced to the camp, it looked like they were ready to draw weapons at any second…If she hadn't stopped it then and there, the whole frontline group could have fallen apart. But…even if he succeeded, how would that help Morte? What could he have possibly gained that would be worth a months-long delay in beating the game—and obtaining everyone's freedom?" She asked it mostly to herself, but Kirito was contemplating the very same question.

The DKB and ALS were so large that they represented nearly the entirety of the game's most advanced players. All the last-attack bonuses from the bosses had been seized by the swordsman in black sitting beside Asuna, but at this point, it was essentially impossible to beat the labyrinth tower without those two guilds.

A motive to make the two guilds fight.

Ordinarily, a good reason would be to ride in during the chaos of the squabble and seize control of both guilds, taking command of the leadership: in short, for glory. Or perhaps looting the money and gear of those players who died in battle, for personal gain.

But was it possible that one's lust for glory or riches could override their desire to survive? No matter your lofty position in this world, no matter how many col you earned or how much elite gear you equipped, it was all worthless if you lost in a fight just once, be it monster or player. You would simply die in this electronic prison, and never return to the real world.

Something didn't add up about Morte's motives. It looked like he was trying to interfere with the efforts to clear the game. But no one should actually think that way. Especially if they were risking death by leaving the safety of town and venturing into the dangerous wilderness.

Asuna's reason for fighting in the danger zone as one of the game's top players was to someday escape this floating fortress. She would return to the real world, get back to her old life, and forget all the fear and sadness she'd experienced here...

Without realizing it, she glanced to her right. Her black-haired temporary partner was gazing into the crackling campfire. The way he was lost in thought removed his usual tense demeanor and actually made him look quite young.

Escaping this world. That would mean...

She forced herself to stop mid-thought and straightened her head with considerable willpower. Her eyes settled on the strange greenish fire surrounding the Fossilwood Branch. Compared to a real fire, there was a touch of artificiality in the way the tips of the flames moved, but it was real enough for Asuna and beautiful, too.

Yes...the world they lived in was a cruel prison, but at times it could also be breathtakingly gorgeous. The city on the first floor, the plains of the second, the forests of the third, and the canals of the fourth...And the entire reason she was able to appreciate these things was due to the influence of the partner sitting beside her.

She was struggling to keep her mind off that fact by pondering Morte's motives further—when Kirito broke his long silence to consider, "Maybe…Morte isn't the same kind of player as us, in the truest sense…"

"Huh? What do you mean?"

Again she looked at Kirito, who was still gazing intently into the campfire.

"If you assume that his motive in interfering with our forward progress itself is an act of sabotage directed by whoever's running this game of death…it does make a kind of sense."

"S…sabotage? You're saying…he's working with Akihiko Kayaba?"

"Yeah," Kirito confirmed. However, he quickly shook his head. "But even still, it doesn't add up. It would be one thing if we were just about to finish the game, but this guy started his activities when we were on the third floor out of a hundred. It's just too early. No, wait…"

Kirito's eyes suddenly gleamed.

"…Right now!"

"Huh?! Wh-what?!" Asuna exclaimed, bolting upright at the same moment that Kirito drew his sword.

The sharp tip of the Elven Stout Sword traced a silver line in the darkness. He pierced the campfire with a thrust that was nearly as quick as Asuna's fencing.

As she watched in bewilderment, a huge storm of sparks floated into the night sky. When he pulled the sword back, something was speared on its tip. It was cooked to a light crisp, emitting savory white steam: a baked yam.

"…Um…Kirito."

"Yep."

"When you were staring intently into the fire like that…"

"Yep."

"…Was it just to monitor how well the yam was cooking?"

"You bet," he answered, straight-faced. In response, she wavered between yelling at him or punching him.

But before she could put either plan into action, Kirito pulled the tip from the sweet potato and placed the sword in the sheath over his back. He tossed the hot potato from hand to hand and eventually split it into two halves. Another burst of steam issued forth, along with a sweet, fragrant scent.

"Here."

He offered her one half. Given that six hours had passed since lunch, she decided she was generous enough to shelve her anger for now.

The hot baked yam was not quite the same as a real sweet potato in color and texture, but it was still delicious. Asuna took a bite and let the soft filling melt like cream in her mouth, the flavor rich and sweet.

After a second bite, then a third, she took a drink of tea, sighed in contentment, and finally asked, "When did you buy this? I don't remember us stopping by a grocer."

Kirito mumbled and said evasively, "Hmm? I didn't buy them."

"...So where did they come from? Don't tell me you picked this up off the ground in the third-floor forest, too."

"Ha-ha, no way. These yams are B-level food ingredients—you can't just find them on low floors like this one."

"So you got them from someone?"

"Hmm, I suppose you could say that, in a general sense...This is a drop from the half-fish, half-human–looking monsters in the fourth-floor labyrinth."

"..."

The unexpected answer left her at a loss for how to respond. If he'd said it was "half-fishman meat," she would have thrown it directly in his face, but a former possession seemed just safe enough to be acceptable. She took another bite quickly, before asking her fourth question:

"...Why would a half-fishman drop sweet potatoes?"

She was counting on one of his usual wry, slippery jokes—but was disappointed.

"Hmmm..."

He groaned, then hummed for three seconds and set down the half-eaten baked potato. He returned her question with another one:

"Do you know where Satsuma sweet potatoes come from?"

"Huh…? Well, Satsuma was the old name for Kagoshima, right? I feel like I learned this in school. Someone named Aoki Konyo brought the seeds from Satsuma province."

Once she finished answering, she realized with a start that she nearly admitted she had been in middle school back in real life. She'd hardly ever talked to Kirito about life out there—never, in fact. This was probably the second time ever.

Kirito didn't seem to think much of the revelation. "Yeah. To be precise, they first came over from Okinawa. But that's only in Japan…What I mean is, where were they first cultivated in the entire world?"

"The world…?" she asked, slightly relieved. "Hmm…I think I heard that potatoes were originally from Latin America…"

"Correct."

"Huh?"

"Sweet potatoes originate from around there. Technically, potatoes were cultivated in the highlands of South and Central America, while sweet potatoes were raised in the lowlands around the coast."

"Ohhh…"

She popped the last piece into her mouth, savored the flavor, then brought the topic back around by asking, "What does that have to do with those fishmen?"

"Well, this is just me trying to force the connection into place," he replied. With a grin, he tossed the last piece of his baked potato up in the air and caught it in his mouth. "But in the mythology of the Aztecs, the world has collapsed four times already. In the first world, people were eaten by packs of jaguars. In the second, people were turned into monkeys. In the third, they were turned into birds. And in the last world, they were turned into fish…"

"…And the people who were turned into fish were the ones

fighting us in the fourth-floor labyrinth?" she responded skeptically. Kirito laughed good-naturedly.

"Ha-ha, maybe, maybe not. But remember what Kizmel said? The various floors of Aincrad were separated from the earth long ago and rose into the sky. There were elves and kobolds and minotaurs in those sections…so who's to say there couldn't have been monsters from Aztec legends?"

"Hmmm…what I want to know is…"

Asuna paused while she finished the tea in her teacup, then looked at him with both exasperation and admiration.

"…how do you know so much about Aztec legends and the origin of sweet potatoes?"

"Ahh…" he hedged, and she realized what she had done. She'd gone beyond the proper bounds of this world again.

But her temporary partner only glanced at her briefly. "The place I lived…on the other side…was famous for growing sweet potatoes. When I was in elementary school, I did my summer vacation report on the history of sweet potatoes. Funny how I still remember that stuff."

"Ohhh…" she mumbled, keeping her face straight while her brain worked away furiously at a new subroutine.

If it was famous for sweet potatoes, that meant either Kagoshima or Ibaraki, but Kirito's vocabulary and intonation were hardly different from Asuna's Tokyo Japanese. So it could be some area around Tokyo famous for sweet potatoes—but did such a place exist? If anything was likely, it would be Chiba or Saitama—perhaps to the west of Tokyo. If she had a real-life phone, she could do a search instantly…

After half a second of this rapid thought process, she closed her eyes and cut it short.

If the game of death was ever beaten, everything in this world would vanish—all the equipment, items, and personal connections. She didn't want that to be a bad thing. It would make her lose sight of her reason to keep pushing onward.

"…Thanks for the potato. And for the potato facts," she said, clapping her hands to drive that lingering thought from her mind. "Now, as for Morte…"

"Hmm? Oh…right," Kirito said, blinking and getting his mind back to the important topic at hand. "We were wondering if Morte was working with Akihiko Kayaba or not. Well, I know I brought it up, but I don't think it's likely. Morte's just an exception to the rule for now, a player working off motives that don't line up with our logic or reason. That's how we should see him for now. There's just one thing that bothers me…"

He paused, his eyes staring sharply into the quiet blaze of the campfire. This time, he did not pull out another set of potatoes.

"…We've already heard a similar story."

"Huh…?" she blurted out, then remembered. "Oh…from Nezha!"

Asuna held her breath until Kirito silently nodded.

They'd met the player blacksmith Nezha on the second floor. He'd used the Quick Change mod to secretly steal her Wind Fleuret, a choice forced upon him by his guild, the Legend Braves.

But the trick in question wasn't his own idea.

"The man who spoke to them in the bar and taught them the trick to that scam for free—the one in the black poncho," Kirito went on, voice low. "I think his true goal was for Nezha to be judged by the rest of the top players. If it weren't for the rest of the Braves getting down on hands and knees to beg forgiveness after the second-floor boss fight, they might have executed Nezha. In a way, that would be PK-ing. Carefully toying with the thoughts of various players, guiding them into ultimately killing each other…You might call it a provocation PK…"

Asuna felt her features twist at the ugly nastiness of the idea.

Monster PK-ing (MPK) and duel PK-ing (DPK) were bad enough, but they also involved an amount of risk on the part of the person attempting it. In constructing an MPK, any mistake might cause the monsters to attack the PKer, and in a DPK, you could always end up losing instead.

But a provocation PK (if it were a common enough concept to have its own acronym, it would be PPK) completely removed any direct risk from the one orchestrating it. The perpetrator just stayed comfortable in the center, guiding individuals and groups into direct confrontation around him.

The chances of success seemed lower than an MPK or DPK, but in every world, there were people extraordinarily skilled at manipulating others. Even at the all-girls school Asuna attended, there were students who otherwise didn't stand out, but could use e-mails, texts, and rumors to manipulate the mood of the class and apply pressure wherever they wanted. They were probably doing it without realizing their skill, but this mysterious man in the black poncho tried to have Nezha killed with clear, malicious purpose.

"…Do you suppose Morte and the black poncho could be the same person?" she asked. Kirito traced the spot between his brows with a finger.

"Hrmmm…Nezha described the black poncho as a man who laughed gleefully. And Morte certainly did enjoy his chuckles, so they could be the same person. If that's the case, then like I said earlier, Morte might just be a unique, solo PKer who refuses to abide by the common logic of Aincrad. But if they're separate people, then the situation is more dire than that…"

The campfire, which was finally losing fuel and strength, popped in a burst of sparks. Asuna flinched, then hesitantly turned to her partner.

"What do you mean…by 'dire'…?"

Kirito took a number of breaths, hesitating to answer, before he finally spoke in a low voice.

"…If they're separate people, we should assume Morte and the black poncho are working together."

"…!!"

"Meaning they're working to commit PKs as a duo…or perhaps there's even more than two. There could be three, four…or an entire gang of PKers out there in Aincrad somewhere…"

The Fossilwood Branch finally reached the end of its durability and crumbled through the middle, disappearing with a large sheet of sparks. As the tiny lights went out, the darkness of their surroundings crept closer, and Asuna unconsciously moved herself a few inches to the right.

"...But if you kill players in *SAO* right now, they can't be revived...They'll die in the real world. Do Morte and his friend not want us to beat the game? Don't they want to get out of this place...?" she rasped, her voice so hoarse and dry that she had trouble hearing herself.

Nearly ten seconds later, Kirito's response was just as strained.

"Maybe...they're not concerned with whether we escape at all... Like you said, when your HP go down to zero, the player dies. So maybe they just want to cause PKs...to commit murder..."

Asuna thought she heard a rustle behind her and spun around.

But the only thing there was a series of dark ruined walls, cold and unfeeling.

2

AFTER SEVEN IN THE EVENING, THE TWO DECIDED to return to town.

The main city of the fifth floor, Karluin, was built in the center of a huge swath of ruins covering the southern end of the floor. It was meant to resemble a settlement of newly arrived people reusing a fallen city of centuries past.

Compared to the crisscrossed canals of Rovia on the fourth floor, there was barely any water here, but thanks to perhaps some busy NPC cleaners, it also wasn't particularly dusty. The buildings, made of darkened stone blocks, were crumbling here and there, but the center of town was full of leather and canvas tents that bustled with chaotic liveliness.

"...It's kind of hard to tell where the safe haven boundary is..." Asuna mumbled, after the words appeared abruptly in her view.

When the notice disappeared, she turned back to look at the path they'd taken to get there, which was surrounded by half-crumbled stone walls. But there were no arches or other visual cues that suggested the boundary of town. It would be important to remember the spot by sight so that they could escape into the safe haven if they ever got into trouble with monsters beyond its borders.

Beside her, Kirito nodded and said, "Yeah, that's the thing. In the beta, people stacked wooden boxes and stuff to serve as the marker, but they're treated as abandoned objects, so they wear out and eventually disappear…"

"Ahh…Couldn't you just stack something cheap and durable? Would anything fit the bill?"

"Sure. The crumbled blocks lying all over the place."

She looked at where Kirito was pointing and saw a number of square stone blocks scattered around the path. But given that they were the same material as the walls, stacking them up wasn't likely to draw her or Kirito's attention.

"…Guess we'll just have to keep our eyes open."

She resumed walking, trying to imprint the view of the area into her brain.

As they approached the center of Karluin, the first sound to arrive was the piping of a flute in the style of some kind of European folk music, followed by the lively chatter of voices. Over a day had passed since they activated the teleport gate, and many players had come through it from the lower floors.

"Hmm…I don't see the DKB or ALS," Kirito muttered as he scanned the crowd from the entrance to the square. That surprised Asuna.

"You're usually the one trying to avoid them. Are you going to invite them to dinner or something?"

"You could say that."

Now she was truly stunned. "Wh-what in the world has gotten into you?"

"Well," he said, smirking with one cheek, then scratching his head with a finger, "I was hoping to catch one of the more reasonable guys, like Shivata or Hafner, and ask them about Morte again. He didn't take part in the third- or fourth-floor boss fights, so he probably left the guilds…but maybe I can learn something about his story and what he did while he was still a member."

"Ahh…" she replied flatly, but deep down, she recognized that if the clumsy, antisocial swordsman was going to these lengths, he really had to be worried about the possibility of a PKer loose in Aincrad. Perhaps she ought to help with collecting information...but then a thought occurred to her.

"Oh, right...Why not ask Argo?"

It was the obvious choice. Argo the Rat, info broker extraordinaire, would surely know all about Morte, down to where he lurked.

But Kirito looked conflicted. "Actually...I bought info on Morte from Argo once already. But that was on the third floor, just before he challenged me to that duel...I doubt she would have undertaken that job if she knew how dangerous he was," he grunted.

"Huh? Why wouldn't she—?" She started to ask it, only to understand halfway through.

Argo was a talented information dealer, with the quickness to slip past all the monsters to reach the boss chamber of a labyrinth, but her (expected) gear and skill choices had to be noncombat focused. Kirito was concerned for her safety.

"...I'm sorry. Of course, you're right. This is a player killer we're talking about; you can't just go asking her to stick her neck into danger," Asuna mumbled. Kirito gave her a meaningful glance.

"Wh-what?" she asked.

"Um...maybe you should repeat that to yourself," he said, a mixture of blunt rudeness and concern. She blinked in surprise.

"Of course, I'm not thinking of doing this investigation on my own, okay?"

"As long as that's clear," Kirito said. His expression struck her as one of a younger boy doing his best to act like an adult. She couldn't help herself from reaching over and knuckling the shoulder of his black coat.

"Wh-what?"

"Nothing," she said, and stretched her hands up overhead. "Ahh, I'm hungry! Show me the way to a restaurant that's good, not crowded, and clean on the inside."

"That's a tall order."

Kirito shook his head in annoyance, thought it over, then grinned.

"All right, I think I know just the place."

After a few minutes of winding through suspicious-looking storefronts left and right, Asuna no longer had any idea where she was. She opened her map screen from the menu, but it was still a new area to her, so the surroundings were grayed out, and the most she knew was that she was on the southern side of the town.

It would be the same for Kirito, but he weaved his way through the maze of alleys without hesitation. Given that the beta was a whole four months ago, his memory was impressive.

"Do you have the layout of all the cities up to the tenth floor memorized?" she asked him suspiciously as they walked.

He shrugged. "Not all of them. My memory of Rovia was pretty vague...but I kind of liked Karluin. I made this my base for about ten days."

"What? Why wouldn't you pick Rovia instead? At least that place was much prettier—oh. Right, in the beta..."

"Exactly. The canals were just roads in the beta. But I still don't know if I'd make my home in Rovia now...I bet I'd get real tired of not being able to get around without a boat."

"I suppose you've got a point..."

She glanced around. At some point the shops had trailed off and the lanterns thinned out, leaving only the ruins around them. There were no players or NPCs on the path with them.

If this were the real world, she would never consider walking alone with a boy in the dark after sunset like this. She'd never had anything like a boyfriend, so the situation normally called for her caution radar to be operating at maximum output, but with the defense of the system's Anti-Criminal Code and her trusty rapier at her side, she was surprisingly unconcerned. In fact, she was even a little excited to see where he was taking her.

They spent another five minutes following Kirito's radar, through wooden doors and arches, until a gentle light appeared ahead.

Set into the stone wall at the end of the narrow alley was a wooden door with lanterns on either side and a small sign planted in front. The walls were too high to tell what was on the other side of the door, but at the very least, it seemed to be a business.

Asuna trotted the last fifty feet, leaving Kirito behind so she could read the sign. It was made of a flat sheet of black stone, with the name TAVERN INN BLINK & BRINK carved into it. The day's special was written in English below the name, with white chalk.

"Blink and Brink...? Let's see, I know the word *blink* in English...but I'm not sure about the other one..." she muttered, glancing down the menu, then noticed a small warning in Japanese at the bottom. It read: WARNING! DON'T RACE INTO THE BUILDING.

As she pondered the meaning of that one, Kirito caught up to her and reached for the door.

"You'll see inside what they mean by 'brink.' After you."

He pulled the cast-iron ring on the door. A cold gust of wind emerged from within, and Asuna turned her face away. When it died down, she cautiously peered in.

A square terrace lay beyond the door. Ahead and to the right were iron railings, while the left side connected to the restaurant. Wood repairs replaced the crumbled stone ruins, and when combined with the large country-style window, the atmosphere felt delightful. But Asuna's gaze was drawn back to the terrace ahead.

She passed through the doorway and crossed the stone terrace, weaving around three cast-iron tables until she reached the edge and grabbed the stomach-high railing with both hands.

"...What...is this...?" she muttered to herself hoarsely. Kirito came up next to her and leaned against the railing.

"Well, it's the sky."

But that was such a simple word for what she saw.

Her vision was full of the night sky, black as ink on the right and transitioning to navy, indigo, purple, and finally the deep red of sunset on her left. Up above was a crowded, starry tableau, looking ready to rain down light at any moment. Below was an endless sea of clouds, glowing faintly with the starlight from above.

She gazed at the stunning sight, feeling a numbing thrill run through her from the top of her head to the tips of her toes.

When she looked closer, she saw a flock of large birds flying slightly above them. They slowly crossed the sky from east to west until they disappeared in the curtain of stars.

Asuna lost track of how long she'd been standing there, but then her brain kicked back into action. She blinked and murmured, "Of course...'Brink' as in the 'brink of a cliff.'"

"That's my guess. I had to look it up in a dictionary back in the beta," Kirito replied.

She glanced around again.

The high walls on either side of the terrace curved gently, each side covering the base of a mammoth pillar that stretched all the way to the bottom of the floor above, three hundred feet away. As the name suggested, they were at the very brink of Aincrad itself.

"...I've never been this close to the edge."

"And not since the beta for me...There's a jutting observation deck down in the Town of Beginnings on the first floor, but I've hardly been back there."

"...Just to confirm—what happens if you jump over this railing...?"

"Hmm..."

He didn't respond at once. Kirito leaned his upper half over the railing to peer down.

"H-hey!"

She instinctively grabbed his coat collar and pulled with all her strength. Kirito gagged and returned upright to the terrace with a strained smile.

"Look, I'm not going to try it."

"Of…of course you aren't! Don't go thrill seeking, now!"

"Sorry, sorry. When I fell from the outer edge in the beta, I got the 'You are dead' notice in midair and then resurrected in Black-iron Palace. Well, I bet it's just the same now, except there's no resurrection. But the fence and terrace are indestructible objects, so they're much safer than they would be in the real world."

"Well…you're right about that, I suppose," she grumbled, letting go of Kirito's coat.

The swordsman held up a finger and added, "Oh, right. In the beta, someone raced through the doors the moment they opened, hoping to order a limited-supply dish with a buff effect, but couldn't make such a hard left turn to the restaurant soon enough and plunged over the railing. So watch out for that."

"…I guess that's what the warning on the sign was for…"

She recalled a scene from about twenty days earlier.

In Urbus, the main town of the second floor, there was an enormous cake with a buff effect called the Tremble Shortcake. Stat effect aside, there was nothing better than eating a massive shortcake with spongy filling, dollops of cream, and scads of strawberries, without a single calorie to worry about.

The memory of the cake activated her sense of hunger, and Asuna pulled on her partner's coat gently this time.

"Come on, let's eat. Since we're here, we might as well eat on the terrace."

"Of course. The outside tables were a huge hit during the beta, mostly for dates. You have no idea how lonely it was to wolf down food for the buff effect surrounded by those types," Kirito grumbled, sitting down at a chair on the table closest to the edge.

Asuna took the seat across from him and replied, "Well, you should be happy, knowing that you finally came with someone else…"

When she saw the odd look on her temporary partner's face, she realized her mistake. Feeling her ears grow hot to the very tips, she smacked the cast-iron table hard.

"I-I mean, not that! This isn't a date, just so we're clear!"

Before Kirito could react to her statement, the door to the restaurant on the western side of the terrace opened. The game probably registered her striking the table as a signal for service. An NPC waitress wearing a black apron hurried over, bowing and welcoming them, then placed two glasses of water on the table.

"Have you decided on your order?"

"Ah, just a minute…"

Asuna picked up the menu of parchment fixed to a bronze plate. The waitress was a virtual NPC, so there was no issue with forcing her to wait—or so Asuna had thought until half a month ago, when she met the dark elf Kizmel. Now she felt like every NPC had its own mind and emotions, whether they were high-functioning agents like Kizmel or simple town NPCs without AIs, like this one.

The menu was written in both English and Japanese, so she let her sight and intuition work for five seconds before making her decision.

"I'll have the chèvre leaf and ten-cheese salad, the piping hot gratin soup, and the poro-poro bird roast, with a bread roll."

She was going to hand Kirito the menu next, but he held up a hand and said, "I'll have the same, plus a bottle of ficklewine, and two blue-blueberry tarts and coffees after the meal."

The waitress repeated it back perfectly, then left. Asuna let out a long breath.

"…When you come up to a new floor, you don't know what all the foods are like, so it feels like gambling when you order."

"You sounded pretty decisive to me."

"I did my best to avoid the new-sounding names," she said, glancing at the menu once more. A question popped into her head. "Did you order that limited-supply buff item?"

"Of course."

"What effect does it have?"

"I'll leave that for you to find out," Kirito answered, grinning. Asuna fixed him with a glare, deciding she'd make him test the dishes first for poison.

Just like that, the food arrived.

To her relief, the salad, soup, and main dish were all largely as she'd anticipated. Kirito pulled the cork out of the wine bottle with his fingers and poured the golden liquid into Asuna's glass.

She'd thought the name sounded weird when he ordered it, but it looked just like an ordinary white wine—except that when Kirito poured it into his own glass, the wine was pink and bubbling.

"…What kind of trick is that?"

"It's not a trick or sleight of hand at all," he said boldly, setting the bottle down with a smirk. "This wine changes at random between red, white, rosé, and sweet, dry, or sparkling each time you pour it. Hence the name: ficklewine."

"So you wound up with a sparkling rosé. I got…"

She lifted the glass, clinked it to Kirito's, and took a sip. The sharp chill and subtle flavor was a pleasant stimulation to her sense of taste. It was a lot like the white wine she'd tried in the real world, but of course, here there was no alcohol content.

"…a dry white. Mmm, that's good."

"Ahhh…" Kirito murmured, watching her closely. She arched a questioning eyebrow at him, and he looked away, clearing his throat awkwardly.

"Er, I…I wondered if you had experience drinking wine."

"Well, a bit, just for the taste…" she started, then stopped when she realized it was bordering on real-world information again. And quite a sensitive topic: If she made him think she had wine regularly, that would mean she was above twenty, the drinking age. Asuna had turned only fifteen just over three months ago, and it felt weird to imagine someone seeing her as five years older than that. In truth, she'd had no more wine than whatever she sipped from her father's or brother's glass at home.

"J-just a bit, really. Didn't you take sips of your father's beer, too?"

"Well, sure. Though it was my mom's beer…"

Kirito looked to the right, toward the night sky. Asuna followed his gaze and, after a few moments, opened her eyes wide with a start.

She hadn't noticed it at first, because there were so many stars in the sky, but now that she looked, she could see a line of three stars: Orion's Belt. That meant the large red star to the left was Betelgeuse, the sparkling star far to the left of that was Procyon in Canis Minor, and two stars below, pale Sirius from Canis Major—the Winter Triangle.

"...The same constellations as the real world's..."

Asuna shut her eyes tight and lowered her head.

The stars were virtually invisible from her home in the Setagaya ward of Tokyo, but the mountain air of her mother's parents' home in Miyagi was clear and crisp, providing a vivid view of the stars. One winter night, she'd gone out in heavy clothes so that her grandfather could teach her the names of the stars. That childhood memory returned in brilliant clarity, shrouded in a painful nostalgia that jabbed at her heart.

She put her hand to her breastplate and sensed that Kirito was going to say something. She shook her head.

"Don't say anything."

"..."

"...I don't want to think about the real world. I'm Asuna, level-16 fencer. If I don't keep believing that, I'll go back to the old me who couldn't fight..."

The words coming from her throat were so faint that even she could barely hear them. After a few moments, a calm voice replied, "Yeah...I get it. Sorry."

She shook her head again, implying that it wasn't his fault. Eventually the pain in her chest left her, and she took a deep breath before raising her head.

"No, I'm sorry...Come on. Let's eat, before it gets cold."

The meal, which they consumed in a bit of a rush, was quite good overall.

The salad leaves contained a faint hint of mayo, and when they took the lid off the soup, it was indeed viciously bubbling away.

The poro-poro bird crumbled into soft pieces with just the poke of a fork, but all told, it was an enjoyable meal. When she finished her third glass of wine—this one a sweet rosé—the waitress brought out the desserts.

"…It looks just like a normal blueberry tart. Is this the…?"

"Yep. The limited-supply buff dish."

The color of the berries seemed a little *too* vivid (probably the source of the extra "blue" in the name), but with the only light coming from the four lanterns hung at each corner of the terrace, it was hard to tell. Once she had seen Kirito happily pack away the first bite without any sign of poison or curses, Asuna worked a triangular piece out and lifted it to her mouth.

"Oh…it's good," she blurted. Under the fresh, sweetly sour blueberries was a layer of thick custard cream, which went well with the crisp tart crust.

Of course, it didn't have the size of the Tremble Shortcake, but it was hard to say which flavor was better. She finished the dessert in a blissful haze, took a sip of coffee, and sighed with satisfaction. As she did so, an unfamiliar effect icon appeared in the upper left of her view.

Inside the square icon was the image of an open eye. It was probably some kind of boost to sight, but she didn't feel like her eyesight or night vision had improved markedly.

"…What is this buff?"

"Look at the terrace floor," Kirito said. She leaned over to look at the stone floor beneath the table. As she scanned it, she noticed something shining dully at the edge of the terrace.

"…There's something over there…"

She stood up and walked toward the glowing object—a small coin.

The glowing effect stopped once she picked it up, but the shine of the reflected lantern light did not go away. It was an old silver coin.

But the image stamped on the side wasn't the familiar icon of Aincrad on the usual hundred-col coin. It was a new symbol of two trees standing next to each other. On the other side was just an odd crest, with no numbers whatsoever.

She returned to Kirito and held up the coin.

"It's just an unfamiliar coin…What is this? Why was it shining?"

She sat down and clunked the coin onto the table. Kirito snatched it up, gave it a quick glance, and nodded, spinning it in his fingers.

"These ruins are made up of remains—the buildings and roads that constitute Karluin—and one other very important element. Do you know what that is?"

She grumbled, feeling like she was being questioned by a history teacher. With her studying mind in gear for the first time in ages, she tried to come up with a reasonable answer.

"…Artifacts?"

Kirito flipped the coin with his right thumb and nimbly caught it in his left hand.

"Close! Well, you're basically right, but the answer is 'relics.' Remains and relics combine to make ruins…By which I mean, Karluin isn't just these ancient roads and walls—it's littered with little relics like this. The story hasn't picked up yet, but within a day or two, there will be hundreds of players from below coming up here to scrabble for relics all over the city."

"Ooooh…"

She couldn't help but look back down at the floor. There was a fresh glow at the base of the south-facing railing, so she rushed over to scoop it up.

"…This one's copper."

The double-tree symbol was the same, but the brown coin was a bit smaller when she placed it on the table next to the first. Now she could feel her body itching to look for more of them. Kirito smirked at her.

"Just be careful of getting hooked on relic hunting. In other games, you'd have a little minimap with the item locations listed, and they'd glow on the screen, but in *SAO*, they're just lying on the ground…It was even hard to find that huge Fossilwood Branch, so you can imagine how difficult it will be to find these tiny coins around."

"Huh? But it was glowing for me…" she started to say, then realized it was the buff effect of the blue-blueberry tart. "Oh. So this eye icon means…"

"Yes. That's a bonus to relic finding, and it only works inside and below Karluin, but it will help you quite a bit by making the coins and jewels glow—"

"Jewels?" Asuna asked, cutting him off.

"Er…y-yeah. The gold coins and jewels are super rare, so even with the buff, it's pretty difficult to find them. Even rarer are the magic rings and necklaces…"

"Rings? Necklaces?"

"…Y-yeah."

Asuna glanced away from the awkward-looking Kirito and down at the silver and copper coins on the table. After five seconds of internal struggle, she admitted, "I want to hunt for relics, too."

It probably wasn't the most ladylike of actions, but when she was in kindergarten, she remembered attending a building completion ceremony, where she trotted around picking up all the ritual mochi dumplings they scattered to bless the finished construction. That had earned her a vicious scolding from her mother, so picking up items in a virtual world was nothing at this point. Besides, they'd paid money for the tart's effect, so there was no point in letting it go to waste.

She stared back at her partner, who was looking more skeptical by the second, and asked, "Is there a problem?"

"N…no, it's nothing…"

"In fact, why do you look so unmotivated to do this? Knowing you, I would have thought you'd recommend snatching them all up before the town got crowded."

"H-how rude…and, well, accurate," the swordsman reluctantly grumbled. "I love doing stuff like this, too, but I have some tragic memories from the beta…Then again, as long as we stick to the town, it should be fine…"

He came to some kind of internal consensus and got to his feet, pointing at the table.

"By the way, these Karl Coins can be converted into col at an NPC exchange merchant in town," he added, scooping up the coins.

When the NPC waitress came to clean up their dishes, they gave her an automatic "thanks for the meal" and headed back through the big door. There were still no players in sight, but once the buff tart was included in Argo's strategy guides, that queue from the beta would return.

"How long does this buff last?" Asuna asked as they departed.

Kirito put on a face like an adult reassuring a small child. "There's no need to panic. We have an entire hour."

"You mean *only* an hour! Oh, right…can you order those tarts for takeout?"

"Unfortunately, the buff only works if you eat it in the restaurant. Just one per customer, thirty made a day."

"Ahh…So you couldn't buy them all up and resell them for a huge profit," Asuna muttered. Kirito pulled away in mock horror.

"Wow, even I wouldn't stoop that low!"

"I…I didn't say I would do it! I'm just saying, it's a good thing that's impossible!"

Even as she poked the shoulder of his coat, she was careful not to take her eyes off the ground. For now, she didn't see any glowing objects.

"…There were two on that terrace earlier, but I'm not finding any out here…"

"There aren't many relics on the pathways. And basically zero in NPC stores and buildings. The places to go are the open plazas

here and there, the temples, and the really ruined spots that the residents don't use."

"Ahh...And when you pick up a relic, that's it?"

"In the beta, they would come back whenever they took the server down for maintenance...but since they started the game for real, there's never been any kind of service period where they stop the server..."

"You know, you're right...When they take online games like this down for maintenance, what exactly are they doing?"

This might be a question more on the real-world side, but she figured it was safe to ask. Kirito pressed his fingers to his temples and strained to remember.

"I feel like I read about this once...They check the software and hardware for damage, then fix or replace it if they find something, update the program with bug fixes, then restart the server...I think?"

"So there's lots of stuff they do. And...that's all necessary, right? How is *SAO* fine running for two months without maintenance?"

"Sadly, I do not know," the swordsman answered, smiling wryly as he looked up toward the floor above. "If they cluster the servers, they can perform rolling maintenance where they switch them out individually without stopping service...but the problem with a game is ensuring that the chronological logic doesn't get mixed up. But in *SAO*'s case, Kayaba clearly designed it knowing he would turn it into a deadly trap, so obviously he had a plan for it all along...I just can't guess how it works from here."

She was starting to lose sight of his train of thought, so Asuna quickly took advantage of his break in speech to say, "Th-thanks. Anyway, at the moment, that means it's possible that any relic that gets picked up will never reappear on the ground."

"Potentially."

"In that case, it's even more important we don't waste our time! Plazas and temples, you said? Let's go!"

"Yeah, yeah, I'm coming. If you turn left up ahead, there's a pretty good ruined temple to plunder…Ah, ma'am, please don't run in the halls!"

But Asuna had already darted off for the unseen ruins ahead.

3

TWENTY-THREE COPPER COINS WORTH TEN COL EACH.

Nine silver coins worth a hundred col each.

Two small gold coins worth five hundred col each.

One large gold coin worth a thousand col.

Three gems of fairly good quality.

One necklace that seemed to harbor a magical effect.

One bracelet of a similar nature.

Two rings of a similar nature.

That was the list of items that Asuna and Kirito found at the temple at the edge of Karluin before their buff ran out. They wouldn't know about the gems and accessories until they had them appraised, but the total had to be well over five thousand col. It was a stunning haul for just an hour's work.

Right after they did one last sweep of the empty temple to confirm there were no more glowing objects, the buff icon stopped blinking and vanished.

"Phew..."

Asuna heaved a sigh and plopped down on a cracked bench next to Kirito. She looked down at the relics—the treasures—they'd collected, laid out neatly on a folded blanket, and sighed again.

"Yes, I can see the dangers of getting addicted to this."

"Right? In the beta, there were people who gave up on leveling altogether and just turned into expert relic collectors. We called them 'hoarders' out of respect."

"...I don't see what makes that term particularly respectful..."

She picked up a red jewel from the blanket and placed it in her palm. It was fun to crawl around the temple searching for glowing spots, but once the magic effect wore off, she was left with a feeling like guilt tugging at her heart.

In a way, to those players who chose to go into crafting or never left the Town of Beginnings, this was one of the few methods to make money in the safe zone. If the relics didn't come back, that made it even worse. They weren't wanting for food or lodging money, so getting a head start on scooping up all the relics before anyone else was nothing short of selfish greed.

She put the jewel back on the blanket. When Kirito spoke next, there was none of his usual ironic snark to it.

"...You're very kind."

He meant it in recognition of her regret, but that message didn't reach her brain at first. Only after three seconds did she squawk in surprise.

"H-huh?! Wha—? I'm not— What do you...?"

Kirito smiled a bit shyly and explained, "You don't need to feel guilty, Asuna. Compared to all the relics in this town, what we picked up is just a tiny pittance."

He awkwardly reached out and very lightly patted the breast-plate connector on Asuna's right shoulder blade.

Before, she might have socked him a counterpunch and demanded he not touch her like that. But this time, Asuna could only hold her breath as she tried to contain the sudden upswell of emotion within her.

She felt guilty for having fun collecting the relics without considering the implications. But she also wanted to argue her case, that she, too, was scared when she went out to fight monsters. The combination of these two emotions blew up within her, turning the feelings she'd been trying to suppress into a powerful urge.

She wanted to bury her face into the chest of her companion, the black-haired swordsman she'd teamed up with for no other reason than to more efficiently make her way through this mortal game, and cry her eyes out. She wanted to cast aside the role of a powerful elite player, an honor she never wanted, to throw out all the limitations placed upon her, and scream and wail like a little child. She wanted to be liberated—and to have that be accepted, forgiven, and consoled.

But it wasn't an option.

She couldn't cling to Kirito in her weakness. She was already taking too much advantage of his knowledge. How many questions had he answered for her in the single day they'd spent on this floor? And the reverse had almost never happened.

If she depended on him too much more, they would no longer be game partners—they would be protector and protected. In terms of game knowledge, that was already true. That's why she had to be his equal in combat and control her emotions.

On her left side, where Kirito couldn't see, she clutched her rapier sheath, withstanding the storm of impulses. Eventually, the high tide of emotions began to ebb, returning to the bottom of her heart where she kept them.

Asuna let out a long, slow breath and turned to smile weakly at her concerned partner.

"Yes…thank you, I'm fine. I don't regret it; I had a lot of fun… but I suppose I'm satisfied with my relic seeking for now."

"…All right," Kirito said, grinning and nodding. He took an empty leather bag from his inventory, placed the coins and accessories inside, and said kindly, "When I said you didn't need to feel guilty, it was true. There are temples and squares like this one all over the city…"

"…Yeah."

"And we don't know for sure that they won't come back…"

"…Yeah."

"Plus, finding relics in town is really more like a simple side product of the real treasure hunt of Karluin."

"...Yeah...yeah?" she asked, pausing in confusion. "What do you mean?"

"Know how we didn't see anyone from the DKB and ALS around the teleport gate or anywhere else? Well, I feel like they're the ones who are going to scoop up all the relics to fund their war chest or whatever."

"...You may be right..."

She watched her partner, wondering where this conversation was heading. Kirito extended his index finger and pointed it straight down.

"I think they're down below."

"...Below?"

"Yep. There's an enormous catacomb beneath Karluin...Basically, a dungeon. It's so wide that it stretches out beyond the boundary of the town, and that's where the real treasure hunt is. The stuff you find in here is small beans in comparison."

"...Wha—?"

"So there's no reason at all to feel guilty about this much. Come on, let's go get these appraised, turned into cash, and split between us. Then we can go to an armory and get our gear souped up..."

"Huh? Huh?! Huuuuuuh?!"

Something else ripped up through Asuna from the bottom of her heart—but unlike before, this was more of a bellow of rage. She clenched her right hand into a fist.

"You should have—! Said that—!! Earlier!!!"

Her right hook tore audibly through the air and would have walloped Kirito in his left flank, if it weren't for the Anti-Criminal Code. The purple sparks that resulted shone brightly, briefly illuminating the ruined temple.

The only way to see the properties of an unidentified item was to take it to a player or NPC with the Appraisal skill. The former wasn't commonplace yet, so the pair went to an NPC merchant in Karluin to have their jewels and accessories identified.

The gems were all D-level stones worth barely five hundred col each, the necklace was +3 to the Recitation skill, the bracelet was +4 to Mixing, and one of the rings added a 1 percent boost to stun resistance—not a great haul. But the other ring had an unfamiliar effect: Candlepower.

As they left the shop, Asuna examined the silver ring with the yellow stone, and Kirito suggested, "Why don't you equip that? It'll be handy."

"Uh…it will? But…"

They'd found it together, so she thought they ought to play rock-paper-scissors for the prize, but Kirito cut her off by holding his hands up.

"Look, I've already got rings on both hands."

Sure enough, there was a silver shine on the index fingers of each hand. The one on his right hand was +1 to strength, a quest reward from the dark elf commander on the third floor. And the one on the left was the Sigil of Lyusula, given to him by Viscount Yofilis.

Asuna had the exact same ring on the middle finger of her left hand. When they received them together, she'd put it on her ring finger without thinking. Even recalling the moment of her belated realization and hasty transfer to the middle finger brought a fresh wave of embarrassment to her cheeks, and she lowered her hand.

"W-well…If you insist, I will."

She put the mysterious Ring of Candlelight on her right middle finger and started to walk off, forgetting to ask him about the magical effect.

They sold the rest of the relics at an item shop closer to the appraiser, and after converting the Karl Coins at the exchanger next door, they had earned 6,480 col in total. Kirito opened the trade window and sent her exactly half, which she accepted.

She hadn't entirely gotten over her guilt at cleaning out a whole temple, but according to him, there were still mountains of treasure around and underneath the town, so the people coming up from below to find relics would have plenty of fun left. Besides, she'd only earned so much in such a short time thanks to the relic-finding bonus effect. Given the limited number of tarts available, the whole town wouldn't be picked clean for quite some time.

Asuna decided to use her sudden influx of money entirely for the sake of advancing the game, a decision that made her feel a bit better. Meanwhile, Kirito was already steering them toward an armory.

"Hey, they said there's no magic in Aincrad, right?"

"Hmm? Yeah...that's what Kizmel said. The elves have their charms from before the Great Separation, but we humans have basically nothing left..."

"In that case, how does that tart effect work? I mean, it's basically a magical effect, right?"

"Ahh," Kirito murmured, grinning, "I just figured that one out today...I think maybe that's why it comes in the form of a blue-blueberry tart."

"What do you mean?"

"You know how they say the anthocyanin in blueberries are good for your eyesight? Well, with two blues, there's twice the anthocyanin, enough to make it possible to see relics better. So you could argue that it's not exactly magic..."

"...Hrrm..."

In that case, she wondered how he would explain the luck bonus offered by the Tremble Shortcake—but decided she'd rather treasure the memory for what it was and held her tongue.

Instead, she looked up at the bottom of the floor above, shining dully with starlight, and muttered, "We'll meet Kizmel on this floor, too, won't we?"

Kirito didn't have an immediate answer to this. Like Asuna, he looked up.

"...The flow of the campaign quest veered way away from how it went in the beta on the fourth floor. Before, General N'ltzahh and Viscount Yofilis didn't even exist. So I can't say anything for sure...but I hope we do."

"Yeah," Asuna agreed hopefully.

"Oh," Kirito continued, "but we might be able to go see her from here."

"Huh…?"

"Remember, we have to go get the viscount's reward before they start tearing through the fifth floor in earnest."

"Oh, right. Of course."

After the battle at Castle Yofel on the previous floor, the castle's master had offered them an eye-popping list of potential rewards, but at that very moment, they got word that the guilds had gone to challenge the floor boss and had to put off their selection and rush to the labyrinth tower. There was no time limit for their selection—they hoped—but they ought to return promptly.

"I don't know if Kizmel will still be at the castle," Kirito added, hoping not to get Asuna's hopes too high. She checked the time: nine thirty at night. It wasn't early, but it also wasn't too late.

"Shall we go back to the fourth floor?"

"Hmm, yeah…I ought to move on to my next sword soon, anyway…"

"Oh? You're not going to keep using that one?" she asked, glancing at the Elven Stout Sword slung over Kirito's back. "Isn't it really tough?"

"Yeah, it is…but I only have one upgrade attempt remaining on it. Even if it's successful, this weapon won't be useful to me for much longer."

"Hmm…So I guess it doesn't always work out."

"Exactly," he said, grinning sourly. "Well! Let's take the teleporter back to Rovia and gather all the ingredients by the end of the night."

"Ingredients…? Oh, right…"

To move on the canals of the fourth floor, they needed a gondola. But their trusty *Tilnel* was still moored at Yofel Castle. They'd need to create a fresh boat to get from the town to the castle again.

"Well…I'd like to see Romolo the shipwright, too…Let's take care of business!" Asuna clenched a fist, burning with enthusiasm.

Kirito interjected fearfully, "We're just making a normal gondola this time, right...? Not one that requires monster bear grease...?"

"Oh, fine. I suppose I'll make do with a normal one."

Her partner sighed in visible relief, but Asuna jabbed his shoulder and picked up her pace.

When they went from Karluin's teleport gate into Rovia, the main town of the fourth floor, they were greeted by the pleasant scent of water and the sound of trickling waves.

It was night here, too, of course, but the sight of the residential lights reflecting off the waterways was as beautiful as a dream.

"We've opened up the fifth floor, but there are still so many tourists here," Asuna noted.

"At this rate, we might have to wait awhile at old man Romolo's place still...Well, let's get collecting those materials for..."

He stopped. A deep baritone voice was hailing them from behind.

"Yo, you two!"

They knew who it belonged to before they even saw him.

It was the bald man who led the team of double-handed weapon warriors—Kirito called them the "Bro Squad"—that retained its independence from the two major guilds.

Kirito turned around and offered a breezy "'Sup."

Asuna followed with a polite bow. "Good evening, Agil."

"Hey."

Agil the ax warrior grinned back at them, but his trademark ax was not equipped. Instead, he was hauling a large tubelike object over his shoulder. After staring for a bit, Asuna recognized it.

That object was a Vendor's Carpet; the very same merchant's item Kirito had received from Nezha the blacksmith and foisted off on—er, granted to—Agil afterward.

"Whoa, are you changing classes from fighter to merchant?" Kirito asked, stunned.

Agil grinned again.

"Well, since you gave it to me, I figured it shouldn't go to waste."

"N-no way..." Kirito groaned. Asuna was stunned, too. If Agil and his three companions put down their weapons, it would be a significant blow to the strength of the frontline group.

But Agil only looked at their concerned faces and laughed, leaning back. "Sorry, don't mean to imply I won't be helping out. But I figured I'd give this thing a shot and see how much better I can do getting rid of excess items with this, rather than selling to an NPC shop. I had a little business going earlier this evening."

"Ahh...How did it go?" Kirito asked curiously.

Agil rubbed his neatly squared goatee and said, "Hmm...it seems to depend on the item. I was able to liquidate the items you need a lot of, like gondola materials, at a pretty good price. But the accessories with food ingredients or noncombat skill boosts didn't sell out. Basically, if you're going into serious trading, you need to keep an eye on the trends in high-demand items and work on your marketing."

"Ahh, I see," Kirito replied, rubbing his own chin with the back of his knuckles. "*SAO* doesn't have one of those auction house features that everyone can access at any time. I guess if you're going to be serious about selling items, you need to put in the effort..."

"Yeah. It'll be hard for a fighter to sell off items he doesn't need at the roadside. It takes time, and the buyers and sellers don't know where to find each other...In fact, the lack of such a thing makes it really hard to set a market price."

"If only there was a major middleman, something like those large-scale recycling shops in real-life Japan, the trading among players would be much busier...but no one has the money to pull off a business like that. Not for a while, at least."

"But that means whoever pulls it off first is going to rake in the cash."

Asuna had been listening to the two men ramble on and on

about moneymaking schemes at a distance, but at this point, she interjected. "Pardon me, Agil...did I hear you say you were selling the materials for the shipbuilding quest?"

"Hmm? Yeah. My inventory was just bulging with wood and ores. Gotta do *something* with them."

"D-do you have any left?!"

Kirito came back to his senses and pressed him. "Y-yeah! Do you have any, Agil?!"

The large man smoothly shrugged his shoulders and held out his empty hands.

"Didn't I just say I sold off all the gondola mats? Not a single item left. But why would you want something like that now? Weren't you the first to make your boat?" he asked curiously. Kirito gave him a quick rundown. The ax warrior nodded, thought it over for a bit, then opened his window, asking the two to hang on a minute. He was sending an instant message to someone.

Agil glanced over the nearly instantaneous reply and said, "My partners say it's all right. You can borrow our boat."

At the eastern dock of the teleport square, Agil loosed the mooring rope of the midsize *Pequod* and stood on shore as Asuna and Kirito waved back, steering the boat south down the main waterway.

Manning the oar at the stern, Kirito boldly proclaimed, "Ahh, there's nothing so rich as generous friends."

"You're going to thank him properly the next time we meet. With a real gift."

"...Which we'll be splitting the cost of, I hope...?" Kirito asked nervously. Asuna only smiled back and turned to face forward.

It had only been a single day since the massive naval battle with the forest elves' fleet on the southern lake of the fourth floor, but it felt like ages since they'd ridden on a gondola. The beauty of the town lights reflecting on the water's surface, the occasional splash and spray, the gentle rocking of the prow as it carved through waves—it was indeed a joy to ride on a boat.

"You were just talking about making money as a middleman earlier; couldn't you make a business selling gondola tours on one of the big models?" Asuna suggested idly. "The NPC gondolas in Rovia can't go outside town, right?"

Her black-garbed gondolier took the suggestion quite seriously.

"Hmmm. I bet there's a demand. But there are monsters in the rivers outside…"

"Oh, good point. You can't run a business that involves any kind of danger to a player's safety…"

"But if you had smaller boats at the front and rear for security…or outfitted your passengers in heavy plate armor…"

"Sorry, forget about the cruising."

As they chatted, the gondola left the south gate of Rovia and made its way into the river that wove through the outer terrain. The rapids took them farther south and through the central caldera lake that had once been the site of their battle with the Biceps Archelon.

They did meet a few urchins, jellyfish, and giant crabs on their trip, but a single sword skill was enough for most of them as the gondola continued onward past the village of Usco, in the middle of the crescent lake, and into the canyon straits of the southern part of the floor. For the next ten-plus minutes, Kirito carefully guided the *Pequod*, which was larger than the *Tilnel*, ensuring it didn't hit any of the rocks, until they finally passed through the wall of white fog that marked the borderline between the regular field map and the instanced area—their own private copy of the destination.

As the elegant manor castle looming dark over the lake came into view, Asuna felt her heart leap in her chest.

It was just yesterday that she'd said farewell to the dark elf knight Kizmel at the labyrinth tower. But she couldn't stop the pangs of her heart with a reunion so close at hand.

The gondola slid onward over the mirrorlike surface of the lake until it slowly docked at the pier of Yofel Castle. If they put the rope around the mooring bitt on the dock, the game would ensure that only Agil, the gondola's proper owner, could release it again, so they simply jumped freely onto the pier instead.

Right next to the *Pequod* was a smaller gondola in white and green—the *Tilnel*, their own boat. Asuna whispered "we're back" to the craft, then looked to Kirito briefly before they set off for the castle gate ahead.

The dark, gleaming gate was still shut tight, guarded by warriors with halberds. But when Kirito brandished the Sigil of Lyusula on his left hand, they saluted him and began to open the heavy gate.

The ring gave them a free pass through the front door of the castle itself, and they headed up the large staircase to pay their respects to the castle owner. When they reached the fifth floor, they knocked on the heavy door to the right.

It was nearly midnight, but a familiar, beautiful voice emerged at once, telling them to enter.

Kirito shot Asuna a brief glance, then pulled the door open.

The first time they had come to this room, it had been as dark as could be, with heavy curtains covering all the windows, but the first thing Asuna saw this time was the warm orange light of a multitude of lanterns and candles. At the back of the office, seated across a large desk, was a tall, thin dark elf.

The master of Yofel Castle, Viscount Leyshren Zed Yofilis.

His wavy black hair was tied in the back, and an old scar running from his forehead through his left eye and down to his chin marred his otherwise beautiful features. He had shut himself in the darkness (supposedly) to hide that scar, which he called "proof of his greatest shame." The battle against the forest elves yesterday had apparently brought about a change of heart.

The viscount smiled at them both, his face a combination of youthful vitality and aged maturity.

"Kirito, Asuna, you have returned."

"Yes. We…er, had an agreement with you, my lord," Kirito said awkwardly. Even for him, it was a bit difficult to admit that they were only there to claim a quest reward. He looked over to his partner for help, but she ignored him and bowed to the viscount.

"Forgive us for intruding so late at night, my lord."

"I don't mind. You protected this castle from great danger; you are welcome at any time. Please sit."

At Yofilis's beckoning, they crossed the office and stood before the desk. There were no other NPCs in the large room.

"Um...where is Kizmel?" she asked, assuming the knight must be somewhere nearby. The viscount fixed her with his gray-green eye and shook his head.

"I'm sorry to tell you that she is no longer within the castle."

"Huh?!" both players exclaimed together.

Yofilis leaned forward and steepled his fingers atop the desk, explaining calmly, "At the order of the priests, Kizmel undertook the task of transporting the Jade Key and Lapis Key to the fortress on the fifth floor. She should have arrived by now."

"...Oh, I see..." Asuna mumbled, trying to contain her disappointment.

Yofilis let a faint smile crinkle across his lips as he said gently, "Kizmel wishes to see you, too, I'm certain. If you have the opportunity, I suggest you visit the fortress. That sigil will grant you passage."

"Yes...we will!"

"We'll go as soon as possible."

Yofilis smiled again and motioned to the right wall of the room. There was a heavy-looking chest sitting there.

"I have not yet given you your proper thanks and reward for saving my castle. As I said before, you each have your choice of any two items from the chest."

Asuna was about to jab Kirito with an elbow, given how openly relieved he looked that the offer was still on the table, but she was distracted by the appearance of a quest reward box with multiple options to select.

She found that she was just as excited about it as her partner.

She thanked their benefactor briefly and scrolled through the lengthy list.

It took an entire twenty-five minutes before both of them had made a final decision on their rewards. The viscount waited patiently, but unless she was imagining things, Asuna thought she saw him stifle a yawn two different times.

They stayed the night in the castle and had breakfast the following morning before taking the *Pequod* back to Rovia. Once they'd moored the gondola to the eastern dock, dropped the anchor, and affixed the rope to the bitt, they sent a message of thanks to Agil. The center square was still packed with tourists, so they had to squeeze their way through the crowds to get to the teleport square.

As she went from watery Rovia to ruined Karluin, Asuna pulled her hooded cape up around her mouth to brace against the cold, dusty breeze. But instead—

They emerged from the gate into an even wetter environment than they'd found in Rovia. And it came in the form of millions of airborne droplets, falling in a sheet from sky to ground.

"...Rain?" she muttered, looking up. Her face was instantly pelted with large drops, and she hurriedly pulled up her hood.

"Yep, this is rain," Kirito muttered in surprise, flipping up the lapels of his leather coat. That wasn't enough to block the onslaught of water, of course, and within moments his black hair was plastered to his forehead.

Wet hair was only an annoyance, but if armor got covered in water, it would suffer a waterlogged effect that made it harder to move.

"W-well, let's find someplace indoors to hide," Asuna suggested, looking around the square. Even despite the early hour of eight o'clock, the weather meant that there were few people around. Large puddles formed on the dark cobblestones, riddled with ripples from the constant downpour.

"But we've already eaten breakfast…And we just upgraded our weapons and don't have anything to buy at an item shop…"

"It doesn't matter where we go, as long as there's a roof!" Asuna hissed. Kirito thought it over for two seconds, then nodded, drops falling off the ends of his bangs.

"In that case, let's start whittling down the quests we picked up yesterday."

"In the middle of the rain?"

"Don't worry, there'll be a roof."

Kirito trotted off through the deluge, and she had no choice but to chase after him.

They splashed through the puddles of the square and into the north side of town, which they had yet to visit. After just a hundred feet or two, they came to another big plaza. In the middle of it was a large, crumbling ruin, but compared to the temple they'd been spelunking in yesterday, this one seemed more creepy and sinister.

Regardless, they plunged into the dark, dank ruins, which finally gave them some respite from the rain. Asuna brushed off the water clinging to her cape and skirt with both hands and exhaled at last.

She looked around to see that they were in a large dim space. The thick stone walls ahead and on either side had no doors, but set into the floor in the middle of the room was a descending staircase. Bizarre holy statues stood on either side, sending writhing shadows about the room in the flickering light of the fires, set in each corner.

"…What is this place?" she asked her partner, who was smacking off sheets of water from his coat. His answer was largely what she expected.

"The entrance to the underground catacombs I mentioned. There are other entrances, I guess, but this is the main one."

"Ahh…And there are quests that we complete here?"

"Oh yeah, a whole bunch."

Kirito swiped his wet bangs out of his eyes and opened his window, setting it to visible mode and showing Asuna his list of accepted quests.

"This one here, 'Little Lost Jenny,' is where you search for the girl's lost puppy or kitty or whatever. 'The Tasteless Collector' involves finding a certain type of relic, and the 'Thirty-Year Lament' is where you have to find some kind of wandering evil spirit—"

"*Nyet!*" Asuna squawked abruptly, covering Kirito's mouth with her hand.

Startled, he tried to mumble something through her palm, but she shot him a murderous look to silence him before finally letting go.

He stayed quiet for several moments, then faintly, hesitantly said, "…What was that *nyet* sound?"

"……It's 'no' in Russian."

"…Why did you say no?"

"…Because…erm…I don't want spoilers," she finished lamely—a weak excuse, in her opinion—but Kirito nodded seriously, quite convinced.

"Oh…yeah, good point. Quests necessary to beating the floor are one thing, but it's more fun to do these one-off quests without knowing the story beforehand…Okay, good idea. From now on, I won't explain or interject comments about quests. You can take the lead, Asuna."

He was so serious and earnest about it that she couldn't correct him now. She cleared her throat and looked down the stairs.

"Ah…yes. I-in that case, I'll go first. Are you all prepared?"

"Of course."

He lifted up his brand-new sword and rattled it at her.

There were two types of one-handed swords on the list of Viscount Yofilis's rewards. From what Asuna could see of their properties, the saber seemed stronger, but Kirito chose the Sword of Eventide instead.

Asuna mentally jotted down a reminder to ask him why at some point, but that wasn't important now. She took a deep breath, surrendered herself to her fate, and turned for the entrance to the underground graveyard.

"...Let's get going, then!"

"Yeah!"

At 8:20 AM on December 29, Asuna and Kirito began their conquest of the fifth floor of Aincrad in earnest.

4

TO ASUNA'S RELIEF, THE STAIRCASE DOWN DID NOT immediately plunge into eerie, ghostly ambience.

In fact, there were already several dozen players in the large room at the bottom of the stairs. They were gathered in little groups here and there, having meetings or eating breakfast— some even curled up in sleeping bags along the walls.

"...Is this a safe room?" Asuna asked, and Kirito turned to her with a baffled look on his face.

"On the contrary, we're still in the safe haven. The notice never appeared, right?"

"Oh...r-right..."

The tension left her shoulders, and she looked around again. With that fact in mind, she saw that hardly any of the players here were frontline warriors. Most of the parties had gear from the second or third floor, and some were unarmed tourists.

"So they're all here to find relics."

"That's what I expect. They've probably picked this room clean and are by now heading down into the subterranean ruins nearby..."

Suddenly, Kirito's face went stern. She prompted him with a quizzical look, and he shrugged his shoulders and mumbled:

"The first underground floor was within the safe haven in the beta. So no monsters and no traps. I'm guessing they've all come here to gather relics based on the news about that, but..."

"Is there something wrong with that?"

"...No, sorry, just overthinking things. C'mon, let's keep going, too."

Kirito started to lead the way, only to stop and motion for Asuna to go first. She swallowed a sigh and looked at the doorways leading out from each wall of the chamber.

Please let me come across the puppy or kitten quest first, she silently prayed, and chose the hallway on the north wall.

The room itself was brightly lit by a number of fires, but it was immediately dark and gloomy in the hallway, bringing a grimace to Asuna's face. Meanwhile, the rain they'd been trying to escape seemed to be seeping down through the walls, dripping here and there and occasionally landing on her head or shoulders.

With things this quiet, she was going to forget they were within the town's safe haven, so Asuna looked over her shoulder to start a conversation with Kirito.

"So I guess it does rain in Aincrad."

"Hasn't it rained a bunch of times before this already?"

"I don't recall it. I know there was snow during Christmas, but..."

"Oh, right. Well, it's true that it happens only rarely. In MMORPGs before this, rains and storms were a regular occurrence, but it's just a lot more unpleasant in a VRMMO. Like you saw, it ruins visibility; makes your gear heavy, your clothes stick to you; and it's real cold...It rained a lot more at the start of the beta, but they lowered the probability when the testers complained."

"Ahh, so that's what happened. It's too bad...I like watching the rain from the inside."

As they chatted, she eventually began to settle down. No matter how it looked, this place was still within the safety of town, and they would never see any monsters. They needed to chip away at the mountain of quests, gain a level, and prepare to tackle the floor for real.

She clenched the hilt of her rapier, feeling emboldened again.

Asuna opened her window along the way and checked her largely empty map, taking a side branch off the main hallway en route to the quest destination. They crab-walked sideways through the foot-wide corridor, then crawled through a tunnel only two feet tall (this time, she made Kirito go first) as they approached the marker.

Eventually they reached a place like a little chapel. There was a line of long pew benches, and next to the wall in the back was an eerie-looking crumbled statue. A number of candles here and there on the floor provided some light, but the corners of the space were plunged into darkness. It looked like the perfect place to find some relics, but there were no other players present.

Feeling a very bad premonition from the place, Asuna whispered to Kirito, "What quest happens in this spot?"

"Huh...? You want spoilers now?"

"Just tell me that much."

"Well, if you just want the title...it's the 'Thirty-Year Lament'!"

"..."

She successfully kept herself from giving away how aghast she was at her terrible luck and checked the quest log.

The quest story was quite simple. The client NPC was a middle-aged bachelor who had recently moved there from another town on the same floor, but he was disturbed by odd rattling noises and falling silverware late at night in his new home. He wanted help, so Asuna and Kirito had checked his basement, but couldn't find so much as a mouse. The log ended at a suggestion that they go farther down beneath the town.

"...So that means this chapel is directly beneath that man's house?" she asked.

Kirito grinned.

"It'll make sense if you switch your map."

"..."

She did as he said, going to her map tab and pressing the arrow buttons that switched between vertical levels, moving from the first underground level to the aboveground level. As he said, the present location marker underground and the quest NPC marker up in the town overlapped perfectly.

"...Ah, I see. So this is where the gho...the mystery vibrations are coming from," she corrected, closing the map and looking around the chapel again. But she didn't see anything that might have any effect on the home above, biological or not.

Normally her partner would take over and tell her the answer, but this time, he stayed back, like a teacher observing his pupil during the learning process. It was the result of a complete and total misunderstanding, but it was also true that she needed to be able to finish quests on her own by now. There was no guarantee that their temporary partnership would ever be permanent...

She made up her mind to solve this one on her own, and went over the information in her head.

A home in Karluin was suffering from ghos— From supernatural phenomena every night. The cause was believed to be subterranean, so they went to the spot in the underground catacombs beneath the house, where they found an obviously spooky and suspicious chapel. In order to find the source of the phenomenon, they could search all over the chapel for the appropriate object—or cause the phenomenon to happen before their eyes. They couldn't find anything, so they would need to attempt the latter.

Once she reached her conclusion, Asuna looked up. "Didn't that man say the house would rattle at around two in the morning?"

"He did," Kirito confirmed.

"Then...we'll need to come here at two o'clock to ascertain the nature of the sound, right?"

"Good thinking. That's the orthodox way to solve this. As a matter of fact, many quests are time restricted in this fashion."

"Look...I appreciate the compliment, but it's only nine o'clock right now. Are we just going to stand around here waiting until two in the morning?" she demanded, exasperated.

Kirito waved a finger theatrically. "We could, but it's also the case that such quests often have a bit of a shortcut. Just wait, and a hint will come along...ah, speak of the devil!"

He started to push her back, but she slapped his hand away. "What do you mean, a hint will come along?" she demanded, confused.

Suddenly, she heard creepy, scraping footsteps from behind her. She desperately held in the scream that nearly erupted from her throat and darted behind Kirito, reminding herself that she was in the safety of town.

Standing silently in the doorway they'd passed through just minutes before was a small NPC, like a child. Its face was hidden behind the hood of a deep gray coat, but its bare feet were extremely large compared to the rest of its figure and its arms equally extraordinary in their length. In its left hand hung a dirty sack, and in its right, a long candle.

The color cursor was yellow, which guaranteed that it was an NPC, but she couldn't be sure as to its humanity. As she watched fearfully over Kirito's shoulder, the small man (she thought) dragged and slapped its feet across the chapel, approaching one of the little candle piles found here and there.

It squatted and pulled a fresh candle out of the sack, lighting it from the tiny, nearly spent one and placing the fresh one on the ground. Then it moved to the next pile and repeated the process. It seemed to be a manager of sorts for the underground chapel, but the species of the thing was still uncertain.

He must have been what Kirito called the "hint." In that case, she had to be brave and get her information. It might look scary, but that was just a design. It was no more than data. She summoned her courage, stepped out from behind her partner, and strode forward to speak to the little man.

"H...hello."

"..."

He came to a dead standstill, then slowly, awkwardly turned to face her. The hood was totally dark, but two eyes glowed dully within it.

"Um…are you the one refilling all the candles here?" she asked for starters. The little man silently nodded. Relieved that they could at least communicate with each other, she continued, "Um, have you ever seen anything strange happen here late at night?"

"…"

The little man did not reply, so she wondered if her question was a little too vague, but his long pause was broken by a rasping voice.

"I don't come here at night. I wake up in the morning and light candles. During day, I add candles. At night, I put out candles and sleep."

He resumed walking away. Once he had put down a fresh candle at the last pile, he shuffled his way out of the chapel.

Once the little man's footsteps were gone, Asuna thought it was over. If his words were to be believed, the candles lit the chapel from morning until evening. She had no concrete times, but it suggested that at two o'clock, in the dead of night, the chapel would be pitch-black.

"Ah…"

She looked over at Kirito. He didn't say anything. She went to the nearest pile of candles, crouched, and blew them out. The chapel got about a quarter darker and eerier than before, but she was certain this was the answer.

"Blow out those candles, Kirito!" she ordered, extinguishing the next pile.

When he finished the last pile moments later, the chapel plunged into total darkness. It was impossible to move around like that, so Asuna was about to open her window to pull out her own lantern when a pale blue light illuminated her hands.

"Th-thanks…" she said, looking up to thank her partner for his consideration, but Kirito was at a distance, his hands empty. She looked around, wondering where the source of light was.

The floor in the center of the room was glowing faintly.

It wasn't the glowing moss from the spider's cave on the third floor, nor was it a magic item with light properties. There was no warmth from it…In fact, the empty light seemed to fill the room with an icy chill.

"*Hyoooo…*"

A sound like the rustling of branches disturbed the chapel air. Asuna bolted upright, her body stiff.

Something was seeping through the floor and taking shape. It was a pale, transparent, twig-thin hand.

…*Pleasepleasepleaseplease, nonononononono.*

Of course, her silent plea did not stop the thing from transforming. It rose from the floor with another wail of hatred—next an arm, then a shoulder. Long, stringy hair, a scrawny body…It was a woman. But where her eyes should have been were only red flickering fires, and sharp fangs jutted from her mouth.

No matter how hard Asuna focused on it, no cursor appeared. But it clearly wasn't an NPC or a player. It was a monster—no, a ghost.

The apparition, which took its sweet time appearing in full to really make the most of its terror, brandished hands with long nails like claws and emitted a third shriek.

"*Hyoooooh…!!*"

Suddenly, the entire chapel rattled violently. The pews fell over, one after the other, and fine pieces of stone fell from the walls and ceiling. She had to stand firm, or she might lose her balance…but her body wouldn't listen. All her senses grew distant, and her stiff body toppled like a stick—

"Whoa there," went a voice in her ear as thin but powerful arms propped up her back. Somehow, Kirito was now standing right next to her.

"Oh…you didn't like it? I thought it was kind of a cool haunted house effect…"

Then he noticed Asuna's abnormal state.

"You okay?"

She tried to reassure her concerned partner, but her mouth wouldn't work properly. He sensed her predicament, slipped his left arm around to cradle her, walking her over to the wall.

The ghost continued to wail as he did so, and the chapel only vibrated harder. It was clearly the source of the quest giver's troubles, but that was as far as Asuna's mind could work. She shut her eyes as tight as she could in Kirito's arms, praying that it would disappear soon.

The next fifteen seconds felt like many times more than that, but at last the rocking began to subside. The ghost's voice calmed, trailed off, and vanished.

As silence returned, Asuna let out the breath she'd been holding in. When her numbed senses returned to her, she realized Kirito's arm was around her, prompting a rise of embarrassment. She opened her eyes to tell him that it was fine, that she could stand on her own...

About a foot away from her nose was a ghostly face, emitting a pale blue light.

"*Yaaaaaaaah!!*"

Asuna let out an ear-piercing scream that far eclipsed the ghost's, clutched Kirito with all her might, and buried her face into his black leather coat.

When had she become so afraid of ghostly things? She didn't even remember the reason why.

Asuna wasn't afraid of anything supernatural. Depending on the type, some kinds of traditional Japanese *yokai* were even cute, and she tended to like zombie movies. But the ones she couldn't handle were anything "ghostly"—the things without a body, that could appear and disappear at will, floating through walls and floors. The unease of not knowing if they were truly there was what got to her.

She'd fought a great variety of monsters since being trapped in *SAO* but had yet to face a single noncorporeal ghost monster. She'd been hoping this meant they hadn't been programmed in, but that was clearly a pipe dream. Kirito had mentioned an "evil spirit" earlier, and sure enough, the source of the rattling that plagued the old man's house was none other than an eerie apparition.

Now that spiritual creature was floating just inches away, watching Asuna with eerie glowing eyes.

With that in mind, there was absolutely no way she could remove her face from Kirito's jacket. She wanted to do this quest on her own to reduce her dependency on her temporary partner, and it took all of a single instant to blow that determination to shreds. It was all she could do to keep her mouth shut and not scream again.

After what felt like ten seconds had passed, her partner mumbled, "Um...Miss Asuna...?"

She kept her face pressed to his jacket so as not to see anything and rasped, "I-is the ghost gone now?"

"Umm...no, it's right here..."

"*Yaaaaaah!!*"

She screamed again, but there was no helping it now. She shook her head back and forth rapidly and pleaded with him like a little child: "Make it go away! Drive it off right now!!"

"W-well, we have to move the quest onward for that..."

"Then move us onward!!"

Kirito tried to break free from her, but Asuna only clutched his coat tighter. "No, stay like this!!"

"G...gotcha."

He tried to keep Asuna's body in place as he turned slightly to speak to the ghost. "Umm, Miss Ghost...why are you rampaging in this chapel?"

After a few moments came an echoing voice that sounded like whistling wind. Asuna felt a scream seize her throat, but she kept it in, just in time.

"...Because...I cannot leave..."

"Why can't you leave?"

"...I am locked...inside of this place..."

It was still scary, of course, but the voice seemed more tinged with sadness than hatred. That recognition helped Asuna's mind work a little smoother, and even with her face pressed to Kirito's chest, she realized something.

When they entered the chapel, the door was a bit out of alignment, but it wasn't locked. And it was a ghost without a body, so it should be able to just swoop through any door or wall as it pleased.

Because Kirito shared the same suspicion—well, more like because he knew the proper conversation pattern to complete the quest—he was able to get through the ghostly conversation quite smoothly.

She (?) had been trapped inside this chapel thirty years earlier, when she was still alive.

The one who locked her inside was the man she had promised her life to.

Her hatred of him was what kept her chained to this place.

Once all of the above information had been related, the ghost's presence faded. Asuna still wouldn't take her face out of Kirito's jacket, so he carefully prompted, "Umm, Miss Asuna…?"

"…Did it go away?"

"Y-yeah, for now."

"…And it won't come back?"

"Y-yeah, for now."

She let out a deep sigh and felt her shoulders relax. With the end of the ghost show, her fear was ebbing away, only to be replaced by a rising discomfort.

After all, she had screamed at the top of her lungs and buried her face into her partner's chest, where it still rested. She had no idea how she could extract herself from the situation and maintain any face.

As she stayed frozen and downturned, she heard Kirito's equally uncomfortable voice say, "Umm, well…sorry for not noticing that you had trouble with the…astral types…"

The unfamiliar term caused her to lift her head a bit.

"…Astral?"

"It's a category of monster. Kobolds and goblins are demihumans, giant spiders and mantids are insects, golems and gargoyles are enchanted, and so on. Specters and wraiths like the one we just saw—basically, undead without solid bodies—are astral types. The other undead with proper bodies like ghouls and skeletons are classified as living dead."

"Ahh..."

When he laid it out and explained it like that, it helped reinforce the concept that this was all just data on a computer, ghostly or not. Asuna counted to three and forced herself to pull away.

Once she had looked around to ensure the coast was indeed clear, she took a step away from Kirito—who was kneeling on the floor—put her hands on her hips, and announced, "I was only startled by how abruptly it appeared. That's all."

"...R-right..."

"Yes, I might not like ghosts...or astrals or whatever, but isn't that true for most girls?"

"...R-right..."

"So let's forget that ever happened and not bother with mentioning it in the future."

"...R-right..."

Having agreed with her thrice, Kirito got to his feet. Based on prior experience, she took the twitching of his nostrils as a sign of an intense internal battle over whether or not to tease her, and she fixed him with a glare.

"And absolutely no childish pranks!"

"Yes, ma'am..." he replied like a scolded boy, and began to relight the candles. At last, Asuna felt comfortable enough to crack a tiny smile again.

They searched the area of the ghost's appearance and picked up a gold pendant marked as a quest item, then returned to town. When they had an NPC identify the pendant, it turned out to be not a relic, but the signifier of a rich merchant family in Karluin. They headed for the family's mansion.

After a brief argument with the guard at the gate, they were allowed to meet the fifty-something leader of the family, whom they showed the pendant from the underground chapel. He broke into tears and admitted to his past sin. He had grown tired of the girl he was betrothed to thirty years ago and lured her into the chapel under the guise of relic hunting. As he locked her inside, she tore the pendant from his grasp.

Asuna wanted to punch him right in the kisser, but Kirito warned her that it would cut the quest short, so she held it in and followed the man back to the subterranean chapel. They put out the candles again, the wraith girl appeared, and the merchant got down on hands and knees to grovel and apologize for his crime. The ghost vanished at last; they escorted the man back to his mansion, received some rewards, and had just closed the door to his office when a terrific rattling started. Upon opening the door, the man was nowhere to be seen...A rather chilling but satisfying end to the "Thirty-Year Lament" quest.

As they left the mansion for the center square again, Kirito idly checking out his quest rewards, Asuna remarked, "You know... that quest seems like a very bad example for children."

"Hmm? Ahh...true. The NerveGear's not for use for kids under thirteen, and *SAO* had a recommended age rating of fifteen and up, so there aren't any actual children here...I think."

"Yes, I suppose..."

Now that he mentioned it, Asuna had turned fifteen just a month before *SAO* launched, so she'd just barely made it inside the rating level.

If she was still fourteen on November 6, would she not have even played the game? Would she have given up on borrowing her brother's NerveGear and successfully escaped the fate of this deadly trap?

...No, she ultimately decided. When she snuck into her brother's room on the day he was unluckily—or luckily—on an overseas assignment and put the already-set-up NerveGear on her head, she hadn't even bothered to glance at the game's age rating.

But she had supposedly given up regretting the past when she left the inn room in the Town of Beginnings. Now the only thing to do was keep her eye on the impossibly distant hundredth floor...and push onward in an attempt to beat the game. And if any astral-type monsters appeared, she would simply have to make a brief detour.

"…Well, let's get going with the next quest…There better not be any ghosts in the puppy quest. Are there?" she asked her partner.

This time, he couldn't help but grin evilly.

"Probably not. But you never know, it might be a ghost dog."

Once they had finished the other two underground quests (fortunately not horror themed) and wrapped up the others in town, it was the evening hour, and they had both gained a level—Kirito to 18, Asuna to 17.

As they walked the same path from the previous night to the restaurant and inn, Asuna grumbled to her partner, "For some reason, I don't seem likely to catch up to you in level at all."

"Huh…?"

"Well, the amount of experience needed to gain a level is higher for you than me, right? So how is it possible that you're always exactly one level higher than I am?"

"Oh, right…" Kirito thought about how to answer the question and awkwardly scratched his head. "Well, there's no party bonus to experience gained in *SAO*, so when multiple people beat a monster, its experience is split among them, but it's not an even split…It takes into account the damage and debuffing inflicted, as well as time spent targeted and stuff like that. Our current battle pattern usually involves me pulling aggro all the time, so…"

"…Ah, I see…"

In that case, she couldn't really complain. When they encountered a monster, Kirito always attacked first and used a sword skill; then, she switched in and did a normal attack, then finished it with a sword skill of her own. But since that order caused Kirito to be the one targeted, it was natural that he wound up with more experience. And given that he had much more knowledge, experience, and technique than she did, it wasn't logical for Asuna to take over that role.

"Hrrm…" she grumbled, unable to accept this fact at face value.

Kirito eventually offered a weak follow-up. "H-hey, we're getting to the point where one level hardly means any difference...
And we're both well within the safety margin, so you shouldn't
worry about it..."

"Rrrmmm," she said, nodding despite her frown.

Kirito was right, of course, and she was not planning to lobby
for a switch in combat duties, but she still felt miserable about it.

Ever since coming to the fifth floor, she felt like her worst qualities were on display. She let her greed come out when searching
for relics; screamed at the astral monster; and even asked for a
personal duel, only to surrender before either of them swung a
single blow. She was at least hoping to catch her partner in level,
but it only served to remind her that she was relying on him even
in normal combat.

Yes, their partnership might be temporary, but she did not
want to be the one always getting helped. She had to provide a
benefit, something she could offer the other.

...I need to think of what I can do.

No sooner had she come to that resolution than she walked
right through the restaurant door Kirito was holding open for
her and scolded herself for not realizing it.

Even on the third night within the fifth floor, the Blink & Brink
restaurant was surprisingly barren. It was the height of mealtime,
but there were no players on the outdoor terrace or inside the
restaurant.

"Huh...?" Kirito exclaimed as he sat at the same table as last
time, examining the menu.

"What's wrong?"

"Well...that blueberry tart hasn't sold out yet...I would have
figured that by now they'd be lining up for it before the restaurant even opens."

"That's surprising...Especially since so many people are hunting for relics underground. Have they been doing it without the
sight bonus, then?"

"I suppose so…"

Meanwhile, the NPC waitress arrived to take their order, so they stopped to handle business. They shared a toast of fickle-wine for a good day's work—white for Asuna, sparkling red for Kirito—and took a sip.

Kirito downed half of his wine in one go, then examined the bubbling flute glass and said, "I like the flavor, but I don't think the sparkling red thing will take off…"

"Oh, that's a real thing. There's Lambrusco from Italy, and Shiraz from Australia, and so on."

"Whaaat, for real? You're so knowledgeable, Professor Asuna," he replied, eyes wide with wonder.

She denied it with a smug smile, then looked down and added, "It's not like that knowledge has any value here…"

"That's not true."

"Huh?"

She looked up at Kirito's dead-serious expression.

"There are plenty of times where real-world knowledge comes in handy when solving quests and puzzles…Besides, Aincrad might look like a fantasy world at first glance, but it's not a true otherworld. We and the NPCs all speak Japanese, and player interactions are all rooted in modern Japanese values. It's a taboo to talk about the other side, but we can't just completely ignore it like that…"

"…Mmm…" Asuna nodded. Her partner looked back at the menu, hoping to change the topic and mood.

"So anyway, knowing they're still selling the blueberry tart makes me want to eat one. The buff's great and all, but I like the taste."

"I agree," Asuna said, recalling the refreshing tang of the blueberries and the thick creaminess of the custard. "But I wonder why it doesn't sell out. You wouldn't find a better buff for hunting relics."

"Maybe Argo didn't put it in her strategy guide? Or, in fact," Kirito noted, looking toward the teleport square, "I don't think

I saw the Rat's strategy guide in the item shop at all. Maybe she hasn't started consigning them yet."

"Now that you mention it…until now, the first volume of her guide has always been out by the following evening after the floor opens."

"Hmm. Well, I'm sure she has her own circumstances…Maybe I should shoot her a message."

Kirito set down his fork and opened his menu, quickly typing out a message on the holo-keyboard. A few seconds later, he frowned.

"…It won't send…"

"Maybe she's on another floor?" Asuna suggested.

Kirito looked away shiftily and muttered, "No…that was a friend message."

This came as quite a surprise to Asuna, who was his temporary partner but not registered as a friend of his. She let out a very long and pointed "*Ohhhhhhh?*"

Kirito hastily explained, "Er, it's just…I buy lots of info from her and offer her my own from time to time, so it's just more convenient to have her registered…"

"I didn't say anything," she noted with a smile, only to consider the new information for a moment.

A regular instant message could be sent to any player whose name you knew (and could spell properly in the Western alphabet), but the space restrictions were severe, and it wouldn't arrive unless you were both on the same floor. Meanwhile, the more expansive "friend messages" could be sent to any registered friend, regardless of floor, as long as they weren't in a dungeon or instanced map.

"So that could mean Argo's in a dungeon right now," Asuna suggested, to which Kirito nodded seriously.

"Yeah…probably. But I don't recall if there was any information in this dungeon important enough to delay the release of her floor guide…"

"What do you mean, 'this dungeon'?"

"Oh…" Kirito glanced down at the terrace floor. "The first level of the underground catacombs we were wandering around in today is within the safe haven, so the message would reach her there. But starting on the second level, it's treated like a dungeon and is technically outside of town."

"Oh…I see. How many levels are there?"

"Three, I think. There's an area boss at the bottom, and if you beat it, that opens up a shortcut tunnel to the next town."

"So it's not just a minor sub-dungeon. I suppose it wouldn't be out of the question for Argo to go collect information from a necessary dungeon…"

Kirito bobbed his head, still wearing an unconvinced frown. "Yeah…maybe you're right. It's a dungeon linked to town, so I'm sure she wants to cover it thoroughly in her first issue."

"I'm sure she'll just pop out of nowhere, like she always does."

"Yeah…C'mon, let's eat."

With a grin at last, Kirito closed his window and picked up the fork again.

Since they weren't sold out yet, the two decided to order the blue-blueberry tarts again and call it a night, renting a room on the second floor of Blink & Brink, which acted as an inn.

In the hallway, they agreed on a meet-up time for the morning, bid each other good night, and opened adjacent doors. Asuna paused for a second, but Kirito yawned hugely and disappeared into his room, so she followed suit and slammed her door shut.

She opened her window to her equipment mannequin, bashed the REMOVE button twice so that she was in her underwear, then dove into her bed. Once she'd buried her face into the big pillow, she grumbled a series of interjections: "Hmph! Fine! I don't care anyway!"

Logically, she understood. There was no merit to friending Kirito at the present time. Given that they were currently a team working together, they wouldn't possibly get split on different floors, so instant messages would serve if they needed to talk remotely.

But emotionally, she couldn't help but wonder why he didn't just ask. All he had to do was phrase it like, *"Well, should we register, too, just in case?"* and she'd be fine with answering a simple *"Sure, I don't see why not."*

As she lay in bed, grumbling away, she played back the conversation with Kirito the previous evening.

How long are you planning to work with me?

Until you're strong enough to not need me.

Maybe that was where Kirito wanted to draw the line. They were partners, not friends…so when the time inevitably came for them to split apart, it would be easier to do so if they weren't registered as friends.

"…No. He's just that inconsiderate and thoughtless," she grunted, then relaxed at last and rolled over. She looked up at the ceiling—flickering with the play of light and shadow cast by the room's lantern—and muttered, "Fine. One day I'll ask you for that friend status…once I'm just as tough as you."

She stretched her arms up, clutching the hands together, then rocked back and used the momentum to bound upward. Deciding to take a bath, Asuna looked around the room but saw nothing resembling a bathroom door. Tapping the wall brought up a reference window for the room, which showed on its map that there were no attached bathrooms; there was only a large one at the end of the upstairs hall.

She panicked briefly, thinking of the great bath hall at Yofel Castle, then realized that unlike that mixed bath, this one was properly separated by sex. However, it wasn't clear if that was actually a rule or merely a directive advising good behavior.

Just in case, she put on her casual wear and set it up so she could equip the swimsuit she'd crafted on the fourth floor if necessary, then headed out. She had just turned the first corner toward the bath, which was on the opposite end of the floor from the staircase, when she heard a door open and close behind her, and instinctually flattened herself against the wall.

When she peered around the corner, a figure was walking away down the dim hallway. She was momentarily relieved, but then her eyes bulged.

It was only a silhouette, but she couldn't mistake that form. It was Kirito. He was outfitted in his usual full garb of long coat and boots, and she could make out the graceful hilt of his new Sword of Eventide over his shoulder.

It was already past nine at night. Maybe he was only leaving for a bit of gear maintenance, but there was something hard and resolute in his walk.

He was probably going to venture into the underground cata-combs to search for Argo the Rat.

"...Why does he have to be so standoffish?" she grumbled, reaching up to open her menu window. On her equipment man-nequin, she activated her breastplate, leather skirt, and Chivalric Rapier. The bath could wait—she was going to follow the man.

Yes, she'd briefly sulked about the friend registration matter, but Argo was also a good friend to Asuna. Aincrad might be big, but Argo was the only one who called her by a nickname like "A-chan." If Argo was in danger, it only made sense to forego her own comforts to help her.

The hallway was empty. She raced down the stairs two at a time, darted past the NPC at the desk—who issued a generic "Have a nice trip"—and leaped out the front door of Blink & Brink.

5

SHE HAD LEFT ONLY A MINUTE AFTER HIM, BUT SHE didn't see her partner at all on the straight path to the main part of town. He must have started sprinting as soon as he'd left.

If it weren't for the fact that he would only pull farther ahead while she typed, she would send him an instant message. So the only option was to run. But no matter how many corners she turned, she never caught sight of Kirito's back.

"…Geez, how hard is he running?" she grumbled as the back alley joined the main road and the number of people in the vicinity grew. She looked around and exhaled in relief when she spotted a familiar-looking shape up ahead.

But she didn't want to yell out to him and draw attention in a crowded place, so she had no choice but to continue her pursuit. Kirito nimbly raced on, avoiding players and NPCs alike, cutting through the teleport square and into the north side of town. When he reached the plaza that contained the entrance to the catacombs, he ran straight into the ruins without stopping.

"Ah, hey, wait a minute!" she called out belatedly, but he didn't seem to hear. Less than a minute later, she reached the temple ruins and stopped at the descending staircase that yawned from the floor.

Briefly, a horrible feeling of anxiety crawled through her chest.

But she didn't have the option of turning back now. She opened her menu, deciding to prioritize meeting up, and sent him a brief message reading, WAIT IN THE B1 ROOM SO I CAN JOIN YOU.

But the window immediately gave her a curt error message: THIS PERSON IS EITHER IN AN INACCESSIBLE LOCATION OR IS NOT LOGGED IN.

"Wha...?"

She gasped, looking up at her left corner, but Kirito's HP bar was still there, a consequence of being in the same party. So the ominous latter option in the error message was not the case. She sent the message again, just to make sure she hadn't misspelled his name, but the result was the same.

The first basement level of the catacombs was treated as inside the town, so she should be able to send him a message. If it hadn't worked, that meant that in the span of less than a minute, Kirito had reached the second level, which was classified as a dungeon.

It was hard to believe, but there was no other answer. She would have to give up and return to the inn.

...*No.*

She had told herself she didn't just want to be a person who was protected all the time. If she turned back now, she would never be an equal partner to him. It would be all right—she'd gained the knowledge and instincts to fend for herself over the last fifty days.

"...I'll catch up to you soon," she swore under her breath, and stepped onto the staircase.

Even at this time of night, the large entry room serving as base camp for the town's relic hunters was dotted with players, but Kirito was, of course, not among them.

She opened her window and checked the map tab. They'd run all over doing quests earlier today, so they'd mapped out about 80 percent of the first level, but there was still some of it grayed out. In particular, they hadn't set foot through the south door of the room.

There were no markers for descending staircases in what she'd mapped out already, so if it was anywhere, it would be through that door. She closed her window, crossed the chamber, and pushed the mossy stone door.

Unlike with the doors to the north, east, and west, there was no hallway. It opened onto a small room with another descending staircase in the middle. The second level of the dungeon had to be down there. No wonder Kirito had been able to pass through the first level in less than a minute.

As Asuna approached, she noticed a small placard set to the side. It had a handwritten Japanese note reading, *Not safe haven below, be warned.* It was probably meant to ensure relic hunters didn't find themselves in trouble.

For an item, a signboard had a pretty long life span, but even that was just twenty-four hours. Whoever had spent the money on this was probably refreshing it each day, but she was going to ignore that warning.

After a final check of her gear and confirmation that her potions were easily accessible from her waistpouch, she carefully headed down the darkened stairs.

Fortunately, the staircase was short, and in just twenty steps she was down on the second basement level. The moment she stepped into the small room below, which was indistinguishable from the one above, a warning reading OUTSIDE FIELD appeared. Beyond this point, the Anti-Criminal Code would not protect her.

The bluish stone walls and cracked floor looked much the same as the first level. But the chill of the air on her skin and the toughness of the stone floor on the soles of her boots felt undeniably different from the floor above.

It wasn't her first experience going into a dungeon alone, of course. She'd spent up to three or four days in sub-dungeons and the labyrinth tower of the first floor alone, battling constantly. And she was much stronger now than she was then.

The recommended level for this dungeon was about 12, and Asuna was currently 17. As long as she could handle the astral types and remained no more than two staircases from the safety of the town, there was no reason at all to fear.

Asuna brushed her bare legs to drive away the chill and began to walk.

The little room had only one exit, so she headed through it into a long hallway. The walls alternated between weak torches that looked ready to go out at any moment and small doors. It was nice to have any light at all, but the thought of checking at least a dozen doors one by one was tiresome.

But if Kirito was down here to search for Argo, he would be looking through all of them. She was only a few minutes behind him, so the possibility was high that she'd open a door and run smack into him.

Perhaps if she shouted at the top of her lungs he would hear, but it would also attract the attention of monsters. She decided to search the slow way, walking over to the closest door and listening through the rusted metal before pushing it open.

The room was darker than the hallway, lit by only a few candles set into nooks in the far wall. She didn't see any players or monsters in the narrow room, but there was a rectangular box placed near the back. It would be quite large for a treasure chest, but upon closer examination, she was still wrong. It was a coffin. But of course—this entire dungeon was a giant tomb.

Asuna simply closed the door, knowing that nothing good could come from approaching or opening that box. She exhaled, carefully walked to the next door, and opened it. Another tomb with a coffin inside of it and no people. She shut the door quickly.

The third and fourth were the same thing. She was beginning to get impatient and was ready to close the fifth door just as fast—when she suddenly froze.

Something was glowing along the back wall.

It wasn't reflecting the light of the candles. The dim white glow was the same as the kind emitted in the temple of Karluin the night before. She checked her HP bar and saw that the buff icon of the eye was lit. She still had some of the Blink & Brink tart effect active.

That meant the source of the white light was a relic that hadn't been picked up yet.

"…"

After a bout of hesitation, Asuna decided to step into the crypt. The relic-finding bonus lasted for sixty minutes, so it probably didn't have much longer. It would be a waste to let it drift away without making use of it…

She snuck across the thirty feet of the crypt, toward the back wall. The glowing object was in a crack in the stone floor, and when lifted up, she found it to be an ancient silver pendant. Asuna wouldn't know its worth until it was appraised, so she put it in her pouch and turned to leave the room.

There was a heavy scraping noise.

Gruk, gruk, like a stone pestle, coming from the right. She glanced aside, overcome by an intense foreboding.

The instinctual guess of a stone pestle was actually not far off. It was indeed the sound of heavy stone-on-stone scraping—in this case, the lid of a sarcophagus, as moved by its body.

"~~~!"

Asuna clamped her lips shut to lock down the scream and pulled the Chivalric Rapier loose from her waist. Meanwhile, a glowing humanoid figure was emerging from the half-opened coffin with a wail like whistling wind.

It was very similar to the ghost of the vengeful girl from the "Thirty-Year Lament." The major difference was a pale red cursor hovering over the thing's head. The HP bar contained the name MOURNFUL WRAITH.

It was a monster. An angry spirit that could hurt her.

"*Hyoooooh…*"

The wraith wailed, spread its arms, and pounced at her. Even knowing in the rational part of her mind that it was just data on a computer, she wasn't able to completely overcome her fear. She scurried backward to the right corner of the crypt as she swung her sword at the thing.

Her boots landed on a particularly large stone, which receded a bit with a tiny *click*.

Under normal circumstances, Asuna would notice the aberration and leap away, even without knowing what it was. But she was so focused on controlling her fear of the ghost that her reaction to the change was late.

Before she knew what was happening, the stone swung downward into a trapdoor. Asuna plunged through the narrow hole and fell without a sound.

Her first thought was the height.

In a way, the only thing scarier than a floor boss, universally capable of instantly killing even the hardiest warrior, was fall damage. It varied based on maximum HP, strength, agility, and the terrain of the landing ground, but even at level 17, if Asuna fell over thirty feet headfirst onto hard ground, she could easily die on impact.

The silver lining was that the hole was narrow, so her body wouldn't rotate in midair. She just had to pray it wasn't a long fall, and brace her feet.

The moment she left the hole, she saw a stone floor much like the one on the second level. It had been about a thirteen-foot fall. She let go of her rapier to brace herself, and when her shoes hit the floor, she bent her legs and rolled. She did two backward somersaults until her back hit a wall, stopping her cold.

The impact was intense, but her HP loss was just under 10 percent. She stayed frozen for several moments, making sure nothing else would happen.

The trapdoor had vanished from the ceiling above, and the wraith's wailing could not be heard. She slowly let out the air trapped in her chest and rearranged her thoughts.

Asuna thought she had conquered her fear of ghosts—or astral monsters, rather—but she'd totally lost her cool and failed to notice that she wandered into a trap because of it. It was pathetic, but the important thing was to react and recover rather than regret her mistake. She had to assess the situation and take the smartest possible action.

Her first priority was to return to the second level of the dungeon from the bottom floor. That meant step one was to examine her surroundings anew.

Asuna slowly got to her feet and looked around in search of the Chivalric Rapier she'd dropped during the fall.

The silver sword was resting about six feet away.

But there was also something else there.

A humanoid creature with bluish skin, just barely a foot and a half tall, with a rodent-like extended snout, and large yellow eyes glowing at her.

The little monster looked up at Asuna and skittered with mocking laughter. Then it picked up the rapier, which was longer than it was tall; tucked it under its arm; and darted off at unbelievable speed.

"Hey, wait!" she yelled, but that had never stopped a robber before. The little creature melted into the darkness, leaving behind only a cursor labeled SLY SHREWMAN.

If she let it pull away until the cursor disappeared, she instantly knew she would never find it again. Asuna tore after the thief.

As she ran, she noted that her surroundings were less of a man-made structure and more like a natural cave. The only light sources were glowing patches of moss on the rock walls, which made it hard to even see the floor ahead. She'd need to pull a torch out of her inventory and light it to avoid tripping, but that wasn't possible at a full sprint. She just kept running, praying that luck would keep her from slipping on the uneven, slippery ground.

Thanks to the Sprint skill that she'd replaced her Tailoring skill with a few days ago, she caught sight of a small silhouette in the darkness ahead after just thirty seconds or so. The Sly Shrewman turned back briefly, then skittered again, a bit more panicked this time.

"You're not…getting away…from me!" she shouted just loud

enough for the rodent thing to hear, and leaned forward as far as she could, stretching in an attempt to grab the thief's twitching tail. Her fingertips brushed the tip of the tail, glanced off it, then finally seized it tight on the third try—when her right foot plunged into a puddle.

The sole of the boot lost its grip and her body toppled forward. She was just barely able to avoid smashing her face into the ground, but she still landed hard on her butt in the water, sending up a large splash. The shrewman darted off.

The light pink cursor vanished silently from her view. All Asuna was left with was the unpleasant sensation of cold water seeping into her skirt.

It took a full fifteen seconds for her to get to her feet.

She made her way to the wall with heavy footsteps, the hem of her skirt and the ends of her hair dripping water. Once she found a dry stretch of ground, she sank down to her knees.

Her sword was gone…Her lifeline in this world, the Chivalric Rapier +5 that harbored the soul of her old Wind Fleuret.

The loss and fear of that shock bounced back and forth in her mind, impeding other thoughts. She needed to regain her wits and take the optimum actions now, but her head felt heavy and dull, robbing her of the ability to even identify what she ought to think.

Her right hand moved slowly in the darkness down her right side, but the only thing the fingers touched was cold rock, and not the partner who was always with her.

Yes…if Kirito were here, he would tell her exactly what she needed to do. He would track down the shrewman through some means Asuna couldn't begin to guess and get her sword back.

"Kirito…"

He did not answer her plea. She looked up at the cave ceiling, lit faintly by the glowing mosses. Somewhere in that direction on the second floor of the dungeon was Kirito. He might be only a few dozen feet away from her at this very moment.

Asuna sucked in a deep breath, preparing to shout out the name of her partner with all her strength.

But when she pulled her lips back to form the "*Ki*," they were trembling.

She wanted to call him. She wanted to scream his name over and over, sobbing like a pleading child. She wanted to cling to the possibility that he would appear out of nowhere and solve her problem like magic.

But she was in the bottom floor of the catacombs beneath Karluin on the fifth floor of Aincrad. As of December 29, it was literally the front line of player progress. The monsters here would be more powerful than any seen thus far, and yelling to draw attention to herself without a weapon in hand was nothing short of suicidal.

She pulled her hand up and clamped it over her mouth. The urge to scream and cry was overwhelming, but she held it in, letting only silent tears leave her.

She was scared. She was alone. She wanted to go back to town right away.

Asuna had never felt fear like this when she had been alone in the first-floor labyrinth tower. She worked her gear down to the breaking point, and if she happened to die, then that was that.

Since then, her gear and stats had grown much more powerful. So was her inability to even stand on her own feet now a sign that her heart had grown weaker? Had meeting Kirito and fighting alongside him caused her to lose that solitary strength?

No.

That wasn't true. The only reason that the old her didn't feel fear was because she had given up. The reason she was so afraid now was because she had found a reason to survive and keep living.

In fact, Asuna had found a new goal for herself just today: to be as strong as Kirito so she could ask him to be official friends with her. She couldn't give up on that now. She would make use of the knowledge he'd so liberally given her and return alive. There was no other choice.

As soon as she swore that oath to herself, she heard her partner's voice echo in her ears.

Kirito had told her about a similar situation once—just after she'd lost her Wind Fleuret to that upgrading scam, and he'd recovered it by using the MATERIALIZE ALL ITEMS button. She could still clearly recall his words.

—So he finds a spot he thinks is safe, then does the "materialize all items" trick, dumping all his stuff onto the floor at his feet. The problem is, there are looting mobs in that dungeon! All these little gremlins come pouring out of the woodwork to grab everything off the floor, stuff it into their sacks, and scamper off. It takes him five whole hours to hunt down each and every one of those gremlins to get his stuff back...I tell you, it brought a tear to my eye...

The "little gremlins" in Kirito's tale had to refer to the shrewman. He'd acted like it was a story relayed to him by another player, but she figured it had to be firsthand experience. Looting mobs had the Robbing skill, which immediately overwrote the owner of an item, so even the MATERIALIZE ALL button wouldn't bring it back, he'd claimed. Trying that again now would be no use. If she wanted her Chivalric Rapier back, she needed to defeat that shrewman.

"...Fine. I'll do it," she mumbled into her palm, then let go and rubbed her eyes with the back of her other hand.

The red in the Sly Shrewman's cursor was quite faint, which meant that its combat ability was much weaker than level-17 Asuna. If she hit it with a single sword skill, that might be enough to wipe it out entirely.

But she needed a weapon for that.

Asuna opened her window and switched to her inventory. She touched the SORT button, praying to herself, and organized it to only show her RAPIER category.

With a little sound effect, it narrowed down and displayed just a single name.

Iron Rapier. The very last one of the pile that she'd bought in bulk from the first-floor NPC and used up without bothering to have them repaired. She'd been meaning to get rid of it for ages, but never did.

She touched the item and selected materialize, and a crude wooden sheath appeared above the window.

She picked it up and stood, put her right hand to the hilt, and slowly drew the blade out.

It was essentially the very bottom tier of that weapon category, the blade dull, and the knuckle guard essentially just a sheet of curved metal. But in this situation, it was Asuna's very last lifeline.

"I'm sorry I wasn't taking good care of you. Please...help me," she whispered to the sword, put it back into the sheath, and hung it from her left hip. Next, she replaced her normal hooded cape with a silver one she was saving. After that, she equipped her rewards from Yofel Castle the day before.

On her ears were the Earrings of Ripples, fashioned in the shape of little shells, with a boost to hearing. And on her legs were mid-length boots with over-the-knee socks called Prancing Boots. They gave her a slight jumping bonus and diminished the sound of her footsteps.

Outfitted in the best gear she had on hand, Asuna looked in the direction of the shrewman's escape.

She wanted to go off searching for it, but obviously, moving meant increasing the risk of encountering other monsters. It was already nearly a miracle that she'd chased so far after the thief without running into any other foes along the way.

On the other hand, it was not going to show up again if she waited in place. Still, there had to be a way to take advantage of a looting mob's habits to lure it out.

Asuna pulled up the map tab and closely checked her surroundings. She was in the southern part of the third level of the dungeon, with essentially a straight corridor mapped out from the spot where she'd fallen through the trapdoor. The passage widened where she'd slipped and fallen and seemed to fork just ahead. She had no idea which of the hallway's two branches the monster had taken.

Asuna closed her window and reached into her waistpouch to pull out the silver pendant that was the original cause of her fall. She didn't know what benefits it held, but it was going to serve as a lure now.

"When the rat thing picked up my rapier, it was barely six feet away…"

She dropped the pendant into the hateful puddle. As the silver light wavered beneath the shallow water, she took one step away, then two, measuring out the six feet that was the shortest distance necessary to pull off a sword skill. She drew the Iron Rapier and waited for the moment the sneak thief appeared again.

However…

"…It's not coming…"

A minute had passed, but the shrewman did not show itself. Either she was too close, or the lure wasn't valuable enough. But from what Kirito said about the "materialize all items" trick in the beta, the shrewmen had appeared from all directions and scooped up every item at his feet. So distance and value didn't factor into it.

What was different about him then and her now?

She thought it over, then looked down at the rapier in her hand. After Kirito had pressed the button in his inventory, he wouldn't have had a weapon. So maybe it came down to whether you were waiting for battle or not…

She put the Iron Rapier back in its sheath at her left side.

Within a few seconds, her boosted hearing detected little scurrying footsteps on the approach.

There it is!

All her nerves on edge, she readied to draw the sword at any moment. Perhaps the one that appeared wouldn't be the one holding her Chivalric Rapier, but she'd just have to depend on her good luck for that.

But once the footsteps got to what felt like thirty feet away, they stopped moving. It was as if the creature sensed Asuna's blood-thirsty gaze.

Actually…couldn't that be the truth, in fact? There was no way to physically *sense* a gaze on one's skin in the real world, but this place was different. The system knew what Asuna was looking at—it was the apparatus sending the image to her brain to begin with. So it was perfectly capable of telling the shrewman that she was looking at it.

Okay, fine. In that case…

She steeled herself and slowly turned around on the spot. Now she was relying solely on her hearing. She placed her hands in front of her ears to catch as much sound as possible, training her every nerve on the creature's steps.

Plep. Plep, plep.

As soon as her eyes moved away, the owner of the footsteps moved again. It approached arrhythmically, stopped, approached again—and then she heard it splash lightly into the water.

"…!!"

Asuna spun around and drew her rapier.

Six feet away, the Sly Shrewman had picked up the pendant from the water and was about to flee.

The rapier skill Asuna knew with the longest reach was Shooting Star, but the motion to initiate it was complex, and the move took too much time to engage. Here, she would use a basic skill, one with short range but the quickest possible burst…

With a motion she'd performed so many times it was like second nature, Asuna pulled her rapier back. Silver light shone at the tip, enveloping the entire blade. As the system assistance took over, she pushed it forward by launching herself extra hard off the ground.

Sha-keeen! The one-part lower thrust skill Oblique tore through the darkness of the cave. As the rest of the world moved in slow motion, she saw the glowing white point of the rapier approach the black of the fleeing shrewman, make contact, and just slightly pierce the skin.

That was all it took for the HP on its cursor to vanish. With a pathetic little crash and a brief squeak, the little humanoid silhouette burst into countless shards.

Just as she landed and stood up again, a little message popped into view listing her experience points, col, and looted items. The XP and money were no big deal—the items were the point. Shrew Tail, Balloon Mushroom, and the Unknown Necklace she dropped. That was it.

"...Hahh..."

There was no stopping that sigh of lament, but she couldn't give up now. It wasn't clear how many Sly Shrewmen inhabited an area at the same time, but if she kept hunting them using the same method, she would have to get her rapier back eventually.

Asuna stretched, then retrieved the pendant from her inventory again, dropped it into the puddle, put away her sword, and turned around.

Over the next fifteen minutes, Asuna lured in three more shrewmen and dispatched each of them with a single blow. But the only items they dropped were tails and mushrooms, with no sign of the Chivalric Rapier. The third even had a Wad of Paper, just to add insult to injury.

"*Hrrgh...*" she snarled, grinding her teeth, as she materialized the paper. She was going to hurl it overhand like a baseball, when— Her arm stopped.

"Rrrr...rgh?"

Asuna stopped and held the paper up to her face. It seemed like something was written on it. She carefully unwadded the parchment, making sure not to tear it.

The standard seven-by-eleven-inch piece of paper did indeed have a line of text written on it. But the cave was too dark to make it out. Even bringing it close to the glowing moss wasn't enough, so she was about to ball it up again out of frustration when she remembered that Kirito would never give up on the trail like that. She put her fist to her mouth, trying to calm her rising irritation. Eventually, her mood returned to normal, and she exhaled a long breath.

Suddenly, to her surprise, a warm light appeared near her hand.

She flipped it over and saw that the stone inset atop the ring on her right hand was emitting a faint but steady light. She heard Kirito's voice in her ears: *Why don't you equip that? It'll be handy.*

It was the Candlepower effect of the ring. Breathing on it made it shine a little bit. He was right: It *was* handy.

She said a silent thanks to her absent partner for ceding that ring to her, then held it closer to the parchment in her other hand. This time the line of writing was clear to see:

29, 22:00, B3F (181. 203).

"…What is this?" she wondered. If it was the start of a quest, the quest log would have chirped with an update the moment she'd read it, but there was no such indicator. So it was a ball of paper a player wrote on and threw away, which a shrewman had picked up and treasured?

22:00 looked like a time, ten o'clock at night. Which meant *29* was the date, and *B3F* referred to the third basement floor of the catacombs. But the numbers in the parentheses were still a mystery. While she puzzled it over, the light on the ring faded away, so she breathed on it and held the gem back up to the paper. At that point, she realized it wasn't a period separating the two mystery numbers, but a comma.

A little light flickered on in her head, and Asuna muttered, "Are these…coordinates?"

She opened her window and brought up the map of the third underground level of the dungeon. When she tapped the cursor that represented her position on the mostly unfilled map, it popped up her name and the numbers of her coordinates. It said, *(181, 235).*

The coordinates in *SAO* were by meter, with the zero point at the upper left corner, meaning that Asuna was currently 181 meters to the right (east) of the upper left (northwest) corner of the dungeon and 235 meters down (south). Based on the map size, it looked like the dungeon was about 300 meters to a side, so her current location was somewhere near the middle of the level, though in the lower right quadrant. The x-value of the coordinates on the paper was exactly the same, so she'd get to the spot by traveling just about thirty meters north from where she currently was.

That all added up in her mind, but it did not answer what this was referring *to*—and why a looting mob would be carrying it.

She breathed on the ring to recharge the light and held it up to the note. Upon examining the handwritten numbers again, she made a new discovery. In the *203* of the y-coordinate, the *2* looked rather roughly written. It might have been a correction from a mistake, but it also looked a little like a *3*. There was a bit of a trick in *SAO* to writing on parchment with a quill, so it was common for clumsy or unpracticed players to make mistakes.

"...So it was a player who wrote this, then made a mistake and tried to rewrite it, but failed, balled up the paper, and threw it away...and then a shrewman came along and picked it up?"

Her partner wasn't around to answer that question for her, but she was pretty sure she was right.

The next question was what these coordinates meant.

If the writer tried to correct the mistake, was unhappy with the result, and used a new parchment anyway, then it wasn't meant for them. And given that it mentioned a time, it was highly likely that the note was indicating a time and place for a meeting.

But there were still doubts.

Why the need to write on a parchment in the first place? That was what instant messages were for. Every mistake could be corrected with the backspace key, and the SEND button would deliver it instantly. So why not use that—was it a love letter? No. Not in a crude, unsentimental way like this.

She glanced at the time indicator in her window. It was 21:45 on the twenty-ninth.

"…Fifteen minutes to move just thirty meters," she justified to herself, putting the parchment into her inventory.

Asuna headed north down the hallway with her map open, deciding the thief-elimination plan would take a temporary break.

She crossed about twenty-five meters without encountering any new monsters and began to hear the faint sound of running water. She squinted and saw there was a little room ahead. A rounded stalagmite rose up from the floor like a bench, and water spouted from the east wall, forming a small spring. She felt a sudden thirst and an urge to rush over and scoop up the water to quench it, but she held this in and stood her ground.

Her current coordinates were 181, 230. The little room was undoubtedly the location of the mystery-note-writer's meeting. She looked around and found a little hollow in a nearby wall that could serve as a hiding spot and squeezed into it.

…If a romantic-looking couple ends up coming along, this totally makes me a creepy voyeur, she realized, and briefly wondered what in the world she was doing—but there was no turning back now. She put her Iron Rapier into its sheath and stuck tight to the wall. If she had Kizmel's invisibility cloak with its 95 percent hiding rate or had at least built up her Hiding skill…But there was no use worrying about it now. Ten minutes passed, leaving just five until the meeting time of ten o'clock.

She closed her window and lowered the hood of her silk cape, listening intently.

A minute later, she heard footsteps approaching. It wasn't the slapping feet of the Sly Shrewman, but the crisp ring of hard-soled boots hitting cavern stone. It most certainly belonged to a player.

As expected, the steps stopped within the little water cavern. Asuna waited a few moments, then poked her head out of the hollow, glancing at the room fifteen feet away.

The visitor carried no light, so the only illumination was from the glowing moss, but the room had more of it than the halls so she could at least make out a figure.

All she could tell was that it was short and thin. A hooded cape covered the figure from head to toe, hiding everything else. There was no shape of a protruding weapon, either, so the person was unarmed or had a small weapon, such as a dagger. Asuna focused hard to bring up a color cursor, but all she saw was that it was green and the HP bar was nearly full.

Given that the person had reached the third level of the dungeon alone, it was probably someone from the frontline group, but she couldn't identify their name without a better look. If it was someone she knew, she could ask for assistance in getting out—at least, that was what she'd hoped, until the sound of more footsteps hit her ears.

A few seconds later, another player entered the room from the north side. This one was also in a hooded cape, but seemed to have a one-handed sword on the left hip.

The first player made a hand gesture like Fleming's left-hand rule, with thumb, index, and middle fingers extended, which the other player returned. The fact that they were communicating with hand signs while wearing full cloaks was quite suspicious. At the very least, it was not lovers on a date, and she had no desire to call out and reveal her presence to them.

Asuna realized her heart had begun beating wildly, and she put her right hand to her chest. She swallowed hard, feeling the sudden onset of nervous energy coursing through her. The sound of her throat was loud in her ears, and she tensed, worried that it might be overheard.

Naturally, the cloaked figures fifteen feet away did not hear the beating of her heart nor the swallowing in her throat. They sat on the stalagmite bench against the wall, facing each other. The latter to arrive spoke first.

"Heya, heya, you're here early today. Waiting long?"

The total lack of care in the voice and its words nearly caused Asuna to slump to her knees. She clung to the wall, listening hard.

"Not that long, but it was a pain in the ass to get here," said the first player. The high-pitched voice seemed familiar, but it was muffled enough by the hood that she couldn't be sure. The only thing she could tell was that both seemed to be male.

"Speaking of pain in the ass, writing down that memo by hand is a royal one. I hate using that damn pen. Can't we just use regular messages?"

"You know we can't. That'll leave the message in your history, y'know."

Despite the light tone, the contents of the conversation were incredibly suspicious. But that answered the question of why the meeting point wasn't just decided with an instant message, at least.

"I'm lettin' things calm down and taking a break from both guilds. If they find out I've been sending messages around, all this trouble'll be for nothin'."

"Fine, fine, I get it."

Based on the way they were talking, the first person seemed to be in a position of higher authority, given that the second spoke with a kind of informal politeness—but for some reason, Asuna got the opposite impression about them. The second player lowered his volume and muttered, "Just in case…you didn't get trailed, did you?"

"That's why we came all the way underground like this, right? Hiding won't work against the astral types on the second level, so anyone following me would get exposed."

"Yeah, good point. Well, let's get down to business…How did the matter go?" the second person asked, opening his window. He started typing on a holo-keyboard, taking notes.

"It went pretty well. Our main force is gonna break out early before the organized countdown event two days from now, and try to just sweep through the labyrinth on its own."

Countdown? Asuna wondered to herself as she listened. Then it occurred to her that in two days it would be December 31—New Year's Eve. A countdown event was certainly possible.

The problem was what they said next. Sweeping through the labyrinth meant beating the floor boss, and there were only two guilds in Aincrad capable of such a feat: either Lind's DKB or Kibaou's ALS. Which meant the high-voiced first player was a member of one of the two.

But a guild's activities and plans were absolutely top secret. If he was coming down here in secret to reveal those to this outsider, that would make him…

"…A spy?" she mouthed silently, then bit her lip.

The first possibility that came to mind was that the first player, the short one who was a DKB/ALS member, was revealing his guild's information to the player with the longsword, who was a member of the other guild. But based on the way he was speaking, it didn't seem like the second one was a member of either group.

But who else could possibly want to go to such lengths for internal information on one of the two big guilds? The only third party she could imagine was Agil and his Bro Squad, but none of them used a single-handed sword, and they had no reason to engage in spying. Agil had shifted to merchant business on the fourth floor when the fifth was already open. It was hard to imagine that he was plotting to sneak past both the DKB and ALS to get to the sixth.

The only other group was the Legend Braves, who had made great strides on the second floor until their scam was exposed and they broke off from the main force. But since they'd had to make amends by handing over all their high-level gear, they probably wouldn't go through such elaborate pains to do this. In fact, it wasn't even they who thought up the trick of the scam, but a mysterious stranger in a bar wearing a black poncho…

"———!!"

Asuna had to clench her jaw shut to avoid gasping aloud in shock.

Kirito's words from the day before echoed in her mind:

There could be three, four…or an entire gang of PKers out there in Aincrad somewhere…

Could this be it? Was the swordsman, who was using the

high-voiced, cloaked player as a spy to gain guild secrets, part of that PK gang Kirito was worried about…?

In that case, Asuna was in much greater danger at the moment than she'd ever contemplated.

She had been nervous earlier, but that was just because she was eavesdropping on a private conversation, and she would feel bad about being exposed. If she lied or apologized about it, she might even get them to help her escape the dungeon.

But if they were PKers—murderers—and their important, secret contact deep in a dungeon was witnessed by someone else, how would they solve the situation? Threats? Bribery? Or…

Her entire body went as cold as ice, freezing her solid. Meanwhile, the lackadaisical second player continued, "Hmm, that sounds nice. Things got a lil' toooo soft between Kiba and Lin on the last two floors. We gotta stir things up and get 'em to clash again to keep it from being too boring."

"Don't act like it's that simple. It's a hell of a job to manipulate a guild meeting into going any particular direction."

"Yeah, I know. But the boss is training us up on that point with that super-coooool conversational technique, you know?"

"True, true. I think I'm finally getting the hang of the exact point where I'm not bein' obnoxious by talking *too* much."

"Ah-ha-ha-ha, I've given up on that."

"Yeah, because the way you talk transcends obnoxious."

The first player chuckled and nimbly sat cross-legged atop the stalagmite, rocking back and forth.

"Still, I just can't tell what the boss is thinking. I know what he wants to do, but it's just so twisted…I think he could get around to it in a much more direct way."

"Ha-ha, we're just sowing the seeds now. Get too hasty, and the fun of our little festival will be over in moments."

"Yeah, I know, I know. Enjoy the process, right?"

"Exactly."

The two chuckled again, and Asuna felt a cold sweat run down her back.

Boss. That was the word the two were using to refer to some kind of leader. Perhaps he was the man in the black poncho, the very one who led the Braves astray.

Kirito's fears were confirmed. At the moment, there was a PK gang of at least three members...and not the kind that just attacked people directly, but one plotting to confuse, agitate, and guide other players and guilds into committing provocation PKs.

But why?

That massive question came to Asuna's mind again.

What did they have to gain by pitting the DKB and ALS against each other, sowing chaos among the best players in the game? What profit could they derive that was greater or more important than escaping this game of death?

If she had her Chivalric Rapier in hand, she would leap from her hiding spot and point it at them to demand answers. She would ask them what they were thinking.

That momentary impulse shifted her avatar's center of balance forward.

The imbalance caused her right foot to step forward an inch or two. It was enough to rebalance herself, but the edge of her boot kicked a tiny pebble that happened to be resting on the spot.

Tak, takak.

The stone skittered forward, the sound echoing off the cave walls. The chuckles from the room, just fifteen feet away, stopped abruptly. Asuna straightened up, pressing her back hard against the wall.

"...Did you hear something?" the swordsman whispered.

The first player replied, "Hmm...maybe it's a mob?"

"It wasn't the sound of a monster popping...What's the hallway like down that way?"

"It's a straight shot for about sixty meters, then a dead end. If anyone snuck in there, we'd see the cursor—it's a dead giveaway."

"Hmm...but in these natural dungeons, even straight passages have little dips and bends. That would suck if someone heard our little secret convo."

Oh no, they're coming to check. Even in this darkness, they'll get close enough to see me. I can't win a fight with this starter rapier.

She had to think. If her brain was sharp enough to imagine the worst-case scenario, she could come up with a plan to get out of this.

A number of thoughts burned through her brain in the span of a second, like sparks, eventually forming an idea.

Her right hand shot into her pouch, pulling out the piece of parchment with the failed instructions on it. She wadded it up and tossed it softly at her feet. It made no sound—it was just a rolled-up piece of paper lying on the ground.

She then turned around and urged, *Hurry, hurry, come quick!*

"...I guess I'll go check it out," came the swordsman's voice. She heard him stand. Footsteps approached over the damp cave floor. One, two, three steps. Then...

"Whoa! What the hell?" the first player shouted, at the same time as the screech of a rodent. A Sly Shrewman had reacted to Asuna's toss of the sheet of paper, running through the little room from the other hallway.

"Get the hell outta here!" he yelled, and the swordsman laughed.

"C'mon, keep that door on the other end closed, please."

There was the sound of a sheath ringing, then a sword skill. Blue light briefly shone on the passage, and the shrewman screamed.

"Stupid ratman, startling me like that. Musta been the sound of it scurrying around."

The sword returned to its sheath, and Asuna let out a long, silent breath. She crouched and picked up the paper at her feet. Meanwhile, the two players continued talking.

"Goddamn annoying little looters...Did they show up in the beta, too?"

"It was terrible if you ever dropped your weapon. The best part was that every once in a while, you'd lift someone else's nice gear from one...and what do you know! No sooner are the words out of my mouth!"

Asuna felt a nasty sensation flooding over her tongue as the swordsman gloated. She heard the sound of an item being materialized, and the smaller player exclaimed in surprise.

"Ohh, no way! That rapier looks mega-rare!"

When the full import of this conversation finally permeated her brain a few seconds later, Asuna felt all the blood in her body run cold.

No, it can't be, she pleaded, but there was no other realistic possibility. The very shrewman that Asuna had called over to save her from her predicament was the one who had looted her Chivalric Rapier to begin with. The two men had killed it and gotten her weapon.

Now that she had accepted that ugly truth, she tried to remember what would happen to the item's ownership and equippable rights now. She heard Kirito's voice again, repeating his lesson during the second-floor upgrade scam uproar.

If someone picks up your weapon or you hand it to them, the weapon cell in your menu goes blank. Including situations like the one where you gave the blacksmith your Wind Fleuret. But here's the thing. The equipment cell might be empty, as though you're not equipping anything...but that Anneal Blade's equipper info hasn't been deleted. And the equipment rights are protected much more tightly than simple ownership rights. For example, if I take an unequipped weapon out of storage and give it to you, my ownership of that item disappears in just three hundred seconds—that's five minutes. As soon as it goes into someone else's inventory, it is owned by that player. But the length of ownership for an equipped item is far longer. It won't be overwritten until either 3,600 seconds have passed, or the original owner equips a different weapon in that slot.

"The original owner equips a different weapon in that slot."

That phrase pounded Asuna's brain like a hammer. After her Chivalric Rapier was looted, she replaced it with an Iron Rapier from her inventory. At that instant, she had overwritten her equipment rights to the Chivalric Rapier.

Actually, the chances were high that the shrewman had

the Robbing skill, which eliminated her ownership rights the moment it was looted. And the cloaked swordsman had beaten the shrewman, so the rights to the Chivalric Rapier were clearly his now that it had dropped.

Devastated, Asuna slumped against the wall. Meanwhile, the first cloaked player was screeching with excitement.

"Hey, let me see that…Whoa, it's heavy! Let's look at the specs…*Shwaa*, you gotta be kidding! Check out the attack value! It might as well be a double-handed weapon!"

"Sounds cool."

"Seriously? That's all you have to say? If you're not interested, then give it to me!"

"Uhh, but you're, like, a dagger user. Do you even have enough strength?"

"If I had a weapon like this, I'd switch to being a fencer! It's called…a Cilvaric Rapier. Damn, that's cool!"

"Look closer—it says 'Chivalric.'"

"Who cares what the name is?! Whoa, and it's already boosted to plus five!"

Asuna fought desperately against the urge to slump down and cover her ears.

She'd carelessly fallen into a trap, dropped her sword—the most valuable item she owned—let it be looted by a monster, lost sight of it, then got beaten to the punch by another player. She had no right to that weapon, and she knew it.

But she couldn't give up on it now. She just couldn't.

If these PK gang members used it, that Chivalric Rapier might take a player's life…a *person's* life. She couldn't possibly stand that.

She would emerge from her hiding spot and beg them to sell it back to her. Even if it meant revealing that she'd been eavesdropping on their secrets and they turned their weapons on her—this was to protect others from what they might do with the Chivalric Rapier.

Asuna took a deep breath, summoning every last ounce of courage. She peeked out a bit from the hollow, looking closely at the players turned away from her, one holding her beloved weapon. She willed strength into her legs, trembling with nerves and fear, preparing to step out into the hallway.

At that moment, the darkness of the hallway on the north side of the little spring room wavered like a watery surface, producing another figure clad in black.

"Mwuh?" spluttered the rapier-holding smaller player as the swordsman tensed. But Asuna barely even noticed what the two cloaked players were doing.

The new member on the scene wore a long black leather coat. A beautifully designed longsword hung across his back. Beneath his long black bangs burned eyes darker than darkness. The sight was so vivid on her virtual retinas that she couldn't even blink.

"...Well, well, well..." said the second cloaked player, still as lackadaisical as before but in a much colder tone. "I always seem to run into you in the funniest places."

The first cloaked player's shoulders tensed as he prepared to shout something, but the second one struck him in the chest with the back of his hand to shut him up. He stepped forward to hide his partner's identity and growled at the newcomer, "Mind if I ask one question...? How long have you been there?"

"I just got here. Heard you two talking," said the black-clad swordsman at last, his familiar voice almost causing Asuna to wilt to the ground with relief. But this was not the time to lose her composure. If needed, she might be leaping out of her hiding spot to come to her partner's aid.

"Well, wouldn'tcha know it. I thought we were keeping it nice and quiet from the main hallway, but I guess we got carried away once I acquired this nice rare loot, ha-ha-ha."

"About that weapon...You said it was a Chivalric Rapier plus five, right? You're sure about that?"

"Wow, you seem to have latched onto that detail for just hearin' it said once. What about it, pal?" asked the second cloaked player, spreading his hands theatrically in challenge.

The other swordsman in black answered coldly, "My partner was using that rapier."

The first player abruptly budged, and again the second one silenced him with the back of his hand. He really did not want his partner to say anything.

Once he was convinced that the other player would reluctantly remain silent, the second made a theatrical gesture of confusion.

"Ohh, is that so? Well, I just looted this off of a looter mob. So do I have this situation right? You want me to return your friend's weapon?"

"No, I'm not going to get on your case about that. It's just…I have no way of judging if your words are the truth or not."

The black-haired swordsman stepped forward slightly, his voice quiet but chilling. "After all, you could have gotten that sword by duel PK-ing my partner. Right, Morte?"

Called out by name, the second cloaked player raised his left hand and slowly pulled the hood back. What emerged was a metal coif, its hem ragged. He shook it, clinking the threaded chains, and laughed in a different tone of voice than what he'd been using previously.

"Ahaaa…All right, I see your tactic here. You mean the way I did to you on the third floor…Kirito?"

Asuna could sense that once the two men called each other by name, the cave grew very, very tense. Neither had drawn his weapon, but she could practically see the sparks between them.

Morte.

The man wearing the coif was the very same duel PKer who had challenged Kirito to a half-finish-mode duel on the third floor and then, just before taking him to the halfway point that would end the duel, attempted a huge critical hit to kill him.

The swordsmen—one in a black coat, the other wearing a black cloak—stared each other down in silence. Even the raucous, chatty dagger user was bowled back, intimidated into holding his tongue by the scene.

Asuna was still partnered with Kirito. So he would see, next to his own HP bar, that Asuna still had about 90 percent of her health left. His challenge that she "might have been duel PKed for her sword" was just a bluff, yet the sheer pressure exuding from his entire body made him seem deadly serious. Meanwhile, Morte wielded his own atmosphere of sheer murder, not backing down a single step.

She was certain that if either of them drew his blade, a battle would result. And not a duel—whoever landed the first hit would become an orange player, unable to enter town until his cursor returned to green status. But both of them had to know that. Each understood the other as a foe whose defeat was worth that heavy cost.

However.

By the act of Akihiko Kayaba, creator of *Sword Art Online*, the game world was no longer normal. It was a cold and cruel game of death, in which the loss of all HP meant the loss of the actual player's life. PK-ing was no longer just PK-ing, it was true murder.

She couldn't let Kirito's hands be stained with blood over something that began with her own mistake. She had to resolve this situation before they turned to battle.

There was probably only one thing she could do: retrieve her Chivalric Rapier from the first cloaked player through means other than battle. At the very least, that would remove Kirito's need to attack Morte, and given that they knew the rapier's incredible power, they would hesitate to begin a two-on-two fight.

The first player had his back to her, unaware of her presence. If this was the real world, she could just sneak up and snatch the rapier right out of his hands, but it wasn't clear if stealing an item that forcefully would work in this world. Plus, just wresting it out of his fingers wouldn't overwrite Morte's system-ordained ownership.

Yes…the floating castle Aincrad was ruled by the absolute laws of the game system, laws that didn't exist in the real world. The most important tool for survival was to understand the system and make it work for you.

What could she do to completely and entirely recover her Chivalric Rapier?

She needed to physically possess the item, then later reset the ownership rights. There was no other way. But she would need to have the item for three hundred seconds for that to work. It was a very long period of time, and it would not be a simple matter to just snatch it out of the first player's hands.

Meanwhile, Asuna's right eye and ear took note of two phenomena simultaneously.

Her eye saw the first player's left hand searching for a weapon on his left hip.

Her ear heard the slight *swish* of a monster popping into being on the south side of the hallway—the direction of the spot where she first fell.

Those two things combined in a chemical reaction, guiding her to a single strategy. It wasn't a sure thing, and it would be dangerous, but she couldn't think of a better idea on the spot.

Kirito and Morte were staring at each other silently, gauging how the other might react, but the impatient first player would be the first to explode. Then, the battle could not be stopped. If she was going to act, she needed to act now.

Asuna sucked a cold breath into her lungs and tensed.

The first player flipped aside his cloak with his left hand, exposing a dagger.

At that precise moment, Asuna dropped the ball of paper from her hand again. Instantly, little footsteps began approaching from the south.

In order to free up his right hand, the first player tried to move the rapier to his left. Just as the sheath was about to move from hand to hand, Asuna leaped out of her hiding spot, drew her Iron Rapier, and expended all the air charged up in her lungs into a deafening scream.

"*Aaaaaaaaaaaah!!!!*"

The scream was so loud, it brought down a patter of sand from the walls. The unnamed cloaked player and Morte both jumped.

The Chivalric Rapier slipped out of the cloaked man's hands and fell to the ground.

In less than a second, it was not Asuna, Morte, or the cloaked player who darted forth to snatch up the weapon—but the freshly arrived Sly Shrewman. As the rodent tried to turn around and slip away, Asuna hit it with an Oblique, her fastest sword skill.

The monster's body burst into blue shards, and the rapier it was carrying disappeared. She jumped as far back as she could and opened her equipment screen. In the main weapon cell, she replaced the Iron Rapier with the weapon that had just dropped. The rapier in her right hand vanished into light, and a reassuring weight appeared on her left waist.

Just over three seconds had passed from the moment she leaped out from her hiding spot.

By the time she landed, Asuna had already drawn the Chivalric Rapier +5. It was much heavier than the Iron Rapier, but the hilt formed around her hand like it was absorbing it. Now that her weapon was once again physically and systematically in her possession, she held it out before her.

The situation was still a dangerous one, but for just a moment, Asuna caught sight of her partner's face between the two cloaked men. Even Kirito was briefly startled, but he recovered at once, grinning and nodding.

The first to speak was the original cloaked player, who still didn't understand what had just happened.

"Wh…what the…? Where did…that come from…?!"

It was a high-pitched falsetto screech. Morte extended his left hand to cover up the mouth of the other player, which was poking out a bit from the hood, as he turned around.

Asuna made sure to stare with all her might at the face of the PKer as she caught sight of it for the first time. She couldn't see much past the hanging chains of his coif in the dim light of the moss, but she could make out some general features. He had a pointed chin and thin lips pulled to one side in a snarl. She burned the image, like that of a joker in a pack of cards, into her retinas.

His lips glistened, curving wetly into a sneer that hid cold steel.

"Ah-ha-ha-haaa, scared by a lil' boo. First Blackie, now you—y'all like to jump out of nowhere. And how long were you hiding over there...?"

She wanted to shout that she'd overheard the entire thing but decided better of it when she saw Kirito shaking his head at her over Morte's shoulder.

"What's wrong, cat got your tongue? You scared a good three seconds off my life with that stunt. I think you owe me one," Morte said, as sarcastic as ever. The other player yanked his hand out of Morte's way.

He moved it to the dagger at his waist, tracing the gleaming hilt, and screeched in a voice like rusted metal, "Listen, I'm really pissed off right now. Is this really the time to stand around and chitchat? We gotta react under the assumption that they heard everything."

Morte shrugged his shoulders in exasperation. "Impatience will get you nowhere, y'know? Besides, you saw that rapier's stats, didn't you? Assuming I take on Blackie over here, do you really think you can handle that on your own?"

"Don't insult me. I can tackle a PvP amateur girl like her," the first player spat.

Asuna realized her breathing had picked up—but only until she heard the next line.

"Besides, I can't go home after having my badass rapier stolen on a lucky ruse."

Since when did this sword belong to you?! You called it "Cil-varic"!! she thought furiously, all hesitation gone.

Perhaps screaming the way she did wasn't exactly the politest of tactics, but it certainly wasn't a stroke of luck. Asuna aimed for that very moment based on a specific, precise logic.

She was certain that the piece of parchment that guided her to this point was written and discarded by the first player. Messing up on the simple act of writing a number was, if not the act of someone with an FNC (full-dive noncomformity) disability, at least the sign of trouble with fine finger movements in a full dive—in short, proof of clumsiness. If she startled him at the very moment he moved the weapon from one hand to the other, he would surely drop it. That was her reasoning for shouting like that.

And she made it so the looting shrew would pick up the rapier so that she could kill it, thus ensuring the sword was officially back in her possession. She would never let it go again and could fight another player to protect her precious weapon.

Asuna pointed the tip of her Chivalric Rapier forward in a display of that will.

The first cloaked player clicked his tongue and squeezed the handle of the dagger.

But at that point, the situation took an unexpected turn.

In the back, Kirito turned and raced past Morte's left side, straight for Asuna.

"...?!"

As Asuna leaned back in surprise, he grabbed her around the breastplate and leaped into the hollow where she'd been hiding. He pressed her flat against the wall, covering her with his coat—and activating the Hiding skill.

Obviously, this was not going to actually hide them.

But the next moment, Asuna heard the reason why Kirito had done it. From the north hallway came a great many sounds of clanking metal, the sign of a group of monsters. But why so suddenly...?

And then it hit her.

Of course. It would be strange for such a thing *not* to happen in a dungeon after the way she'd shouted.

She couldn't see the cloaked men anymore, but she heard the first one hiss, "Shit, they brought a buncha mobs down to MPK us! The dirty bastards!"

"Ah-ha-ha-ha, coming from you?" Morte laughed, but it was not as confident and cocky as before. She heard them drawing their weapons, but as the monsters approached, his order to his comrade was tense and worried. "Never mind, it'll suck fighting this many of them. We oughta pull back."

"Tsk, fine."

"Whoops, that's a dead end down there. We gotta sprint to the staircase, so do your best to keep up, bud."

"H-hey, wait!"

Two sets of footsteps raced away, eventually eclipsed by the raucous pursuit of the monsters. The sounds gradually, gradually died away, and disappeared at last.

Silence.

No, not quite. There was one sound left, tirelessly throbbing in her ears in a bass register...the sound of her heart. The sound of blood rushing from her virtual heart. Or perhaps it was her real heart, beating so loudly that it got through to her ears. As she listened, the pulse slowly, slowly calmed, gradually pulling her away from the absolute state of tension.

For just a moment, she felt her wits grow distant, and she nearly dropped her rapier. But she would never let that happen again. She willed strength into her fingers and returned the sword to its sheath from her spot beneath the coat that covered her body.

In response to that action, Kirito let out a long breath and prepared to stand up from his crouch over Asuna. But she unconsciously lifted her right hand, pulling on his left as he rose.

There, right within reach of her arms, was the reassuring presence of her partner.

Yes...it was all right now. There was nothing to fear.

Asuna trembled powerfully, overcome by the sudden upsurge of all the emotions that had been pressed and compacted inside of her from the moment she fell through the trapdoor. Heat gathered in her eyes, and something roiled up into her throat. The strength went out of her knees, and she nearly slumped down to the floor.

But Kirito's hand propped up her back. His voice said in her ear, "...You did well. I'm glad...you're all right..."

Those words permeated her mind instantly, removing all self-control.

The demand that she had to be stronger.

The admonition that she was always getting help.

And the fear that if she showed any weakness, she would be left behind.

All these emotions were temporarily set loose, and she pressed her head against Kirito's chest. Through trembling lips, she blubbered like a young child:

"…I was scared…I was so scared…"

She squeezed her eyes shut, letting her emotions do the speaking.

"There was a ghost, and I fell into a pit…then I got lost, and dropped my rapier, and I thought I was done for…I thought I was going to meet my end in this horrible dark cave…I was so, so scared, so scared…I really mean it…"

Her whole body trembled intermittently. She clutched at Kirito's shirt, craving direct, if virtual, contact.

Suddenly, a pleasing, gentle sensation enveloped her.

Kirito was rubbing the top of Asuna's head. He repeated the awkward but heartfelt motion over and over.

"It's all right…You're all right," he whispered, barely audible, but the steadfast will contained in those words was more trustworthy than anything else in this world.

"If we ever get split up again, I'll find you and come help. You're…my partner, Asuna."

"………Yeah."

Like the flipping of a switch, Asuna stopped trembling. But she didn't let go of him, and Kirito didn't stop rubbing her head. They kept a long, silent embrace in the little corner of the catacomb dungeon.

6

11:00 AM, SATURDAY, DECEMBER 31, 2022.

Asuna stood in Shiyaya, a small village on the northern side of the fifth floor of Aincrad.

It was a Non-Code village, meaning that the Anti-Criminal Code did not work here. But Asuna was in a state of utter relaxation, without her sword equipped and without her armor on—without a stitch of clothing, in fact.

She could do this without fear because Shiyaya was an instanced map that allowed only party members within its borders.

And the reason she was not wearing clothes was that she was submerged to her shoulders in bathwater.

"Hufhuwhee..."

She stretched out her arms and legs as far as they would go. The water temperature was a bit on the lukewarm side, but the floating bundles of fragrant fruit and herbs filled her nose with a pleasing scent that permeated her core with pleasant warmth.

Not only that, but the bath was quite large. Not as big as the great bathing chamber in Yofel Castle, but the granite bathtub could easily fit at least ten at once. It was clear that the dark elves truly loved their baths.

"I wonder if the forest elf village has baths this big..." she speculated idly, trailing her fingers in the water. Her answer came from a short distance away.

"Not so, apparently. The forest elves have tiny baths, but their food's supposed to be phenomenal."

That was Argo the Rat, floating freely on the surface of the water. Naturally, she wasn't wearing her trademark short hooded cape, but even in the bath, those whiskers on her cheeks didn't wash off.

"Oh, I happen to think the dark elf food is quite good on its own," Asuna remarked, but Argo only chuckled without changing position.

"They bring out feasts like they came out of a three-star restaurant. But after experiencing this bath, I'd have to say that I personally prefer the dark elf side. Thanks for letting me into your party, A-chan."

She looked up to the left. Instead of the usual two HP bars, there were now three.

"Don't be silly. I wanted to thank you properly, Argo, for camping out in the catacombs for an entire day to nail down the boss's attack patterns."

"Not at all, not at all. I didn't do much. In fact, I should apologize for lettin' you and Kii-boy worry about me. And I hear you got yourselves into a bit of trouble when you came lookin' for me?"

The events of two days prior returned to Asuna's mind in vivid detail, and she felt her face grow hot.

It's not red, right? If it is, I can always blame it on the bath...

She glanced over to her right, where the floating information broker chuckled in all-seeing delight. Asuna lowered herself down to her nose and blew bubbles in the water to hide her embarrassment.

After Kirito's rescue on the third level of the catacombs two nights ago, Asuna resumed activities with him—he had been on a search for Argo, after all—once she had regained her composure.

Fortunately, they found Argo less than an hour after that, but the reason she couldn't be reached by messages was not nearly as ominous as they'd imagined.

Argo was camping out in a small safe room right in front of the area boss's chamber at the end of the dungeon. It turned out the boss's name and appearance were totally different from in the beta. At first she was planning to mark the location of the chamber, then go back to town and put out her first issue, but when she noticed the boss was entirely different, she figured she might as well collect some info while she was there—a process that was harder than she expected and ended up taking an entire day.

The boss was an enormous zombie far too large to have been a human in life, heavily resistant to slashes, thrusts, and piercing damage, but by manipulating levers scattered around the chamber and solving a stone puzzle in the ceiling, sunlight could be let through to weaken the boss—assuming it was daytime, of course. Argo ran into trouble solving the puzzle, and at one point was basically just trying combinations out of sheer trial and error.

Thanks to that, the boss was defeated handily by a chosen group of top players on the thirtieth, but Asuna still didn't rest easy during the fight. Not just due to the openly competitive DKB and ALS, but even more so due to their reliance on Argo's information as a whole—and the dangers that Argo was putting herself through to get that intel.

It wasn't polite to comment too heavily on others' playstyle, but there wouldn't be a better opportunity, so Asuna pulled her head out of the water and hesitantly asked, "Um, Argo…?"

"Hmm? What is it?" the girl replied, sitting upright at Asuna's serious tone.

"…It was thanks to your work that we were able to beat the catacombs boss that easily, and I'm very grateful for that…but I think it's too dangerous for you to be collecting data on an unfamiliar boss all by yourself."

Based on her experience at an all-girls school, Asuna knew that offering (what might be seen as) patronizing advice could easily blow up in her face, but Argo maintained a slight smile, prodding her to continue. Feeling emboldened, she chose her words carefully.

"I used to spend lots of time in the labyrinth alone, so I can't really act blameless here…but your information is helping not just the top players like us, but also the mid-level players who left the Town of Beginnings later on. It's such a help that if something happened to you, it could completely stop us from proceeding in the game. Therefore—actually, just speaking for myself, I'm worried that you might be putting yourself through too much. Um… as a friend…"

They were difficult words for her to tell a friend in the real world. Ironically, it took being trapped in a virtual world for her to finally speak her mind like that.

She was half expecting Argo to be upset by this, but the Rat's whiskers only rose in a smile. Perhaps it was just the echo of the bath, but her voice seemed louder than usual as she said, "Thanks, A-chan."

Those big eyes of hers, usually hidden behind the long brown curls, stared Asuna full in the face. When she continued, she spoke slower than her usual rapid-fire pace.

"It makes me happy that you're so concerned for my sake. To be honest, I was wonderin' if my stakeout was pushing it a lil' bit, too. But…I got a duty to continue risking danger to provide information."

"Because…you're an info dealer…?"

"Nope," Argo said, drops flying as she shook her head. "Because I'm a beta tester."

"…!!"

She had sensed for herself that this might be true, and Kirito seemed to believe it as well, but it was the first time she'd heard Argo admit it aloud. Asuna was taken aback briefly before she followed up with, "But…even if that's the case, it doesn't explain why you need to take on that dangerous role by yourself. Kirito's a fellow beta tester, and he takes part in the frontline group's raid parties for all the floor bosses…You could join us as a support scout, Argo…"

"I don't like how long and cloying that 'frontline group' term is. I think 'front-runners' is a much cooler name."

Argo chuckled to break the mood, then poked at a banana-like fruit floating in front of her.

"Hmm…The reason you're so worried about me is because I play a noncombat build, am I right?"

"W…well, yes…" Asuna admitted.

Whenever she met Argo out in the field, she was equipped with minimalist armor and combat claws, but her skill lineup and proficiency couldn't possibly be suited for battle. If she focused on Hiding, Search, and Eavesdropping, she wouldn't be able to spend much time on weapon skills, and she was most likely sacrificing max HP and other stats to raise her agility as much as possible. She could dart her way around wimpy monsters, but that raised the danger of scouting a boss, who held a variety of attacks…

Argo smirked again, sensing Asuna's concerns, and picked up a floating bundle of herbs to toss at the other girl. Asuna caught it by reflex; then Argo grabbed the banana and stood up with a forceful splash.

"Proof is what we need, not arguments. Wanna try it, A-chan?" Argo challenged, emerging onto the side of the granite bath.

Asuna stared at her, baffled. "T-try…what?"

"A duel, of course…Well, I guess that's a bit dramatic. A little sword fight, let's call it."

She descended to the open washing station, twirling the banana deftly in her hand.

So Argo meant for them to have a mock duel—she with the banana and Asuna with the herbs. She was willing to accept the challenge, but the problem was that both Argo and Asuna weren't geared up with a single item. It was already embarrassing enough to be bathing together, but having a play fight? She wasn't sure she could concentrate properly.

"Umm...can I wear a swimsuit?" Asuna asked. The information broker was taken aback, then looked down at her avatar, and her cheeks puffed out.

"Listen, I'm here baring what minimal assets I've got, so how can you be so ashamed when you've got much better?!"

"Th-that's not the issue!"

"Well, fine..."

"And I want you to wear a suit, too, Argo..."

"Huh? But I don't have a swimsuit."

"Then I'll make you one right now!"

And after a brief demonstration of Asuna's Tailoring skill, the two faced off in the bath of Shiyaya village.

Asuna was wearing a simple white one-piece.

Argo was wearing, upon her own request, a yellow tankini.

Asuna swung the bundle of herbs in her hand, idly wondering how in the world they'd come to this point. Her weapon was three fairly thick stalks about two feet long, which made it surprisingly firm. It couldn't be compared to an actual rapier, but that wasn't the point. And besides, Argo only had what looked like a banana.

"So, um, what are the rules...?"

"How about whoever whaps the other first wins?"

"G-got it," Asuna said, pulling her left foot back into a stance. Argo, however, was standing still, arms dangling at her sides.

"Okay, whenever yer ready."

With an invitation like that, it was hard to get into the spirit, but she wasn't going to make light of an honest competition. She glanced to her sides, surveying the area.

The bathing chamber was about thirty by twenty-five feet. On the right was the tub, lowered down into the floor, and on the left wall was a line of wooden chairs. The floor was polished granite and appeared very slippery where it was wet.

It would be difficult for Argo to take advantage of her footwork here. It would turn into a flat-footed jab fight, Asuna thought...

and then she realized just how much her brain had switched into combat mode. She took a deep breath.

"All right…here I go!"

Asuna took a sharp stride forward with her right foot.

Poof! Argo disappeared, leaving only a puff of white steam behind.

She's fast!

Faster than any monster Asuna had fought before. Even the strongest elite mob she'd ever faced, the Forest Elven Hallowed Knight, hadn't been able to move faster than Asuna's eye could follow. But Argo was so quick that it seemed she had teleported. The only reason Asuna was able to raise her left hand and lean to the right was her sense of hearing: She caught a single footstep hitting water on her left side.

A yellow blur grazed Asuna's side and passed behind her, producing a tiny little smacking sound.

"Kah…!"

Did it hit?! Asuna jumped as high as she could, spinning around in midair. She slid her feet back when she landed, taking advantage of the slippery floor to create extra distance between them.

As she took position with the bundle of herbs in front of her, Asuna saw, on the other side of the bathroom, Argo twirling the banana in her fingers, left hand on her waist.

"That was really good, A-chan. I figured I was going to win it in one go, but that was more of a lil' smack than a whap."

"…So the fight continues?" Asuna asked. The broker gave her a toothy grin.

In a sense, the display of that light-speed movement served the purpose of the duel in the first place. But being startled and letting it end would be a waste of Argo's invitation.

Huh? What am I…?

For a brief moment, she realized she was thinking something strange, so she cast that thought aside to concentrate. She couldn't keep up with Argo's speed, but speed alone was not all there was to fighting.

The experience in the catacombs was so terrifying that she never wanted to think about it again, but it had also taught her something very valuable. Battle wasn't just something that happened between you and your opponent. It also inevitably involved the surroundings. When Asuna fell through the trapdoor, and when she used the shrewman to recover her rapier, it had been the surroundings that had dictated the circumstances. In fact, the only way she had dodged Argo's swipe was the water on the floor telling her the direction.

Just as with the rapier, she could take that extra step and utilize her surroundings to her advantage.

Without taking her eye off the distant Argo, she confirmed the state of the arena. They'd switched spots so that the bath was now on her left side. She began to inch toward it, sliding the soles of her feet over the wet floor.

There was no extruding lip or boundary between the sunken bath and the floor of the washing area, and the water continually flowed up and out onto the floor, so it was hard to tell where the surface of the bath started. As she kept inching her way sideways, keeping the tip of the herbs pointed carefully at Argo, Asuna's toes eventually found the corner of the bath. But she didn't stop there—she continued sliding a further six inches to the left.

Asuna's left foot was completely off the floor, touching the surface of the bathwater. All her weight was supported on her right foot, in a pose that made it look easier than it actually was. It was an impossible pose to keep in the real world, but muscle fatigue was handled differently here. Any action that exceeded one's strength stat—carrying items that went over the weight capacity, trying to lift very heavy rocks—would cause a hidden fatigue parameter to rise. When that number reached its peak, the player's limbs or entire body would enter a weakened stun state. But it didn't necessarily show until that point, which made it hard to gauge when a player was attempting more than they could handle.

Based on how her right leg felt, Asuna guessed that she could

keep her left leg steady there for another ten seconds. She waited for Argo to move.

The steam gathering at the ceiling formed a large drop of water that fell and dripped onto the floor.

Once again, white steam billowed from Argo's feet.

This time she charged straight forward, not to the side. It was so fast that if she'd been standing normally, there would be no chance to react. Asuna tried to intercept Argo with the herbs, but her opponent simply slid past the tip toward Asuna's side.

Suddenly, the yellow swimsuit tilted to the left.

"Mwah—?!"

Argo's right foot sank through the water. That was Asuna's trap—resting her foot on the bath to make it look like she was standing on firm ground. As she hoped, Argo stepped off the bathing room floor, plunging her leg into the bath.

Got her!

She lowered the bundle at the sinking Argo. It wasn't a sword skill, of course, but it would be enough to whap her helpless opponent.

But instead of sinking down into the bath, Argo's body reacted unnaturally.

One of the leaves at the end of the herb bundle softly brushed the shoulder string of the tankini. Asuna lost her balance and toppled as she turned with Argo's momentum.

As she landed on her bottom at the lip of the bath, Asuna could not believe her eyes.

Argo was running on top of the water.

Before her right foot started to sink, she pushed off the water with her left, and before that one sank, she pushed again with her right. She got through four steps across the water, splashing uproariously, before plunging face-first into it and eventually rising out.

"…Nya-ha-ha-ha!"

The sight of the information agent laughing heartily with her face poking out of the water was somehow extremely funny to Asuna. She snorted and joined in.

After a good dozen seconds of laughing, they both got to their feet. Argo walked through the water normally to get out this time, tossed the banana into the bath, and stretched luxuriously.

"Mmmmm...Well, that was fun. I guess we'll say that each of us got in a smack and call it a draw?"

"Uh...y-yes, of course," Asuna agreed, dropping her herbs into the water. After watching the ripples spread across the bath, she looked up at Argo and asked, "Um...was that some kind of skill effect, the way you ran across the water...?"

"Well..." Argo started, tugging on her wet curls and rolling her eyes. "Normally I'd charge ya for that info, but I don't mind. It's not a skill, just a lot of hard training. Remember how I used those Floater Sandals on the river in the fourth floor?"

"Yes..."

"I had a lot of fun with those. I ran all over with 'em, and by the time I was good at it, I went into the water without them on. Well, I sank in, of course, but the first step I stayed on the water... Remember trying that as a kid at the pool? The theory that as long as your other foot moves while the first one hasn't sunk, it's like you're running on water."

"...M-maybe I did try that..."

"Well, when it occurred to me that maybe that's possible here, I couldn't hold back. Since then I've been practicing it in rivers and baths, until I was able to take about four steps. I guess you might call it an unofficial skill."

"..."

Asuna wasn't sure whether to be impressed or exasperated by this. Eventually, she decided to ask, "Do you think I could do that?"

"Mmm, I dunno. I was able to do it, so it's not that the game doesn't permit it...but it might be hard unless you put all your points into agility and have a lightweight avatar like mine. With your ample endowments..."

"Th-they're not that ample!" she shouted, crossing her arms in front of her. Argo hissed with laughter again and opened her window. She removed the yellow swimsuit and sent Asuna a trade window.

"Thanks for the suit. You can have it back."

"No...take it as payment for the info."

"You sure? Well, thanks."

Argo canceled the trade, and Asuna removed her own suit. She sank her chilly body back into the bath and exhaled.

Once every last cell of her body was relaxing in the crystal-clear water, a thought floated to the surface of her mind like a little bubble.

I was...enjoying that duel.

Well, they were using a banana and a bundle of herbs and never officially challenged each other, so it couldn't be called a duel, but they were two players competing in a fight. And at the very least, partway through Asuna had been a hundred percent serious about trying to land a good hit on Argo. And Asuna didn't shrink away. She enjoyed the excitement of the challenge.

"...Do you have a lot of dueling experience, Argo?" she asked, looking over to see the mousy brown curls swish sideways.

"Mm, not really. And definitely not since the retail game started."

"Well, you seem very used to it to me..."

"Izzat so? Given the trick you came up with on the spot, you seem a lot more comfortable in battle than me, A-chan. Ya tricked me good."

Asuna hunched her neck, embarrassed by the mention of her impromptu one-legged bath boundary ruse. "Th-that was just a spur-of-the-moment idea..."

"I'm not complainin'. It was a real good trick. Mind if I copy that one?"

"P-please do, I insist."

"Nee-hee-hee! Thanks. Well, I oughta pay you for that idea," Argo offered, grinning widely. Before Asuna could reply, she abruptly asked, "Are you afraid of dueling, A-chan?"

Only a truly talented gleaner of information could have seen through Asuna to the issue eating away at her heart.

"…Yes, if you can even say that. I only tried it once, here on this floor with Kirito. In fact, I couldn't even officially start the duel. The countdown ended, and we were facing each other with our weapons, and my body just refused to listen to my commands…"

Despite being in a warm bath up to her shoulders, she felt a chill trace her back in thinking about that moment. She clutched herself with both hands, trying to explain what was going through her mind at the time.

"…It wasn't that I was afraid of Kirito. He was very serious, but not in a threatening way. I was the one who asked him for PvP tips…and the duel was first-strike mode, but I was still terrified. And it made me horrified to think of moving onward…"

She lowered her mouth into the water and let out a little sigh. The stream of bubbles popped under her nose, filling her nostrils with a citrus scent.

"…I'm not sayin' I don't understand that feeling. But a silly sword-fight game and a real duel are different things. Even in a first-strike duel, you're losing HP," Argo offered. Asuna nodded, lifted her face out of the water, and turned to the other girl.

"To get back to the topic…when you go on solo recon missions, you can do that because of the incredible speed you showed me just now, right? You can handle a dangerous dungeon on your own, having the confidence to evade any attack that comes your way. Is that what you were trying to tell me with this duel?"

"When ya put it that way, I sure sound full of myself," the broker chuckled, shrugging, "but I'll admit that a part of me knows if I need to, I can sprint outta there. I've just got to be more careful about where I'm steppin' from now on."

She winked at Asuna, who grimaced and asked, "But having extreme AGI means low HP, and you can't equip tough armor to protect you, right? Don't you worry about what would happen if you take an unlucky heavy hit from a monster or get immobilized by a trap…?"

"I do worry about that, of course," the Rat said, smiling in a way that was more transparent than her usual smirk. "I'm scared of losing HP. Ya can't just respawn like in the old Aincrad...If I was thinking about survival and nothing else, I'd join a big guild and put all my points into strength to be a tank. In fact, maybe never leavin' the Town of Beginnings would be the smartest option. But...I happen to place a bit higher priority on what I'm doin' now rather than sheer survival."

"Because...you're a beta tester?"

"True, but not just that." Argo grinned and winked again. "Sorry, but any more than this will cost ya. Still, in thanks for inviting me to this incredible bath, I'll give you one piece of intel on the house."

"Uh...o-okay..."

"Earlier, you said that I didn't need to do this dangerous reconnaissance alone, that I could do like Kii-boy and join the frontline gang."

Asuna nodded, and Argo held up her index finger, waving it back and forth.

"But I think the reason Kii-boy doesn't brave the dangers of solo adventuring isn't because this way is more safe."

"Then...why?"

"Ain't it obvious?"

Argo's finger moved through the air to gently poke at Asuna's collarbone.

"Because he's got you."

7

"NEW YEAR'S EVE..." I SAID TO NO ONE IN PARTICULAR, lying in the grass and staring up at the bluish bottom of the floor above.

The date was indeed December 31, but it was still the bright daytime, the breeze wasn't particularly cold, and there was no house to clean, so it didn't *feel* like the end of the year. I closed my eyes and tried to remember what last New Year's Eve had been like.

I had wanted to participate in the New Year's Eve event of the MMO I had been playing at the time, but on my father's orders after his return for the holidays from America, I had to join the huge house-cleaning effort. I remembered the cleaning of the little kendo dojo in the corner of the yard being exhausting, so I had to bow and scrape to my sister Suguha, whom I hardly ever spoke to anymore.

When I returned to the living room, exhausted, my mother had brought out the sweet mochi rice cakes early, which were so tasty they hurt. I gave up on the MMO event and watched TV with my family, ate the special New Year's soba noodles, listened to the bells, then went to the nearby shrine for the customary first visit of the year...

I lifted my eyelids, ending the reminiscence.

All I saw was a lid of steel and rock, looming three hundred feet overhead.

Was my family in the real world cleaning at this very moment? Would Suguha be struggling to wipe the dojo clean without my help?

Fifty-five days ago, when Akihiko Kayaba announced that the game of death had begun, I never imagined that I would spend New Year's Eve in this world. I didn't have a vision about how many days it would take in total to clear all one hundred floors of Aincrad. And I certainly didn't expect that nearly two months later, we wouldn't even have beaten the fifth floor.

Assuming our pace remained the same, we would be here for New Year's Eve not just next year, but the year after as well. In fact...that was just a hopeful calculation. If I kept participating in the frontier group, I might not even survive to see the next New Year's Eve.

Until now, a part of me felt that if I died fighting monsters, I would have no regrets. Just after the game began, I left the Town of Beginnings before anyone else to make use of my beta knowledge and experience and up my chances of survival, but that wasn't all. In a way, I was afraid of other players being stronger than me. As a level-based MMORPG, once someone else got ahead of you in level, there was no catching them again. I was pressured by that fear playing on my ego. If I wanted to stay one of the best players, I had to continually risk the dangerous boss fights...It was a paradoxical thought process.

However...

Two days ago, I realized a new motive had appeared within me.

Even relaxed in the safety of the dark elf village, thinking about that moment made my guts churn uneasily. As I was rushing through the second level of the catacombs beneath Karluin to the next staircase in search of Argo the Rat, I saw Asuna's HP bar suddenly drop 10 percent in the upper left corner of my vision.

At first, I had no idea how my temporary partner could have

lost HP while asleep in her bedroom above Blink & Brink. The first possibility that occurred to me was that she accepted someone's duel within the city and was fighting them. But that was unlikely, given that it did not rise or fall any farther for many seconds afterward.

That left only one answer. Asuna had come into the catacombs dungeon after me. I had to overcome the urge to start sprinting madly and force myself to think about where she might be.

The toughest monsters on the second level were the poisonous Moldy Mummy and the astral Mournful Wraith. Both were tricky, but neither could take that much HP from Asuna at level 17 with one hit. Since her HP didn't change after that, it was most likely from a trap, not combat. This dungeon didn't have any traps that caused direct damage, which meant it was a trapdoor. And the only trapdoor was in one of the crypts right at the start of the second floor.

It would be more direct to go down the same trap to find her, but I was already deep on the second level, and the stairs were closer to me. I raced to the third level, cut down any monsters I saw, and raced straight for the area where the trapdoor let out.

Eventually I sensed people ahead, but all I saw were two unidentified cursors. They were both green, but I hid just in case, approaching the little room in the cave until I saw the two men in black cloaks.

Soon after, I heard one screech about a Chivalric Rapier +5. As soon as I saw the silver sword in his hand, I felt all the blood in my body freeze and boil simultaneously, a sensation I would never forget.

Asuna's HP bar was still displayed in the corner, yet I couldn't stop myself from imagining that they'd PKed her to get the rapier. Perhaps the cyclical updating process of the HP information was behind, and when it refreshed, it would instantly drop to zero. My body trembled at the thought.

At that moment, in the cave on the other side of the little room, Asuna saw me emerge and face the cloaked men, assuming that it was a bluff on my part, but I was half-serious. When Asuna abruptly emerged from her hiding spot and retrieved the rapier with brilliant aplomb, I thanked the god I assumed did not exist in this world.

It was time that I admitted it. The reason, the motive that I had for fighting at the very edge of human progress, was no longer just a yearning for numerical strength and superiority. The words I'd aptly spoken on the stairs to the fifth floor echoed through my head.

How long are you planning to work with me? Asuna had asked me. I'd responded as soon as the words popped into my head.

Until you're strong enough to not need me.

To my surprise, that had turned out to be a very honest answer. I wanted the fencer, always no more than my temporary partner, to survive through the end of the game…and I wanted to do everything in my power to see that through. It was a true and ongoing sentiment.

If she continued growing at her present rate, Asuna would undoubtedly surpass me in both knowledge and ability in the not-too-distant future. The moment when "she didn't need me" would come one day. When it did, I could not hold her back. Unlike me, she had the talent to shine in a group. She would eventually grow to be one of the true best players in the game, capable of leading a major guild that would free us from this prison.

My duty was to protect her until that time and give her all the information she needed to know.

That was everything, and nothing more.

Or so I told myself as I got up from the grass and heard a voice calling me from over my shoulder.

"The bath is ready for you, Kirito!"

I turned around and saw that same fencer climbing the little hill in the center of Shiyaya. When she reached the top of the hill next to me, she plopped down on the grass.

Her dark red hooded cape—the hood wasn't down now—and leather skirt were the usual, but there was a slight wetness effect remaining on her long chestnut-brown hair, shining with the reflection of the midday sun. In the moment, I was seized by a desire to touch it; I didn't, of course. Instead, I looked in the direction of the large bathhouse and asked, "Where's Argo?"

"She said she was going back to Mananarena. But she said hi to you."

"Oh..."

Just then, the third HP bar hanging from the left corner of my view disappeared without a sound. Argo had disengaged from the party as she left the village. The Rat hadn't been taking part in the Elf War campaign quest, so we invited her into the village to deliver the appropriate information, and she spent almost all her time in the bath with Asuna.

"That was a real long bath. What did you talk about?" I asked nonchalantly. For some reason, Asuna looked away in a panic briefly.

"Y-you shouldn't pry into girls' conversations."

"Eh...? So you're saying *the* Argo and *the* Asuna got together to have a little girl talk...?"

"I just told you not to pry! Besides, what do you mean, 'the' Asuna?!"

"S-sorry, sorry. I was just taken aback..."

"And I'll have you know that we were not engaging in 'girl talk'!" She snorted, opening her window to check the time. "Oh, it's already midday...If you're going to bathe, you should be quick about it."

"Nah, I'll do it next time. We've got to get moving on this..."

I looked to the north, toward the labyrinth tower looming a mile or two away. Asuna followed my lead and nodded.

"You're right. But...do you think the ALS is serious about tackling the floor boss early on their own...?"

"Hey, it was your intel, Asuna," I pointed out.

"I know, but..." she replied noncommittally.

As I suspected, Asuna had fallen through the trapdoor in the Karluin catacombs, which made her unfortunately fortunate enough to overhear a massive secret that even Argo didn't know. One of the two best guilds in the game, the Aincrad Liberation Squad, led by the spiky-haired Kibaou, was going to skip out on the expected year-end countdown tonight in Karluin to take on the floor boss by themselves.

At this minute, the ALS and the other major guild, the Dragon Knights Brigade, would be staying at a village called Mananarena, not far from Shiyaya. The village was in the center of the floor, half a day's travel from Karluin, but less than two hours if using the underground tunnel. So as I understood it, the guilds planned to return to Karluin by nightfall, preparing food and music, then throwing Aincrad's first New Year's party at nine o'clock.

But if the ALS was heading from Mananarena straight to the labyrinth tower in the northeast, to challenge the boss and head to the sixth floor—and it was the result of the agitation of Morte's mysterious PK gang, that was a development I couldn't ignore.

Asuna, Argo, and I spent much of the previous night discussing how to react to this plan. Ideally, the ALS would give up on their reckless plot and join the New Year's party in Karluin as planned, but they weren't the kind to take such well-meaning advice to heart. More likely, Kibaou would turn on us and demand, *"Where'dja hear that info from?!"*

We could leak the ALS plans to the DKB on the sly as well, hoping they would also try the tower...but it would mean canceling the big party.

The countdown party had been proposed and planned by the more relatively peaceful members of the DKB like Shivata and Hafner, together with the similarly cooperative officers of the ALS. If it was a success, the guilds would be on better terms in the future. That was what Morte and his cohorts were trying to prevent, so if the party never happened at all, their goal would be at least partially successful.

I sighed, wondering what we ought to do, when I heard Asuna whisper, "If only Kizmel was with us..."

Puzzled by this, I blinked and asked, "Uh…why?"

With a completely straight face, the fencer suggested a rather alarming plan. "Isn't it obvious? Together with Kizmel, we could beat the floor boss first. Then the ALS would have no reason to rush ahead of the others."

"…Uh…right…That is a good point," I hesitantly agreed at first, then switched gears and shook my head violently. "A-actually, no, not a good point at all. Even with Kizmel, that would be insane."

Kizmel the dark elf knight had visited Shiyaya yesterday to our delight. But unfortunately—if you saw it that way—the fifth-floor chapter of the Elf War quest was quite brief, so after a few short quests and a battle against a Fallen Elf officer, Kizmel moved onward to the sixth floor.

Thinking back on our fun but brief quest with her, I continued, "We were only just barely able to beat the hippocampus on the fourth floor with Kizmel, Viscount Yofilis, and an entire full raid party. And the fifth floor is a milestone floor, so we'll have a tougher boss than usual…"

"Oh…What kind of boss was it in the beta?"

"It was a gigantic golem, the guardian of the ancient ruins. However, the area boss in the catacombs was completely different from the beta boss, so they could have totally changed the floor boss as well. We won't know anything until we scout it out…"

"Good point. Speaking of which," Asuna wondered, staring pensively toward the tower, "the ALS haven't done the boss quests, have they? And they're going to attempt the floor boss on the first try without any of Argo's strategy guides? Where are they getting the confidence to try this…?"

Boss quests were a series of quests related to the boss of each floor. Doing them earned you hints about the boss's category, strengths, and weaknesses. But because the quests were heavily story based, time-consuming, and offered poor rewards, the ALS and DKB preferred to wait for the info to get out—in other words, for Argo to put out the boss issue of her strategy guide.

Asuna and I had been busy enough with the Elf War campaign that we hadn't gotten around to the boss quests yet, so we couldn't act too high-and-mighty about it, but Asuna was right that the ALS was being reckless. Even if an insider from the PK gang was inciting them on, we needed to figure out what sort of criteria was causing this heedless plan to be accepted by the group…

"Hmm. Do we know anyone in the ALS who understands enough to share more information?" I wondered. Asuna looked pensive.

"I don't think so. Most of the current frontline group is made up of Diavel's raid party from the first floor, right? Since he died in that fight, Lind took over and created the DKB. Then Kibaou resisted the hierarchical structure of Lind's style and formed the ALS based around solidarity…Given that history, the DKB members will feel that they are the 'original' group, while the ALS feels like the underdog that has to seize the reins from the DKB."

"Aha…So it's like majority and minority political parties," I noted, impressed. But Asuna's troubled expression didn't fade.

"It's just that the difference in strength between them is minor. In that sense, the ALS is working really hard. The problem is that you and I are, if anything, members of the Diavel team. The ALS seems to think we're both DKB leaning."

"Uh…*what*?! Who would believe we're DKB leaning…?" I shook my head, gaping. "In fact, along those lines, wouldn't Kibaou be considered part of Diavel's team? He seemed to really look up to Diavel, in fact."

As I spoke, I recalled the scene of the very first strategy meeting we held in the town of Tolbana on the first floor. That had been December 4, so it wasn't even a full month ago. Yet the image seemed so distant now.

A blue-haired young man standing at the lip of a fountain. Silver armor gleaming in the setting sun, and a friendly smile.

My name's Diavel, and I like to think of myself as playing a knight!

With that cheerful greeting, Diavel seized the hearts and minds of the players present. And when he met a heroic, fateful end against Illfang the Kobold Lord, boss of the first floor—no matter the circumstances behind the scenes—Diavel the knight became a sort of holy figure to the players of the front line.

Asuna echoed this opinion by saying, "I think that's why. Kibaou really respected Diavel…so he believes that by leading the DKB, Lind is trying to use Diavel's image for his own purposes."

"Yeah, you could be right. Ever since the first meeting, Kibaou expressed his anger with the former beta testers. I'm sure he can't stand the thought of a small percentage of players monopolizing the best resources like in other MMOs, now that *SAO* is a game of death. In that sense, you can see why he can't hang with the DKB, given the stark differences in how they treat their officers and normal members…"

"Uh-huh," Asuna agreed, looking down at the brand-new boots she was wearing. They were magic boots she'd received as one of her rewards from Viscount Yofilis.

They were items that everyone had the chance to earn if they made their way through the Elf War campaign, so it wasn't truly a monopoly, but there was clearly a kind of conflict between their gradually growing layout of elite gear and Kibaou's mantra of redistribution.

I reached out unconsciously toward Asuna's knee to break her gaze on the boots below. "It's true that Kibaou's assertion that we should share what we gain equally, whether information or items, has a kind of merit. Now that this game is deadly, the most valuable resource of all is player life, so it only makes sense to maximize our protection of it. But in an extreme situation like a boss fight, it's impossible to treat your own life and others' lives equally. First, you protect yourself; then the next closest player… That's why I want you to put the most effort into keeping yourself safe, Asuna. Including equipping yourself with high-level armor."

"…Yeah."

She nodded timidly, then cleared her throat.

"I get it. You don't have to press so hard. I happen to like these boots; I'm not thinking of giving them to someone else."

"Okay," I said, relieved. Then I noticed that through her socks, I was firmly gripping Asuna's shapely knee.

"Wuhoah!" I yelped, removing my hand at light speed and hiding it in my coat. "S-s-s-sorry! I wasn't doing that to cop a feel or anything, it was your boots..."

"What about my boots?"

"I was trying to...touch your boots..."

"That's the same thing!"

I withdrew my argument, properly scolded, and fortunately Asuna did not let that distract her from the topic at hand. "At any rate, from the ALS's viewpoint, we are targets for correction. I doubt that any of them are just going to reveal sensitive guild information to us. Actually...wait a second..."

She frowned, then glanced at me.

"...It wasn't *just* the DKB members who planned tonight's countdown party, was it?"

"I think so...Shivata and the DKB led the planning, but the goal was to bring the two guilds closer together, so a member of the ALS was going to cooperate, I think," I said, recalling the instant message that Agil sent us four days earlier.

Asuna thrust her face forward. "So maybe that person on the ALS side will talk to us? I mean, the big party they were planning could be ruined by this sneaky boss plan, right? It might be their guild, but they can't be happy about that."

I was recalling the note about "inviting my partner" at the end of Agil's message, so it was a second later that I finally processed what Asuna was saying. I smacked my knee.

"Ah, good point...If their early boss plan was forced by the hard-line members, then the moderate party planner would have been overruled. They must have some private thoughts about that...but then..." I trailed off.

"But then what?" Asuna asked, suspicious. I avoided meeting

her gaze by pulling up strands of grass nearby. When I continued my thought, it was in a darker tone.

"Unless I'm just thinking too hard about this…the party could have been just a part of the plan. If they proposed the New Year's event to distract the DKB and keep them tied to the city, that would give them a better opportunity to jump ahead. If that's the case, then we won't learn anything from the planner on the ALS side. Instead, they'll be suspicious, and it'll make things worse…"

"…"

Asuna didn't respond for a while. Her left hand began pulling grass next to mine, starting a little competition. Tiny plants like grass weren't treated as separate items by the game. They disappeared as soon as you pulled them loose, but did not vanish from the ground, so you could keep pulling them indefinitely if you wanted.

For most of a minute, we yanked and yanked on the blades of grass, until Asuna finally spoke.

"…I don't want to imagine that the ALS would go that far. The non-Morte player on the third floor of the catacombs was definitely a spy within the ALS. Even if he's agitating the hard-line faction to give them an edge, there must be players in the guild that want to be on peaceful terms with the DKB."

Now it was my turn to fall silent.

In all honesty, my "party planner is agent of sabotage" theory and Asuna's "ALS moderate faction" theory could coexist. If the planner was a secret hard-liner, the plot could have all been happening behind the moderates' backs.

But no amount of thinking in this situation was going to bring us an answer. Ultimately, it came down to whether or not we believed in the good nature of *SAO* players.

I knew I didn't have the right to believe in that. On the day that *SAO* began, the moment that Kayaba's welcoming tutorial ended, I was the first to race out of the Town of Beginnings. I couldn't imagine a future in which ten thousand players banded together as one to defeat the game. I sought to make myself more power-ful, so I could avoid the malice of some unseen fellow player.

But Asuna was different. She didn't pick up her sword and leave the safety of town to be stronger than others. After we ate black bread with cream in the backstreets of Tolbana, I asked her why she left the Town of Beginnings.

So that...I can be myself. If I was going to just hide back in the first city and waste away, I'd rather be myself until the very last moment.

Asuna was battling herself. She believed in the strength within her and was trying to prove its existence. That strength was radi-ating out of her now, shining upon me as I sat next to her.

"...Let's go ask," I said, giving the grass a break. I sensed Asuna looking over at me. I glanced into those hazel-brown eyes, feel-ing the powerful light within them, and continued, "The ALS's plan to jump the boss is too dangerous, and even if they succeed, it will create a huge rift between them and the DKB. If there's a chance we can stop them, we should act, not sit here. And if he were able to see us now, I'm sure Diavel would scold us..."

"...You're right," Asuna said, a faint smile on her lips. I thought I heard her say "*thank you*." I stood up without reacting—not knowing how I should respond anyway—and clapped my hands.

"In that case, let's go back to Mananarena for lunch!"

"Sure thing. But...how will we identify the member of the ALS that was responsible for planning the party?" Asuna asked as she got to her feet, brushing the backside of her leather skirt.

I smirked.

"We could ask Argo for help, but she's probably tackling the boss quests about now...We'll do it the orthodox way."

As befitting an elf village, Shiyaya was full of water and greenery. By contrast, Mananarena was a dusty place built in the remains of an ancient mine. Stores and homes lined the sides of a mortar-like depression that extended down into the earth, with the yawning mouth of a mine-shaft dungeon at the very bottom. In there were ores and fossils, as well as a rich assortment of relics, but for now, Asuna and I headed to the biggest restaurant in town.

If we kept following the downward spiral path, we would eventually arrive at our destination, but we were in a hurry and used staircase shortcuts here and there. At about the middle of the descent, we came into view of a large building exuding lively music and pleasant smells.

The fragrance of cooking meat hit me directly in my empty stomach, but first I had to check the interior through the window. As I expected, the place was full of players, but most were DKB members. The ALS would be staying in town, too, but they were likely congregated within a different restaurant lower in the town.

From what I could tell peeking through the window, the DKB looked cheerful. Even through the window, the jostling of mugs, cheers, and raucous laughter were obvious. The fulfillment of ample money and experience earned from the dungeon and the excitement about the upcoming countdown party in town were bringing those smiles to their faces.

"...I don't think I've ever seen Lind and the others smiling like that..." Asuna noted. I glanced at the table in the center of the restaurant.

The man at the head of the table with the long blue hair tied back and his mug in the air was undoubtedly Lind, leader of the DKB. The man most recognized for the ever-present disapproving wrinkle between his brows was smiling wide.

"Maybe he got hit with a curse that causes him to keep laughing," I suggested. Asuna elbowed me in the side.

"This isn't the time for stupid jokes."

"Yes, ma'am..."

I tore my eyes from Lind and continued scanning the room, then found the person I was looking for. A tall, thin man ordering from an NPC at the back counter, standing apart from the rest of the group: Shivata.

"Here we go!"

I opened my menu and moved to the messages tab, typed up a quick instant message made out to the player named Shivata, and sent it.

Through the window, Shivata reacted instantly. With his back toward us, he checked his menu, then glanced around surreptitiously. Once he saw me looking through the window, he made a face of obvious displeasure, but left the counter, said a word to one of the other members, and left.

By the time he got outside, Asuna and I moved away from the window and into the shade of the adjacent building.

"Over here," I called quietly, and Shivata walked over to us but kept going without slowing down. As he passed, I heard a faint "Follow me," and we let him go before following at a distance.

Shivata climbed the spiral path for one or two hundred feet, then walked into an empty dwelling. Once we were certain no other players were in the vicinity, I opened the same door and set foot inside the dark interior.

As soon as Asuna closed the door behind me, a voice of pure, 100 percent irritation shouted, "What are you playing at?!" from the darkness.

Leaning against the back wall with his arms crossed was Shivata, his eyebrows angled in a way that would be impossible in real life. Asuna prodded me forward and whispered, "What kind of message did you send him?"

"Uh...I just asked which ALS member had been involved in planning the countdown party with them..."

"And that's why he's so angry? You didn't put anything else especially insulting in there?"

"I-I didn't! I think."

As if he heard us, Shivata's brows began to change angles. They started at a V for maximum fury, then shot past horizontal and ended in a slight reverse slope of miserable concern.

"...You...you didn't contact me because you knew about me and my partner?" he asked.

I frowned. "Partner...? We know that tonight's party was joint planned between you and the ALS, but nothing more than that..."

For some reason, Shivata clamped his mouth shut, looking guilty. His eyes started wandering suspiciously over the ceiling, and he cleared his throat evasively a few times.

I had no idea why the DKB officer would need to react in such an inexplicable way, but Asuna had latched onto something. "*Oh-ho*," she gloated, stepping past me and pulling back her hood.

"It's all right, Shivata. We just want to know how the party was put together. If you simply tell us that, we won't pry into anything else, and we won't tell anyone what we learned here."

That seemed to bring some calm to Shivata's nerves, but the suspicion in his eyes hadn't disappeared entirely. The tall man leaned forward a bit and grunted, "How can I be sure of that?"

"We just want the party to happen as it was planned. Now, I'm just guessing, but...have you perhaps received a foreboding message from the planner on the ALS side?"

"H-how did you know...?" he asked, stunned.

Asuna took a step forward.

"We'll help you solve the problem. So will you tell us in more detail? With your ALS counterpart, if possible."

I panicked a bit, thinking she had gone too far, but Shivata's athletic features only contorted with indecision. He grunted, "You're certain you'll keep our secrets?"

"I swear on my blade," Asuna replied theatrically, which seemed surprisingly effective on Shivata. He nodded his head in defeat and opened his window.

While the DKB member tapped awkwardly at his holo-keyboard, I leaned in toward Asuna and asked, "What in the world just happened?"

The fencer chuckled smugly back at me and whispered, "You'll find out soon."

However, when the door opened again three minutes later and a smallish ALS member entered, I still hadn't found my answer.

He was probably a tank, outfitted with a full steel plate that was rare at this early floor and a heavy armet helm that covered his whole head. A long mace was slung over his back. Even in town, the helm's visor was down, so the face behind the vertical slit was invisible.

If our bad suspicions were true, this man was a hard-line saboteur of the ALS and was in an ongoing play to deceive Shivata. In the worst case, he was the second companion of Morte, infiltrating the ALS. In fact, he might even be the same man Morte was meeting in the catacombs.

If that was the case, he might start swinging that mace any second now. The man glanced in our direction as I went into full vigilance mode—then he turned back to Shivata.

"What's this about, Shiba?"

The man's words were distorted by the metallic effect of the closed helm, so I couldn't tell if it belonged to the cloaked partner from a few days before.

Shivata scratched at his short hair and gave his excuse. "Sorry for calling you out like this. But they said they're going to help with the party. Plus…I think the fencer's figured it out."

I looked at Asuna in disbelief, but I still had no idea what she had figured out. The man in plate armor budged, clanking from the joints as he looked up at Asuna.

"…Really? How could you tell?"

Asuna returned a very confident smile and said, "From the way Shivata reacted. It was obvious."

"…"

After a long silence, the metal helm creaked in Shivata's direction.

"I told you, you let too much show on your face, Shiba."

"I-I can't help it. The NerveGear just takes your emotions and puts them out there."

"Then you ought to wear a face-covering helmet, too."

"C-come on, you know I can't…"

As I listened to the plated man and Shivata talk, an indescribable feeling began to eat away at me. I tugged on Asuna's cape.

"Hey...what's going on here...?"

But the fencer merely grinned back, then took a step forward and said to the plated man, "Listen, I don't mean you any harm. We're looking forward to tonight's party, and we know there's a problem on the ALS side. We just want to know more so we can help solve the issue."

"..."

After a full five seconds of silence, the man nodded slowly at last.

He lifted his right hand, clad in heavy gauntlet, and opened his window. He placed his finger against the top slot of his equipment mannequin and flicked.

The armet vanished in a brief spray of steel-colored particles.

What emerged was orangish hair cut neatly above the brows and the cute, doll-like facial features of a girl.

No way, you can't determine sex in SAO *by the features alone. You can't say for sure that a guy would never look like this...*

That thought was cut off by the very cute sound of a female voice nothing like the metallic echo I heard earlier.

"We believe you. I...I have a lot of respect for you, Asuna. Plus, Shiba and I put a lot of work into this party, and we want it to succeed."

Shivata's track-runner features took on an expression that should've been accompanied by the sound of an angelic chorus.

So that was what it meant. The plate-armored man from the ALS was a plate-armored woman. And she and Shivata from the DKB were more than strangers, though it wasn't clear when it started...

"...What the hell?!"

It was all I could do to hold my head in my hands and shout.

The woman, whose name was Liten, sat down in an old chair with her helmet off but the rest of her heavy armor still on.

Shivata sat next to her, and Asuna and I took seats across from them. The chairs had been abandoned in the old house long enough that I was concerned for their sturdiness, but the furniture from NPC houses was all essentially indestructible, so even the weight of full-body armor wasn't enough to break them.

I leaned across the similarly ragged table and asked the first question.

"So…Liten. How long have you been in the ALS?"

"December twenty-second," she said instantly, her bowl-cut orange hair totally still. I consulted my mental calendar.

"So the day after the fourth floor was opened…Did you enlist? Or…"

"I was scouted. Because of this."

Liten spoke frankly, glancing down at the suit of armor covering her body.

I'd felt earlier that the type of steel plate armor she was wearing was rather rare for the fourth or fifth floor. NPC shops did not sell the complete set, and I couldn't think of any monsters that dropped it.

Which meant it had to be crafted, but it was a difficult task to commission NPC blacksmiths or players with metal armor crafting skills for something like that. Just seeing a list of the crafting ingredients you'd need would be enough to put you off the task.

Collecting metal materials started with mining ores with a pickax from the walls of caves and the sides of rock boulders.

Once the player's inventory was full of the heavy, bulky ores, they needed to return to an NPC smith to have the ores refined and forged into metal planks or larger ingots. It took two ores to make a plank and six to fashion an ingot.

"Iron" in Aincrad was what we would call pig iron in the real world, just a rank above bronze in quality. But iron ingots could be used to produce the more-valuable steel ingots. It was a simple process to melt down iron ingots, but the yield was poor; it took four iron ingots to make one steel ingot, meaning four times the iron ore.

And to create a full set of steel heavy armor required at least sixty steel ingots. That meant $60 \times 4 \times 6$ iron ores, or…1,440 in total.

I couldn't imagine how many days it would take to mine that much ore. If things hadn't changed since the beta, ten ores was the maximum extractable from a particular vein, and on the lower floors, such veins were few and far between. So crafting seemed to be ruled out. Then how did Liten get this armor?

Yet that suspicion of mine was flatly denied by the first female voice I'd heard in ages that didn't belonging to Asuna or Argo.

"This armor was player made. Of course, I didn't make it myself."

"R-really…? Which means you mined out a thousand-plus iron ores? How long did that take you, if you don't mind me asking…?" I said, aghast. Liten only grinned and shook her head.

"You don't have to be so polite with me, Kirito. You're my senior among the advanced group."

"Er, right…"

I glanced beside her, where Shivata was nodding, his athlete's mask cracking to reveal some other kind of emotion.

"Yeah, that's fine. You and I are on pretty equal terms, so it would feel weird for you to act formal around Liccha…around Liten."

"W-well, if you insist…"

I really wanted to bust his balls about the nickname he had nearly given her, but my sense of propriety prevailed.

"So about the topic at hand…" I prompted.

Liten pursed her lips for a moment, then spoke heavily. "Well, this is something I've told only Shiba, so I'd appreciate it if you kept it between us…"

"Of course. That was our promise from the very start," Asuna intercepted. I agreed. Satisfied, Liten resumed her explanation.

"It was about a month ago that I left the Town of Beginnings. Of course, it was my first time playing a VRMMO, but I'd tried online games before, so I didn't want to just wait around in town for someone else to beat the game. I wanted to join the fight and help out. It was a late start compared to Shiba and Asuna, but I had chosen the Heavy Armor skill just after the game started, and it was a huge task to put together my armor..."

"So you were always planning to be a tank?" Asuna asked.

Liten immediately answered, "Yes. I usually played a defensive role in the other games, too. I hunted the boars and such outside the Town of Beginnings, and when I finally got a store-made Copper Mail, I thought I could finally proceed upward. But then I found that no parties would accept me. I know it's not something I can help, but I kept hearing that they couldn't trust a woman to be a tank."

"Even though it has nothing to do with your fighting abilities," Asuna added, incensed.

Liten's eyes narrowed.

"I should have told them that...but instead I got very stubborn and said I'd make the front line as a solo tank and started mining ores for my armor and grinding levels..."

"I know tanks have high strength, and thus high carrying capacity, but mining a thousand ores is still incredible work," I commented, impressed, but Liten looked down for some reason. Meanwhile, Shivata muttered to her that she didn't have to mention it if she didn't want to, but the bowl-cut girl shook her head.

"Yes, I gathered all the ores to make this armor myself. As you said, I had to mine at least fifteen hundred iron ores. But...it's not something to be proud of at all."

"What do you mean?" Asuna asked in a calm, gentle tone meant to reassure—sadly, a sound I almost never heard from her.

"I was grinding levels near the town of Marome on the second floor," Liten went on. "I found a vein of ore in a little valley, so I switched my mace for a pickax and started chipping away like usual. Normally I would get seven or eight and that would be it, but this spot just kept producing and producing without running out. At first I just thought I had found a lucky spot, and was very excited, but eventually it got scary…By the time I had pulled out over a hundred, I finally figured it out. That it was…"

"An infinite bug?" I asked, stunned. Liten nodded. Asuna looked confused, so I explained, "It's a bug in the program that causes monsters or items to continue generating past their normal limit. I've never heard of one in *SAO*…but I guess everything is prone to them…"

"Oooh…so you could just keep mining the same vein for ores as long as you wanted. It's like winning the lottery or something," Asuna said innocently. The rest of us grimaced. Shivata spoke as representative for the hard-core gamers.

"It's not that simple, Asuna. Taking advantage of such a bug is called glitching, and whether or not you take advantage of it in a single-player game is up to you. But in an MMO, if the management finds out about it, they can roll back your status or even ban you."

"So Liten…didn't give up on it? I mean, you have the armor, after all…"

The short hair bobbed up and down in affirmation. "Yes…I was conflicted, but I couldn't stop myself. With an infinite supply of iron ore, I could skip right past iron armor and go to steel. It was all I could think about…"

"I don't blame you. If I found a spot like that, I'd go crazy mining it," I reassured her.

Shivata said, "I'd do it too!" in an oddly competitive way.

Steeling myself against the look I was certain Asuna would give me, I asked, "And, um, just out of curiosity, this infinite-generating point is still active…?"

"No…" Liten said, shaking her head sideways this time. "I mined it nonstop for about thirty minutes, until suddenly the rock texture seemed to fail. It came back to normal right away, but no ores dropped from it anymore."

"So the devs noticed the bug and fixed it…? I mean, if there even *are* any devs…" I wondered.

Shivata shrugged. "Well, the bug was fixed, so what other possibility is there?"

"But none of the Argus staff can tamper with the *SAO* server now, right? The only person with administrator privileges is Akihiko Kayaba..."

"Then Kayaba fixed it."

At that point, I had no grounds to deny it. I mumbled that maybe he was right and got back to the topic.

"Meaning that you made your plate armor from the ores you mined there. I'm surprised you could carry over a thousand ores, though...I remember that iron ore has a pretty long decay period, but even then, it had to be a monster task, right?"

Liten shook her head again. "No...I didn't transport it all myself. In fact, even after I brought it to the village, it wouldn't all fit into the storage at the inn..."

"Oh, good point..."

If you rented out an inn room, it would come with its own chest, which could be used for external storage, but the ones at the budget-rate inns were small in size. Of course, it was enough for extra gear, food, and potions, but not hundreds and hundreds of metal ores. Storage for heavy ores was an issue for everyone and the biggest initial challenge for a player who wanted to be a blacksmith.

"In that case, what if you brought a portable forge to the mining spot and melted them all down? You can carry way more as ingots. And if that wasn't possible, you could go straight to an NPC smith to do the job," Asuna suggested.

I had tried that idea in the beta, a fond memory of my early trial-and-error days. I explained why it wouldn't work: "Unfortunately, you can only use a portable forge to craft gear and upgrade it. Ingots have to be cast at a large, fixed forge. You could take them to a blacksmith, but that could lead to trouble if other players saw you. A combat-centric player hauling in tons of ore to melt down is practically advertising that there's a huge stack of it outside town..."

"I was afraid of that, too...It was right around the time of the big fuss about the upgrade scam on the second floor, so I was worried about dangerous people following me around," Liten admitted. It seemed that this was news to Shivata, who had lost his main weapon to that very scam. He turned to her in concern.

"Licchan, there was a lot of stuff that went on behind the scenes with that scam, and I can't go into specifics, but the people who did it weren't just plain bad people. They apologized to the victims and compensated them for the loss, so there's no bad guys anymore."

"Oh…Thanks for letting me know, Shiba."

If I was a kid in grade school, I might have gotten away with whistling and taunting, *"Hey guys, things are looking so hot between you, the South Pole's gonna melt!"* but I was going to be in the third year of middle school next year and needed to be more mature than that.

Sadly, Shivata's words were already being proven false. Perhaps it was known only by Asuna and me among the front line, but there was a *true* group of bad guys, a PK gang, working in the shadows. The entire point of setting up this meeting was to help fight back against Morte's plot.

I wanted to get right to the point, but it wasn't clear yet if Liten could be absolutely trusted. It was a surprise that she was female—and that she and Shivata were *like that*—but that brought its own suspicions to the plate. I didn't want to think about it, but I couldn't rule out the possibility of a honey trap in play. At the very least, I needed to hear the story of this steel armor to the end.

"Then…how did you move the ore?" I asked. Liten straightened up and resumed her story.

"Ah…well, before the physical transportation even entered into it, I wasn't sure if I should use the ore. As a tank, I was desperate for it, but it was obviously an infinite supply bug…so I wasn't sure if I should use armor I got through a glitch, because I was afraid of what would happen if I got banned…So I decided to ask a friend who was helping repair my gear on the first floor for advice."

"Repair...? So your friend was a blacksmith?" I asked, envisioning the face of Nezha, the blacksmith at the center of the very upgrading scam we'd talked about a minute ago.

Liten nodded. "Yes. She's not really a smith—not with her own shop—she just was putting a bit of work into the weapon- and armor-crafting skills. We got along, both being girls, and so I started asking her for help with maintenance and crafting a bit."

"Oooh, a female blacksmith..."

That alone confirmed that it wasn't Nezha. It was at this point that I was reminded there were still players in the Town of Beginnings who were taking on the game as best they could.

"I sent her a friend message about the ores, and she replied at once...She hadn't had much MMO experience before *SAO*, but she was absolutely decisive."

A little smile appeared on Liten's lips.

"She said I shouldn't hesitate, that the most important thing in this world was to survive, then to beat the game, in that order, so you should use whatever bugs you need to in order to get stronger. And that even if I got banned, it would mean getting out of here, so I shouldn't be afraid in the least...I realized it was totally true, so I asked her to help me carry the ore, and we got the blacksmith at Marome to turn all of them into steel ingots without being detected by any other players."

"So it wasn't an NPC that made your armor, but a friend of yours?" Asuna asked.

Liten nodded proudly.

"Yes! It was just barely within her skill level, and she said I should pay an NPC for it, but I insisted she try...She failed over and over, turning it back to ingots, then pounded away again, throughout the night, until she had made me all five pieces: torso, legs, gauntlets, boots, and helm."

"Wow...she must be a good friend and a good blacksmith..." I said admiringly. This time, Liten's smile was clear and undeniable. That moment was enough to convince me for good that she was not Morte's saboteur.

* * *

The rest of the story was short. With a five-piece set of steel armor that was rare even among the best players, Liten leveled up against the treants of the third floor until the ALS recruited her, which she accepted on her blacksmith friend's advice. On the fourth floor, she met Shivata from their rival guild, and they ended up hitting it off...And the fine details of that part of the story would be unbearable without alcohol.

At any rate, as they continued to grow closer in secret, they started planning to bring the guilds together in harmony—the first step of which would be tonight's countdown party. On the DKB side, Lind was surprisingly enthusiastic about it, and the others seemed to be eager as well. The problem was the ALS.

Now that the story was finally up to the present, I pulled four little bottles of lime water out of my inventory. Sadly, they weren't chilled, but they served to quench the dried throats of everyone present before we got to the most crucial part.

"Umm...first, how much have you told Shivata about the problem within the ALS, Liten?"

Shivata reacted to this question before Liten did. "Exactly. You sent me that message yesterday saying a problem arose but you were going to handle it, Licchan. I was worried about what that meant..."

"I'm sorry, Shiba," Liten said, but it was obvious from the look on her face that she was caught between a rock and a hard place.

No doubt the ALS had issued a stern gag warning to all members about their plan to jump the boss early. As a member of the guild, she had a duty to obey, but Liten was also an executive member of the countdown party-planning committee with Shivata. Her distress was palpable.

"If something happened, why won't you tell me? I know I'm in the DKB, but more importantly, we're both *SAO* players. The ironic thing is, you were the one who helped me realize that..." he pleaded, placing a hand on her armored shoulder, but Liten only stared down at the floor.

I made eye contact with Asuna and cleared my throat. "If Liten can't explain it to you, then I will. Listen carefully to what I say, Shivata...The core members of the ALS plan to ditch tonight's countdown party and attempt the floor boss on their own."

Shivata wasn't the only one who looked shocked. Liten leaned back with a metallic clank, nearly falling out of her chair. Her topaz eyes, close to her orange hair in color, were bulging.

"K...Kirito, how did you know that...?!"

"Sorry, I can't tell you yet. But I assure you that it wasn't a leak from within the ALS, and I didn't buy it from the info broker."

"...Oh...I see...W-well, it doesn't matter. I'm sure players like you two have your own top-level information gathering abilities..."

"Y-you're getting the wrong idea about us," I pleaded after an awkward look from Asuna. "I'm an outsider within the group, and I just do my own thing, so I'm not in a position to give any orders to the ALS or DKB. But...Asuna and I really, truly want to make sure the two guilds don't engage in hostilities. Sure, a reasonable rivalry might help advance the pace of conquest... but this act of going behind the other's back is crossing a line. If they succeed, it will totally ruin relations with the DKB, and if it fails...it could result in the total collapse of the ALS. I mean, they're going after the milestone fifth boss as a single guild..."

Shivata had his head in his hands. He groaned, "But...why would this happen? Kibaou is gruff and rude, but he's not stupid. He should know full well how reckless it is to challenge a floor boss on his own..."

Asuna and I had come to Mananarena to find an answer to that mystery. With three sets of eyes on her, Liten bit her lip in indecision, then finally made up her mind.

"...If you already know about that, then I will tell you what I know."

The newest tank in the ALS took a sip of lime water, stretched, and began to speak.

*   *   *

"The ALS stresses equality among members, so meetings are held with full attendance, as a basic rule. But the meeting about the boss strategy in question was held among only a dozen or so of the oldest members. I was still a fresh new recruit, so I wasn't called to join. So everything I tell you came from my group leader.

"The meeting was held three days ago, on the night of the twenty-eighth. One of the senior members got crucial info from a beta tester. Because the topic was so sensitive, Kibaou made the decision to limit attendance to just the senior members.

"The info was about an incredibly important item dropped by the fifth-floor boss…something that would change things dramatically depending on whether the ALS or the DKB got the drop. My group leader and some other officers argued that if it was that important, they should bring it to the DKB's attention and propose joint management before the fight. The party would be the perfect setting to hash things out.

"But joint management of the item in question was apparently impossible by nature. That led to the opinion that they should defeat the boss while the party was happening, to ensure that they got the item…otherwise, the ALS might end up being absorbed into the DKB. Ultimately, Kibaou didn't have any choice but to approve the boss strategy. That's everything that I know about this."

When Liten finished, Shivata turned to his left, twisting at the waist, and rasped, "Licchan, what in the world is this item…?"

But she could only shake her head sadly. "Sorry, Shiba. I learned about the boss plan just this morning. I asked my group leader for more information, but that was top secret…The group leader was all for our party, but there was nothing they could do about this. I'm new, so what could I do? I talked with the rest of the group, and we'd just decided we should state our case to Kibaou directly, when I got Shiba's message."

"...I had no idea..." Shivata groaned. He looked up, straight into my eyes; swallowed; and asked, in a deadly serious tone, "You're a former beta tester—so do you know it? What's this crucial item the fifth-floor boss drops?"

"Um...errmm...?"

I crossed my arms and tilted my head as far to the side as it would go. "Crucial item from the fifth boss...? I took part in that fight, but I think it was a two-handed swordsman who got the centerpiece drop...I mean, any boss drop is going to be great, but I don't recall something so powerful it would destroy the balance between guilds. Besides, a weapon can just be joint managed..."

I pulled my head back to a normal angle, shut my eyes, and replayed distant memories.

The fifth-floor boss in the beta was a huge golem made of blue stone, much like the ruins. Naturally, it had tremendous defense and was nearly tall enough to scrape against the ceiling of the boss chamber—a considerable challenge, but at a time when you could laugh off dying. With the sheer suicidal force of nearly a hundred players, we crumbled the stone golem to dust, and ten or so items dropped for a lucky few. After a brief assessment of the loot, we climbed the stairs to the sixth floor. It was just the usual excitement after beating a boss.

No...wait.

There *was* an odd item that dropped for someone. It looked like a fancy polearm, but it had extremely low attack power, which we all laughed about in puzzlement, so the winner tossed it aside angrily. Someone else picked it up and, within a few days, displayed its true worth to the shock of all—a story that I just barely recalled in the corner of my mind. In any case, it was an item that meant nothing to me, but if my memory was correct, it was...

"A flag..."

The other three looked at me.

"A flag? What about a flag?" Asuna asked. The image of a tricorn pennant flapping over a battle flickered into my mind. I sucked in a sharp breath, clutching my hands together, and I rose slightly out of my chair.

"Oh...*ohhh*...Yes, that would be bad!"

"Wh-what is it, Kirito?! When you say 'flag,' do you mean a switch? Some condition that will prompt a change in the game?" Shivata shouted, also out of his chair. It was probably the first time the athlete had called me by name instead of "you," but I didn't even register it. I shook my head.

"No...not a programming flag, I mean a literal flag..."

"Why would a flag be an ultra-powerful item?"

"It's not just an ordinary flag. It's a guild flag. If you carry it around, every guild member within fifty or sixty feet gets a buff to all their stats..."

Shivata's narrow eyes went round. He gaped.

"Wh...what...?"

8

I WASN'T SURE IF IT WAS BASED ON THE SPIRAL structure of the town, but Mananarena's local specialty was a jumbo roll cake of thin sponge and heaping helpings of banana-flavored cream. I was determined to have one when I got here, but now that the moment had arrived, I'd lost my appetite.

The eight-inch-long spiral of cake stared me in the face from the middle of table. Meanwhile, on the other side, Asuna looked deadly serious.

"...So I wonder if they're officially a couple."

"...Huh?"

It was not at all what I'd expected her to say. She continued, her manner still completely serious.

"Shivata and Liten, I mean. How they got together and what's happened between them since— We missed out on all the important details."

"Y-you've got a point..."

I honestly didn't know how I would be expected to react to a story of that nature, so for my part I was relieved that Shivata abridged the details, but Asuna seemed quite interested. I forked a large piece of banana cake and brought it to my mouth, choosing my words carefully.

"But...that deadly serious track athlete was calling her 'Lic-chan,' so I'd say they're going out."

"Ohh? Shivata's on the track team?"

"No, that's just what I imagine."

"And to think I actually believed you for two seconds!"

She raised an eyebrow at me skeptically and stuffed a big bite of cake into her cheeks. The miraculous power of the specialty dessert eased the crease between her brows, and I decided it was safe to present a concern of mine.

"But...what exactly does 'going out' entail in this world?"

"What does it entail? Well, it's the same as in the regular world," she said matter-of-factly. I would be lying if I said that didn't make me more than a little curious about her real-life experience in that field, but I couldn't very well ask, so I deleted that question from my mind and moved on.

"Anyway...I would think that doing the same stuff as the regular world is impossible here..."

"Huh? Oh...right. Because of the protective code," Asuna muttered, glancing around.

After the two of us parted ways with Shivata and Liten, we moved to this café, a secret landmark in Mananarena. Unlike the restaurants where the DKB and ALS hung out, it didn't face the main spiral road, so you had to know where it was first. As I hoped, there were no customers inside, but we were still in the mood to speak in hushed voices.

The Harassment Prevention Code in question was the most uncomfortable of *SAO*'s many in-game systems to discuss.

I knew why it was necessary. Without it, there would no doubt be some male players who exposed enticing female NPCs to unsavory behavior. The system worked in very simple ways: Any inappropriate contact with an NPC or player of the opposite sex over a certain length of time would elicit a warning and a repelling force, and repeat violators would be automatically teleported to the prison within Blackiron Palace in the Town of Beginnings. I myself was momentarily terrified of being spirited away in the workshop of old man Romolo, the shipwright on the fourth floor, when I shook Asuna's shoulder in an attempt to wake her from a rocking chair.

Asuna was rubbing her left shoulder and glaring at me, clearly remembering the same situation. She cleared her throat.

"Well…yes, you might not be able to touch the other person… but you could still be in a relationship."

"Ah, r-right. But the conditions of the code are too vague to grasp…How do you know where the fine line is on inappropriate contact? In my case, I didn't get a warning or a shock or anything before you got the forced teleportation window…Maybe a bit of research is in order…"

"So if I'd pressed the YES button, you would have gotten very valuable data."

"Er, never mind…" I said, shaking my head. Asuna glared at me again, then thought something over.

"But on that topic, I didn't even get a teleport window this last time…"

"Last time?"

"You know, after we escaped from those guys in the catacombs, you—"

She suddenly stopped still, so I looked up from cutting myself a fresh piece of cake. The fencer turned away just before we would have made eye contact, but upon seeing the tinge of red to her cheeks, I remembered.

"Ahhh, r-right…"

She had a point there. After Morte and his companion were chased by the swarm of monsters, Asuna was so overcome with the release of her tension that I had to hold her and stroke her head to calm her down. Thinking back on it now, I was impressed with myself. The contact lasted for at least three minutes, much longer than the contact at the workshop. So it was a mystery that Asuna hadn't received a window prompt to teleport me away.

"Hmm…Maybe the shoulders are a no go, but the head is okay…?"

"But if the one being touched doesn't like it, there's no difference between the head and shoulders. Besides, you were also touching my shoulder at the time."

"Oh, I-I was...? Hmm, it's a mystery...Maybe it's because on the fourth floor, you were asleep..."

"That wouldn't be it. Why show a window to a sleeping player? They can't press the buttons."

"Very true...Oh! We should just ask Shivata next time."

"Ask him what?" Asuna wondered.

I unveiled my brilliant idea: "Well, if that track athlete tries to make physical contact with Liten, then he should inevitably be collecting data on the limits and conditions of the Harassment Code, right?"

Suddenly, the fork in the fencer's hand shot audibly forward toward my nose. If it had been a knife, she might have successfully pulled off a Linear.

"L-listen to me! You are absolutely not allowed to ask an indecent question like that! I don't care about the guy, but it's not fair to Liten!!"

"I-I understand. I won't suggest it again, so please put the fork down..."

Once it was safely resting on the surface of the table again, I breathed a sigh of relief and leaned back in the chair.

"Hmm. The only other thing I can figure is that it evolves depending on the target player..."

"What do you mean?"

"I'm saying that it could be triggered most easily between two strangers who have never had contact before, but that it gets eased as the players' relationship grows...I just can't imagine how they track and quantify the emotional closeness of the two players..."

I looked down from the ceiling, and the fencer was quiet, her expression flat. I worried that I might have said something stupid again, but for whatever reason, I noticed that redness was rising on her skin, from the collar of her cape up toward her mouth and nose.

Anticipating an eventual eruption, my legs tensed, prepared to dart away in escape, but to my considerable fortune, the jingling bell at the door rang at that moment, cutting through the thick tension.

The visitor to the café was none other than Argo, who had set up in Mananarena before we arrived. It wasn't coincidence, of course; I had sent her a message as soon as we were done with Shivata and Liten.

"Heyaaa."

The tired-looking whiskered broker walked over and sat in the chair next to Asuna. She ordered a roll cake, triple thick, and let out a long breath.

"You dragged me outta my own business, so I hope this is more important than the boss quests, Kii-boy."

"O-of course," I reassured her. For a brief moment, I considered breaking the ice with a silly question about the Harassment Code conditions, then decided it wouldn't be worth it if nobody was going to laugh.

"Umm, I think we figured out why the ALS is planning to sneak ahead on the boss."

As befitting a creature that fed on information, Argo's face immediately brightened up.

"Wait, really? Even I haven't caught that morsel in my net of intelligence. This is quite impressive."

"Rather surprising, isn't it?" I asked.

"...What is?"

"Well, I would have thought you knew already...Don't you remember anything about an item from the fifth-floor boss causing trouble in the beta?"

"Trouble...?"

Her painted whiskers twitched—I had successfully tweaked her pride as an informant. Argo pursed her lips for a while, consulting her memory, then eventually lifted her hands in surrender.

"I hate to admit it, but I can't remember. If I can make an excuse, I wasn't an info broker in the beta. I also wasn't a front-runner, so I didn't take part in that boss fight..."

"Oh, you didn't? Well, I won't hold it over your head, then…I think the ALS is after a guild flag."

"Guild…flag? Why would they want a flag?"

"As an object, it's no more than a low-powered long spear…but if you do this…" I stood the fork in my hand straight up and struck the base of it against the table. "When the player with it equipped sticks it into the ground, all guild members within fifty or sixty feet get increased attack and defense, as well as extra resistance against debuffs."

"Wh…what…?" Argo said, the same as Shivata's stunned reaction. She pointed at the fork in my hand and asked, in rapid succession, "C-can the player with the flag move around? How long does the buff last? Is there a limit to how many players it affects?"

"The answer to your first question is a half yes. If you take the flag out of the ground, the buff shuts off, but once you move and plant it again, it kicks right back in."

"…Hmm."

"The answer to your second question is: as long as the flag is planted."

"…Hmmmm."

"The answer to your third question is: no limit, as long as they are guild members."

"…Hmmmmmmmmm."

Argo crossed her arms, grunting, as a piece of banana cake three times as thick as mine and Asuna's arrived. At eight inches long and over two inches wide, it was nearly the size of a small whole cake. Argo split a quarter of it off with her fork and stuffed the entire mound into her mouth.

"…That is indeed very big trouble, Kii-boy."

"Exactly…"

"The statistical boost is one thing, but the effect on the players' mentality is especially dangerous…If the ALS gets that item and plants it during battle, their morale is going to skyrocket, and the DKB's will plummet. The same would hold true for the reverse…

It's more than powerful enough to crush the uneasy balance that exists now."

"You can understand why Kibaou would decide to attempt the boss prematurely once he learned about it," I murmured, bringing a piece of cake up to my mouth. In the meantime, Argo had made another quarter of her own cake disappear. She glanced over to her left.

"...You seem pretty quiet today, A-chan."

"...Er...uh, no, it's nothing!" Asuna insisted, finally getting her conscious brain back in motion. She scrambled to eat more cake, and Argo blinked in surprise.

"So...how'd that spiky-haired buffoon manage to get word about this item? It's kind of a shock to me that they got this intel before I did."

"W-well, you and I aren't the only beta testers, Argo," I pointed out.

I hadn't told Argo about the PK gang lurking in the shadows of Aincrad, a decision that Asuna was holding me to. Naturally, we were afraid that if she learned about them, she would attempt to collect information about them on her own—and that was a job far more dangerous than compiling boss intel.

I didn't doubt Argo's ability. I knew that she had the speed to dart out of the most dangerous locales. But the ability of the man in the black poncho, the suspected leader of Morte's gang, was a total unknown. Until I could find out what kind of danger he represented, I didn't want Argo to get involved with them.

The informant smiled in an all-knowing way and nodded, giving in. "Well, ya got a point there. What's important now isn't where the deets came from, but what to do about 'em...If it's really that huge of an item they can loot, the ALS won't be deterred by direct arguments."

"Um, I was thinking..." Asuna started. She had finished her cake a bit later than I did, and took a sip of tea before suggesting, "What if we simply share the information about the guild flag with the DKB? The reason the ALS is being so reckless about looting it isn't because they want it that bad, but because they're afraid the DKB will get it, right? If Lind proposes a fair way to split the loot…"

"…Yeah…That's not a bad idea…"

I thought of Lind's deadly serious face. If Shivata was an imaginary track-and-field athlete, then Lind belonged to a martial arts club or even a calligraphy club.

"No matter what, Lind can be reasoned with…He might be able to force a conversation with the ALS. It's just…joint managing the guild flag is impossible, much less sharing its power. Once the item is registered under a guild, I can't imagine that you can alter it, and it wouldn't be possible to split the flag and the staff apart, either. Ultimately, they're going to come down to a rock-paper-scissors match, or a roll of the dice, or even a five-on-five group duel."

"…I can't imagine that Kibaou would accept that proposal…" Asuna muttered. Both Argo and I nodded.

It was an ironclad belief of Kibaou that all resources should be shared to hold the casualties of the game to a minimum: gold, items, information. It was the foundational philosophy of the guild he started.

Lind and DKB held that the top players with the deepest knowledge and greatest power should fight bravely at the front line and serve as a symbol of hope, thus generating the energy and inspiration to defeat the game.

I didn't know which was right. All I could say was that both were successors to Diavel the knight. And both would strongly desire the guild flag to further their respective causes. Neither would dream of ceding it to the other.

Why did you have to die, Diavel? I asked the departed knight, leaning back in my chair and staring up at the boarded ceiling.

There was no answer, of course. But somehow, I heard his final words repeat in my mind.

You have to take it from here, Kirito. Kill the…b—

His avatar had blasted into pieces before he could finish his sentence. Yes—I, too, had inherited something from him.

Kibaou inherited the knight's sense of fairness, and Lind had taken on his heroism. And what I took, as a fellow beta tester... was his sense of realism.

I opened my eyes slowly, looked at Argo and Asuna in turn, then spoke.

"...Let's beat the boss."

The words melted into the air of the room, echoing and vanishing, but the info dealer and fencer did not speak.

Argo's fork, which had been hovering in the air for several moments, finally stabbed into the remaining half of the thick roll cake, then lifted the mass of sponge and cream, which disappeared as if it was a magic trick. In true rodent fashion, the Rat's cheeks bulged comically as she chewed away at her meal.

At last, she asked, "You mean the three of us?"

"Oh, not at all."

After all, when Asuna suggested the same thing, I stated that it was impossible, even with Kizmel the elite knight on our side. Asuna turned to me, curious.

"Then who are you going to ask for help?"

"Well..."

I started to list the candidates on my fingers.

"First, there's Agil and his three friends; then, Nezha might help us..."

".........That's it?" Asuna wondered, staring down at my folded thumb and fingers. I coughed and cleared my throat awkwardly.

"...Um, Argo, do you know anyone...?"

"Come on, don't be ridiculous, Kii-boy," she said. But even my safety net, with her entire intelligence network, could only shrug. "Well, I keep an eye on the people trying their best to join the front-runners, but that very potential means I can't invite 'em on a dangerous mission. Why do ya think I've been handing out those strategy guides on lower floors for free?"

"Yeah, good point...Well, even if Nezha says yes, that's me,

Asuna, Argo, Nezha, and the Bro Squad for eight in total...I'm going to say we need at least twelve for two parties..."

"No way, even with two parties, that would be hard enough," Asuna said, waving her hand in front of her face. "You were the one who said we just barely beat the fourth-floor boss with a full raid, Kizmel, *and* Viscount Yofilis. If the next boss is tougher than that sea horse, how is a group of twelve going to win...?"

"Hmm...In numerical terms, every fifth boss is always going to be especially tough. Assuming that each boss grows stronger at the same equivalent amount..."

I made imaginary slices along the edge of the table, setting aside four chunks, with the fifth being slightly larger.

"...then I imagine that the fifth-floor boss is going to be close in strength to the sixth-floor boss. But a boss's strength isn't measured in just attack, defense, and HP. If that giant golem hasn't been altered since the beta, there's a way for even a twelve-man raid to beat it. Depending on the information from the boss quests and recon of the boss chamber, of course..."

Only when the sound of my own voice hit my ears and I processed what I was saying did I remember that on the other side of the table, Argo had been doing those quests already.

"Oh, r-right. What kind of hints were the boss quests giving?"

"Kii-boy, are you forgetting that I deal information for a living?"

I quickly opened my window to propose a trade, but the Rat was already smirking at me.

"I'd thank ya for the transaction...but I'll give it to you in return for that tidbit about the guild flag. Speaking from conclusion first, it seems like the boss is still a golem."

She opened her own window and switched to the memo tab, designed for saving notes and such.

"Let's see here...Remember what you told me from the elf quests, the secret of Aincrad's creation, and whatnot?"

"Oh...the Great Separation, you mean?"

I had already given Argo a rough outline of the elf legend that Kizmel had shared with us.

It said that the hundred floors of Aincrad hadn't always existed as they were now. The various elf, human, and dwarf realms had been cut in circular chunks from the earth and summoned up to the sky to form the floating castle. In that moment, all the powers of magic had been lost. But that story hadn't played any part in the game yet, outside of the elf campaign quest.

Argo grimaced and explained, "Well, in a shortened form... this floor was originally an industrial area for a human kingdom. They dug up metal and magical ores with spells and mass-produced arms that were sold into a regional conflict elsewhere. But the king of that land didn't export the truly powerful magical ore, saving it up to build a massive war weapon...the golem. When the golem was finished, he was going to use it to invade the dwarves that were his trade rivals when the Great Separation occurred, and the golem and king were summoned up into the sky. The power of magic was lost, so they couldn't mine or refine the material...and that's the story."

"Ahhh, I see..."

Across from me, Asuna realized something and spoke up.

"Um...now that I think about it, when we fought that zombie boss in the catacombs...wasn't he wearing a crown of some kind?"

"Yeah, since you mention it...So that giant zombie was the king from the past? But he wasn't human-sized at all."

Argo chuckled at my bafflement. "Hey, it's customary for all those evil king bosses from video games to magically grow in size."

"Either that or being in a damp place for eons made him bloat from all the moisture. Zombies always seemed highly absorbent to me."

I had to move on quickly once the two girls wrinkled their noses at my sizzling-hot sense of humor.

"Anyway, back to the floor boss...If that's what the boss quests said, then it seems like we can rest assured that the golem from the beta is still in place."

"In a basic sense, yes," Argo confirmed. She closed her window and downed the rest of her tea. "It's just...even the bosses that have looked the same as their beta form have been changed in some way. The minotaurs on the second floor got an extra companion, for example..."

"That's something we won't know until we scout it out...Also, we should plan out an escape method from the boss chamber," I said, switching to concrete boss strategy topics when Asuna cut me off.

"Wait, Kirito. You just said a twelve-man raid would be enough to handle the boss, but that still leaves us four short. And we don't even know if Nezha and Agil's group will help us..."

"If the Bro Squad says no, we're plain out of luck. If that happens, we can tell Lind about the guild flag and pray that his talk with Kibaou reaches a peaceful conclusion. As for the four other members..."

I paused, then went with my gut.

"Let's ask Shivata and Liten."

"Wh...what?!" Asuna blanched, leaning back. "Y-you know that won't work...They're members of the DKB and ALS!"

"That's exactly why. If they were members of the same guild, they wouldn't assist a plan that ultimately undercuts their group...but since they're each from one, I think there might be a chance."

At that suggestion, Argo perked up and grinned. "Liten's the one in the plate armor who just joined the ALS? So she and Shivata from the DKB...Ahhh, that's a new one to me."

"Hey! No, Argo, you can't sell that to anyone."

"Nya-ha-ha, I know. But like Kii-boy says, if they're that close, they might help us out. Love is stronger than guild regulations, as they say."

That line was so out of character, I had to hold myself back from commenting on it.

"A-anyway...if Shivata and Liten can each bring a partner, that will make twelve. Fortunately, they're both members of the party-planning committee, so they should be moving from Mananarena to Karluin soon. If we can catch them before and head straight for the tower, their guilds won't find out about their participation in the boss battle…I think…"

"You'd better be certain about that. Also, assuming Shivata and Liten even agree to help us, how will we help them if they get kicked out of the guild for what they do for us? I can't agree to bring them into our plan if you can't give me a proper answer to that," Asuna stated decisively, leveling me with a determined gaze.

Our insane plan to attempt the floor boss with just two parties was meant to prevent either the ALS or DKB from taking an unstoppable lead, and it seemed likely that if we couldn't carry the plan out, Shivata and Liten would be forced to choose between their guilds and each other…but Asuna wasn't talking about logic, she was talking about loyalty. They had trusted us with their private information, and it wouldn't be right for us to use them like disposable pawns in our game.

"…Agil's party has exactly four. I'll ask them if they mind letting the other two join up. If that's a no go…we'll invite them into our party," I said, displaying no small amount of determination. Asuna smiled and nodded.

Agil and Shivata were on the fifth floor, so we could contact them with instant messages, but we'd last seen Nezha on the second floor. If he wasn't up here, we'd have to take the tunnel back to Karluin, then teleport down to lower floors and send messages there. If he happened to be in a dungeon, even that wouldn't work, and we'd have to forget about him. With a silent prayer, I decided to attempt contact with him first.

LONG TIME NO SEE. WHERE ARE YOU NOW? I wrote simply.

Just fifteen seconds later, he replied.

IT'S A PLEASURE TO HEAR FROM YOU. I'M COLLECTING RELICS IN THE DUNGEON BENEATH THE CITY.

I pumped my fist and thanked my lucky stars that the relic-hunting festival was still ongoing in Karluin.

"I'm going back to the main city to meet Nezha. Asuna, can you get in touch with Agil, Shivata, and Liten?"

"M-me?"

"Your Persuasion skill is a lot higher than mine."

"Uh, it is…? Hey, there's no such skill in the game!" she pouted, even as she brought up her holo-keyboard. Meanwhile, Argo smirked.

"And what should I be doin', Kii-boy?"

"I want you to stock up on consumables for us. Budgeting isn't a variable here, so just get as many of the good potions as you can."

I brought up a trade window and sent Argo more than enough money for the trip, then left the café.

The underground tunnel that connected Mananarena with the main town of Karluin had a fair amount of monsters and treasure, so the trip might take an hour or two for a party battling its way through, but that time could be compressed significantly by a single player racing through it.

It took me just over twenty minutes to finish the three-mile route, evading groups of monsters and dispatching singles with a good thrusting sword skill. I emerged into the large waiting room on the first basement level of the dungeon and searched for Nezha.

Before I could spot him, I heard someone call "Kirito!" from behind me. No sooner had I turned around than my hand was being clasped warmly.

"It's been so long. I'm happy to see you again!" said the very same blacksmith—well, former blacksmith—I'd met on the second floor. But unlike before, there was no shadow of timid fright in his smile.

I couldn't help but grin and squeeze back. "It's good to see you, too, Nezha…or should I call you Nataku?"

The other man's smile dimpled shyly as he said, "No, just Nezha is fine. My companions still call me Nezuo, anyway."

"Oh…they do?"

I glanced around the chamber, but caught no sight of the other Legend Braves. Nezha let go and looked up.

"I was doing the whole relic hunt thing with the guild, but they went back up into town first."

"Ahh…"

That was a relief; I felt bad about it, but I was planning to ask him to do that anyway. We wanted as many people as possible, but given that we forced them to give up their powerful gear to make amends, it wouldn't be fair to make them fight a deadly boss now.

"…Anyway, sorry about the sudden message."

"No, not at all. What did you want to discuss?" Nezha asked curiously. I tugged his arm to move him to a corner of the room. The base camp for relic hunting wasn't as packed as when the town first opened, but there were still a good dozen players hanging around.

Once we were a safe distance away, I kept my voice low and got right to the point.

"Nezha…I hate to be so abrupt about this, but I need to ask you a favor."

"Anything, as long as it's something I can do."

"Okay, I'll just say it…I want you to come help me beat the fifth-floor boss right now."

Beneath his evenly parted bangs, his eyes grew as wide and round as thousand-col gold coins, and he sucked in a sharp breath. I clamped a hand over his mouth before he could shriek in shock.

"Mrrrgh?!"

Once the muffled yelp was over, I let go. The former blacksmith heaved a few deep breaths before turning on me with as quiet a bellow as he could manage.

"Wh-what are you talking about?! The two big guilds are the ones who manage the floor boss battles. Are you doing this with their knowledge?!"

"Nope, not at all."

"Not at…"

I grabbed the speechless blacksmith's shoulder and pulled him closer so I could explain.

"For reasons I won't get into here, we need to beat that boss before the DKB and ALS. I'm not going to put you in direct danger. You just need to hang out in the back and hit the boss's weak point at the right time…Please. Will you help us?"

"…"

He took a deep breath again, let it out slowly, then glanced down at his waist. On it hung a thin metal circle about eight inches across. It was a rare chakram that belonged to the Throwing Weapons category.

Fingers that had once gripped a hammer traced the side of the chakram instead. He clenched his fist and raised it to chest level.

"…They're very important reasons, I assume?" he whispered. I nodded.

"That's right. Important enough to determine the future of the frontline group…of *SAO* as a whole."

"All right, then," Nezha said, clapping me on the shoulder. "Since you seem to be in a hurry, I'll let you explain as we go. Just lead the way."

"…Thanks," I said, and turned toward the stairs I'd just taken to get here.

It wasn't as if I had no misgivings about this. Based on his gear, I estimated Nezha's level at around 12 or 13. It wasn't completely beyond the safety margin for fighting the fifth-floor boss, but it definitely wasn't well above it, either.

I wasn't planning to have Nezha front and center, of course. I wanted him to provide long-range attacks from the rear. The golem boss used physical attacks only with its limbs, so with enough distance, there was no worry about losing HP…

But the previous four bosses had taught me that in their battles, there were no absolute guarantees.

Illfang the Kobold Lord, boss of the first floor, used Katana skills that weren't there in the beta to end the life of Diavel the knight.

Asterios the Taurus King, boss of the second floor, nearly

wiped out the entire party with a lightning breath attack that had never been seen in the beta.

Nerius the Evil Treant, boss of the third floor, made use of a new wide-ranging poison attack that would have destroyed the raid if we hadn't stocked up on tons of antidotes.

And Wythege the Hippocampus, boss of the fourth floor, flooded the boss chamber with water, which nearly drowned the entire raid.

It was clear that the golem boss of the fifth floor would also be different from the beta in some way. We needed to observe these details carefully ahead of time to eliminate all unexpected dangers. Now that we were bringing Nezha into this, "we didn't notice" wasn't going to cut it anymore.

"I've contacted my team. I should be fine for the rest of the day," Nezha said after a long stretch of keyboard tapping. I looked at him closely—he really did look different than he had before.

"All right. Let's go."

9

IN A FOREST CLEARING A SHORT DISTANCE FROM Mananarena, the other members had already congregated ahead of us.

Thanks to Asuna's formidable Persuasion skill, I saw Agil's Bro Squad, Shivata, Liten, and one other player from each guild, wearing their respective colors. I'd asked the two of them to recruit members if possible, expecting it to be futile, so this was a pleasant surprise.

Nezha went off to pay his respects to Asuna and the others, so I approached Shivata's group.

"Sorry for being so..."

"*Late*," I was going to say, but the large DKB member with Shivata spun around ferociously and grabbed me by the collar.

"Hey there, Blackie," said Hafner, a greatsword user and subleader of the DKB, calling me by a nickname that referred to my outfit. He leaned in with a menacing face that made me think of a soccer team member and growled, "I'm going to clobber you if it turns out that you've told a single lie about any of this."

Setting aside the fact that the Anti-Criminal Code in town and the threat of going orange out of town prevented him from *actually* clobbering me at all, I nodded obediently. Shivata grabbed Hafner's shoulder with an awkward smile and pulled him back.

"Haf, this idea came more from our side. All Kirito offered was the info about the guild flag, and I don't think he's lying. Why would he? There's nothing for him to gain by it."

"...Well, you might have a point there. But why would he put together such a dangerous plan? Does he have a good reason to keep the ALS from getting that flag thing?"

"Hang on," I interrupted, waving my right hand to cut off the DKB officers. "First of all, the point of this operation isn't just to keep the ALS from getting the guild flag. When the flag drops, we can't give it to the DKB, either. If either guild gets the flag, it might spell the collapse of the other."

It seemed that Shivata had explained this premise to Hafner already. The soccer player scowled but fell silent, so I took the opportunity to ask, "What about you, Hafner? Are you sure you should be taking part? We're extremely grateful for your help, but as a subleader of the DKB, you'll be betraying your own guild."

Hafner ruffled his long blond hair, which was held back at the hairline by a string, and grumbled, "Yeah, I'm not thrilled about it, but beating the game comes first...and we need both the DKB and ALS to get out of this shitty MMO. I can't betray the thousands below who are waiting for freedom, even if it means betraying Lind and my guild. That's why you're here, too, right?"

That last question was directed toward Liten and the other ALS member, who were standing a short distance away.

The midsized, mid-build older man—he looked to be in his thirties—carrying a halberd on his back drew his faintly whiskered lips together and nodded.

"That's right. Our plan to charge ahead is the reckless result of a few hard-liners playing on the fears of the officers. Kibaou knows that, but he was forced to approve the plan to keep the guild from fracturing. But if getting that flag means destroying the already-unstable relationship with the DKB, then it means nothing," the halberdier said calmly. He walked over to me and stuck out his hand. "We've met a few times in boss battles. I'm Okotan, the leader of the ALS's recruiting team. Good to work with you, Kirito."

"Uh...th-thanks for being here..."

I was momentarily surprised by the name, which was rather cute for a scruffy-faced dandy like him, but I recovered in a timely enough fashion to shake his hand.

However, a thought occurred to me.

"So if you're the head recruiter, does that mean you were the one who scouted Liten for the guild...?"

"Yes, that was me."

The look on his face as he turned back to appraise the plate-armored macer was fatherly. It made me wonder if he realized Liten and Shivata were a couple, but that wasn't for me to bring up.

With our greetings out of the way, Hafner slapped me heartily on the back.

"Well, Blackie, me and Oko have explained our motives to the group. Before we get this shindig on the road, why don't you tell the group why you're leading the charge?"

"Wh-what?"

I tore my eyes away from the soccer player and saw that Asuna, Argo, Nezha, Agil, and the Bros were all gathered around, waiting to hear my answer. There was no escape. I cleared my throat.

"Well, it's the same as Hafner and Okotan...and probably everyone else here. The ALS and DKB are the two wheels that run our progress forward through the game. If they aren't attached by a center axle, or we lose one of the two, the whole cart grinds to a halt. I figure the only way to prevent that situation is to beat the boss before the ALS does...And that's why I gathered you all here."

Of course, that was barely half of my true motivation.

Okotan described the ALS's plan as the rampage of a hard-line minority in the guild, but there was a darker side to the story he didn't know about. There was an external evil that had infiltrated the guild and was fanning the flames of conflict with the DKB—the mysterious poncho man and his provocation-PK gang. Stopping *them* was my true motive.

But I couldn't reveal that yet. Until I at least knew the names of the other members aside from Morte, bringing the subject up would only lead to distrust and paranoia within the guilds.

Fortunately, everyone aside from Asuna, who already knew the truth, seemed to be satisfied by the speech. Even Hafner, though disgruntled, nodded in agreement.

At that point, Liten raised her right hand with a *clank*, her features hidden once again by the metal visor. She spoke in that androgynous metallic echo.

"Um, Kirito, I've been meaning to ask you...if you're so concerned about the state of the group, why don't you join a guild? I'm certain that given your skill, you'd be placed as a party leader in either guild immediately..."

A murmur ran through the group. It was an honest question from someone new to the scene, but given that she probably didn't even know the word *beater*, it would be very difficult to give a detailed explanation of the touchy situation between me, Kibaou, and Lind.

After about a second and a half of frantic thinking, I decided to lay the blame for that question at the feet of the two guild masters.

"Well, you see, Lind and Kibaou said that if me and Asuna were going to join guilds, we'd have to join them separately."

Another murmur ran through the group, which gave me a brief moment of panic that I'd said something stupid. Red-faced, Asuna wailed, "Wh-why would you say that?!" and Liten followed with, "Ah yes, I understand...That's beautiful!" Meanwhile, Agil bellowed with laughter and Argo cackled.

In the end, I wasn't given the opportunity to plead my case against her misinterpretation.

By the time Argo had divvied up all the potions, and everyone had lent and borrowed gear until each slot had the highest stats possible, it was just getting to be three o'clock in the afternoon.

According to Okotan, the ALS would leave Mananarena for the tower—pretending to be leaving for the party in Karluin—at around six o'clock, which gave us a three-hour advantage. Even with a scouting run, it wouldn't likely take three hours to fight the boss, so we had plenty of time. Still, it didn't hurt to ration it carefully.

So I left Argo to be our guide and ran along at the back of the group with Asuna, jotting down a loose, estimated breakdown of the group according to level.

1. KIRITO, level 18, one-handed sword, leather armor
2. ASUNA, level 17, rapier, light metal armor
3. AGIL, level 16, two-handed ax, light metal armor
4. HAFNER, level 16, two-handed sword, heavy metal armor
5. SHIVATA, level 15, one-handed sword, heavy metal armor, shield
6. OKOTAN, level 15, two-handed halberd, light metal armor
7. WOLFGANG (Agil's squad), level 15, two-handed sword, leather armor
8. LOWBACCA (Agil's squad), level 15, two-handed ax, light metal armor
9. NAIJAN (Agil's squad), level 14, two-handed hammer, heavy metal armor
10. LITEN, level 13, long mace, heavy metal armor, shield
11. NEZHA, level 12, chakram, light metal armor
12. ARGO, level unknown, claws, leather armor

"Hmmmm..."

It was a very short list for a floor boss raid party.

The path through the woods was lined with the bluish rock that made our group's footsteps ring loudly, but Asuna still heard me mutter and looked over for clarification.

"What's the 'hmmm' about?"

"Well..." I made the memo visible and showed it to her. "We need to figure out a formation before we get to the labyrinth tower, and I'm noticing that we have an awful lot of DPSs..."

"What's a DPS?"

"It means damage dealer, an attacker. Out of the twelve on this list, me, you, Agil, Hafner, Wolfgang, Lowbacca, and Naijan are attackers—that's more than half. Shivata and Liten are our only true tanks, and Okotan, Nezha, and Argo are CCs…"

"CC?"

"Crowd control, responsible for controlling the enemy mobs. These are mages in most other games, but since there's no magic in *SAO*, it mostly comes down to using debuffing sword skills that freeze or weaken monsters."

"Ah, right. Most of the longer-reaching weapons have debuffing skills," noted Asuna, who deftly crossed her arms to think, even as she ran, the momentum pulling her body forward. She murmured to herself the same way I had earlier.

"…It's just two parties, so we can ask Shivata and Liten to be a tank in each, then split the DPS and CC between the two, right?"

"That would be the orthodox method. The thing is, the golem only has direct attacks with its hands and feet, but they're all extremely powerful…The normal attacks are one thing, but even a shield isn't going to stop the skill attacks. So we have to avoid them no matter what. Shivata's experienced, but…"

"…But Liten just joined the guild, and it's a bit scary to push such a difficult role on her," Asuna finished. We groaned together, my arms crossed, too. I glanced at the list again.

Even with a simpler lineup of twelve total, there was no single correct answer. If it was a full raid of forty-eight, the possibilities were limitless. And Lind and Kibaou were doing this process for every floor and field boss.

That realization brought a wave of newfound respect for the two, but the goal here was to beat them to the punch. As we grumbled over the quandary, the dead forest around us thinned out, revealing a long stone wall snaking ahead.

Its length and breadth was on a scale that reminded me of the Town of Beginnings, but it was not a city on the other side of this fortification. Instead, it was the largest maze of the fifth floor, which had to be maneuvered before you could reach the labyrinth tower.

There were monsters, too, of course, so it would take more than a day or two to map it all out. However, as long as you solved a few environmental puzzles, you could take shortcuts on a virtual straight shot through the maze, and we had a helpful companion with us in that regard.

I unfolded my arms and sped up to catch Argo, who was at the head of the right column of the group.

"Um, Miss Argo, is there a map to..."

"The maze? You bet."

I sighed in relief. The information broker glanced over at me and grinned. "And it's piping hot an' fresh, so it's worth five thousand col, I reckon."

"Wh-what?! You're gonna *charge* me?!"

"Argo the claw wielder'll fight the boss with you for free, but Argo the information dealer needs to earn a living."

"Hrrrgh..."

I gnashed my teeth, wishing that I had done more relic hunting back in Karluin.

"Nya-ha-ha-ha! No worries, I just thought I'd tease you a bit for that lovey-dovey stuff back there," Argo cackled, and winked at me. "Yes, I mapped the labyrinth, but you won't need it."

"Uh...what do you mean?"

"You'll see when we get there," she hinted, and turned us to the right.

The fifth-floor labyrinth was in the northeast corner of the floor, and the maze, which was a third of a mile in radius, surrounded it in a semicircle. That meant that at either end, the looming stone wall intersected with the outer aperture of the floor.

Argo was leading us toward the southeast end. It took us off the path, so we ran into a few mobs, but with twelve members, each battle would be over in an instant if we fought full strength. Instead, we used a bit of time to allow for a show of our combination work, and it was about three forty-five when we reached our destination.

"Nice work, everyone. That ends the trekking across the wilderness, at least," Argo noted, and we gratefully came to a stop.

I stretched and glanced around us, taking in the rather desolate sight. To the north loomed the sixty-foot wall, and to the south and west were barren gray wastelands without a blade of grass on them. Beyond that was the dead forest we'd just traveled through, dyed in monochrome by the lengthening rays of the winter sun.

When my eyes rolled to the east, they beheld an expanse of endless sky through the nearby aperture, but the faded, grayish-blue color struck me as ominous, not the sweeping majesty of the starry sky that Asuna and I saw at Blink & Brink. I turned back to the dark stone wall and looked up.

According to the legend that Argo told the group on our trip, at the middle of the giant maze was the secret development center of the ancient kingdom, and the maze was built to deter outsiders from infiltrating it. That only made the massive wall even more foreboding, but to do anything, first we had to somehow get past it somehow.

"So...where do we go in?" I asked our guide as she chugged lime water, wiped her mouth, and grinned. Argo pulled something shining out of her cloak. It was a giant key about six inches long.

"Whoa...did you get that from the boss quests?"

"'Zactly."

Argo strode over to the stone wall, spinning the key around her finger with the leather cord it hung on. She leaned close to the rough, weathered blocks, searching for something, then stuck the key into a particular gap and turned it with a click.

Everyone else murmured in admiration. No doubt a part of the wall would open as if by magic, revealing a hidden passage inside.

Instead, the stone wall rumbled, a few of the blocks sank into the wall by six inches or so—and that was it.

"Uh...Argo, where's the hidden door?"

"There's no hidden door."

She stuck the key back into her cloak, put a hand into one of the sunken gaps, then lifted herself, *hup-hup-hup*, ten feet up the wall. I looked up, stunned, to see that the pattern of sunken blocks continued straight up the wall to the top, like an unconventional ladder.

"W-wait, we have to climb over?" Agil noted in panic. Argo looked down, hanging on by one hand, and grinned cheekily.

"Uh-oh, does this mean the biggest tough guy in the front-runners is actually afraid of heights?"

"I-I'm not saying that...but you can't laugh off a fall from that height," Agil retorted, and he had a good point. There were many sources of damage in *SAO*, and the one that everyone agreed was the scariest was fall damage. Next to me, Asuna trembled, no doubt thinking about her fall through the trapdoor in the catacombs.

The stone wall was over sixty feet tall, and the ground was dirt mixed with gravel. Anyone who fell from the top and had lower amounts of HP was in danger of instant death, I decided, and was about to ask Argo to wait so we could set up a lifeline, but she spoke up first.

"Oh, well, here's a special little gift, just for you," Argo said, one eye closed, and she started generating several large items from her inventory. They fell and bounced softly on the ground: large cushions for player homes, which hardly any player was yet rich enough to start bothering with. They were quite light for their size, so she must have packed her inventory with the things.

We stacked the cushions high next to the handhold ladder, and Argo fell backward onto them. She landed with a hearty *bafoom*, but hadn't suffered any damage. With the demonstration concluded, she popped up and glanced at me sidelong.

"I'll go last so I can pick up the cushions before I go. You're up first, Kii-boy."

"Uh...m-me? Well, okay..."

I looked over at Asuna, who made a silent *You first* gesture.

The only skirt wearer present certainly was not eager to climb up with all the gentlemen below. I nodded, stepped onto the pile of cushions, and grabbed onto the wall.

Once I got climbing, I noticed the alternately spaced handholds were quite deep and easy to grip, which made the physical process fairly simple. The real problem was the mental pressure that arose once you were halfway up. I knew that with the cushions stacked below, there was no way I'd die if I fell, but that didn't prevent the cold sweat from forming on my limbs.

I scaled the last of the wall, wondering if that sweat was just a virtual sensation from the NerveGear or if my real body was seeping liquid from my pores, too. On the other side of the wall was a narrow walkway set a bit lower. I hopped over, heaved a sigh of relief, and called down to the group below.

"It's not that hard, just stay calm and you'll be fine!"

"A-all right, I'll go next!" called out Hafner, beginning a ten-minute process that ended with Asuna and Argo. No one ended up falling, but that was probably thanks to the mental reassurance offered by Argo's cushions—it occurred to me that it was a good idea to keep two or three of those things in my inventory, just in case. I grabbed Argo's hand as she finally made her way to the top and pulled her over.

With the wall-climbing phase concluded, we traded high fives and turned our gazes north.

"...You weren't kidding when you said this labyrinth would be a big deal to tackle," muttered Wolfgang from the Bro Squad. He used the same greatsword category that the DKB's subleader did, but while Hafner looked like a heavy knight in his metal armor, Wolfgang's skintight leather gear gave him the air of a veteran mercenary.

As he said, it was hard to imagine an easy route through the massive maze stretching out before us, even with a map. The layout seemed different from the beta, so I couldn't even use my old memory as a guide.

"And the ALS were going to charge through this place at night, without scouting it first?" Shivata asked Okotan skeptically. The halberdier, who appeared to be the oldest of the group, nodded awkwardly, his whiskered mouth twisted into an abashed smile.

"It's rather embarrassing to admit, but that is their plan…From what I understand, we have information on the puzzles and traps from a beta tester. The schedule called for the entire process to take an hour."

Asuna and I shared a look.

It had to be the same beta tester that told them about the guild flag. From the way Okotan spoke, it sounded like this wasn't a fellow guild member, so it was likely to be one of the cloaked men we ran across in the catacombs: Morte. Which would mean the other man was undercover in the ALS.

Given the circumstances, I really wanted to tell Shivata, Hafner, and Okotan about this plot, to help identify the spy, but that was difficult to do with Argo and Agil's team present. Not only that, but we had an urgent quest on our plates.

If the boss battle went well, I'd suggest a celebration and find the time to bring it up, I told myself. My eyes swung right, to the massive tower looming over the labyrinth's center.

They were always categorized as "labyrinth towers," but each floor's tower had a different scale and design. The only unifying feature was the three-hundred-foot height, so while some were fat and squat with uniform width, others were narrow and willowy. The fifth floor's tower was an orthodox cylinder, about a third as wide as it was tall, which put it on the small side. There was a grand entrance door at the base, but the wall we were standing atop stretched from the very edge of the floating castle all the way to the tower itself, ending in a small door. In other words, we were getting a shortcut that put us 20 percent through the tower just as we entered. Thanks to Argo's tedious work completing the boss quests, we were going to shave a good two hours off our time.

"Thanks, Argo," I said softly. Her curly haired head swung toward me, blinking in surprise. But it was quickly replaced by her usual sardonic grin.

"Don't be silly, we're only getting started."

"Good point…"

I took a deep breath, preparing to move the group forward once more.

We traveled in a line down the walkway atop the stone wall and took a short break at a small observation deck where the wall connected with the exterior of the tower. The toughest dungeon on the fifth floor was on the other side of the door, so we needed to prepare ourselves.

"Here you go, everyone."

Asuna was pulling one of those massive cakes out of her inventory. It was the only famous local confection of Mananarena, but given that you had to know about the secret café, it was new to most of the group. Hafner and the Bro Squad stuffed handfuls of it into their mouths, grunting about how "damn good" it was, while Liten and Shivata got cozy with some forks against the wall. I looked around in alarm for Okotan, but he was already chatting mirthfully with Nezha—which caused a different kind of alarm to fill me, when I imagined the former blacksmith being recruited into the ALS.

With the cake all distributed, Asuna brought me my piece and glanced up at the tower looming overhead as she ate.

"…So it's time…"

"Yeah…"

I picked up the cake with my fingers and took a bite. The banana flavor, which had been so thick when I ate the same item hours earlier in the café, hardly seemed to register on my tongue this time. That made me realize just how nervous I was.

This was supposed to be our only option to defeat this game of death and escape the electronic prison that bound us. Whether the ALS's plan to race ahead was successful or not, it would cause a major rift in the group of advanced players and disperse the collection of energy that had been driving our pace and speeding us along. We would slow down, and players like Liten who were doing their best to catch up to us from below would lose hope. Despair would settle upon all of Aincrad. It would be like an eternal night, without glittering stars or the rising morning sun…

I put the half-eaten cake back onto the plate, surrounded by a sudden waft of music. I knew it was an illusion, but I shut my eyes to hear it nonetheless.

An eerie sight appeared on my closed eyelids.

Three dancing silhouettes lurching against a bloodred sunset to a mad, racing, mocking melody. The hems of pitch-black cloaks and ponchos flapped like bat wings. The mouth of the figure on the right turned visible, displaying a familiar, twisted leer.

What if even my own actions here are an intended result of their provocation…?

The sudden thought caused my limbs to freeze to ice.

Here on the milestone fifth floor, we would fight a floor boss that was far harder than any previous. I'd warned Asuna about this again and again, and I believed I was preparing myself accordingly. And no matter how I rationalized my current actions based on what was happening in the game, I was leading a tiny group of twelve against that boss.

There was a way to win. We were going to scout it out vigorously.

If there was a problem here, it was that my choice and actions were not based on absolute, rock-solid belief.

When I left the Town of Beginnings, I prioritized my own survival above all else. Asuna and Argo were with me now, but I hadn't developed a new, grand ideal like protecting all the captive players of *SAO* or beating the game with my own two hands.

Meanwhile, the other players here were participating in this impromptu strategy out of their own strongly held beliefs, with full knowledge of the risk.

Hafner, for example, was a man who was moved by the priority of beating the game above all else. He pushed his way brusquely to the front of the line waiting for the gondola ride in Rovia on the fourth floor, but that was surely because he'd been irritated at the tourists. He was the kind of man who would chastise them for having the energy to go enjoy themselves, rather than helping attack the game. I understood that feeling, and his current actions spoke to the strength of his beliefs, given that he was prioritizing this over his guild's profit.

Then there was Shivata, whom I could only speculate about, but seemed to be here for Liten's sake. I didn't know how it was that they had come together, but they had drawn their swords to ensure their guilds did not come to blows. That was an admirable motive itself.

Agil's group, Argo, and Nezha all had searched their own feelings for their own answers as well. So why was I—the guy who spurned the guilds and prioritized his own personal gain—going against my own beliefs not only by participating in this group, but also by leading it?

The answer to that had to be my antagonism toward Morte and his provocateurs.

They had attempted to duel PK me and put Asuna through a terrible fright, and now I was moved by a furious determination to keep them from continuing their ways.

In that case, I had to admit that it was they who had stoked the fire within me. Was I losing my cool? Was I letting my antagonism and hatred guide me into a reckless strategy that would end up sending me and the people I cared about into certain death...?

I realized I was gritting my teeth and staring down at the half-eaten cake. But suddenly, my cold, numb hand was enveloped in a pleasing warmth.

I looked down to see that in a spot hidden from the rest of the group behind my black leather coat and a silk cape, a small, pale hand was gripping my own. I looked up to catch the side profile of the fencer's face.

Her expression was the usual aloof, vaguely hostile one, but the undeniable warmth that covered my hand was like touching the spring sunlight. I stood there dumbly until her pursed lips finally opened.

"...That's for giving me that buff at the camp on the third floor."

"Uh.........oh, right, I forgot about that..."

I recalled the moment when she'd melted down her Wind Fleuret to create her Chivalric Rapier and squeezed her hand back.

Why had Asuna agreed to this plan, anyway? The story about the guild flag and the competition of the two guilds couldn't have meant this much to her. If she was here out of her own unyielding personal belief, what could that possibly be...?

I wanted to know, but it didn't seem like the right moment to ask.

If we defeated the boss and made it back to town alive, then I'd bring it up. I would make that my biggest motivation to fight and win.

With that determination in mind, the foreboding music that had been ringing away in the back of my head finally faded, along with the eerie dancing silhouettes.

Without letting go of Asuna's hand, I lifted the paper plate up to my face and flipped it over to dump the rest of the cake into my mouth. I chewed and looked up at the tower again.

It was a darker shade of the stone that made up all the ruins here, the left side lit by the midwinter sun, gleaming coldly. It was as if the countless monsters inside and the menace of the floor boss was being exuded like frost.

But the heat of Asuna's hand flowed through all my veins, keeping the chill at bay. I squeezed it one last time, then let go and lowered my face to its normal level.

Immediately, I met the smirking gaze of Argo and had to cough awkwardly and clear my throat before I could step forward to address the group.

"...Well, everyone, I think it's time to announce my idea about our group formation."

Once the party had finished eating its cake and gathered around, I explained, "A-Team will be Hafner, Shivata, Okotan, Lowbacca, Naijan, and Liten. B-Team will be me, Asuna, Agil, Wolfgang, Nezha, and Argo. What do you think about that split?"

This apparently ran counter to their expected groups, and a murmur ran through the gathering before Shivata cut through to ask, "So…A-Team is the tanks, and B-Team is the attackers?"

"That's right."

"That goes against common theory. Why didn't you split us up evenly?"

"We didn't quite have enough tanks to pull that off. Shivata and Liten are the only ones with shields, so if we put them in separate parties, they might not hold out long enough for potion rotation. In that case, we should have one party with high defense maintain boss aggro, which should make it easier to manage HP. Of course, that will create a heavier load for our tanks…"

Shivata shook his head at that last statement and said, "Don't worry about that," before continuing with his rebuttal. "But if we have all the tanks together, we won't be able to handle wide-ranging simultaneous attacks. Won't that be a problem?"

"Well, just going off of the beta, the golem boss of this floor doesn't have any area attacks like Breath. It mostly punches and stomps, with different timings for either side. So as long as we manage its hate levels, a single party should be able to continually defend for us."

"Ahh, I see," Shivata murmured.

I looked around at the other members of the group and added, "Of course, I'm going to scout out the boss first to make sure there aren't any unexpected attack types. Once we start for real, we'll make sure there's a clear escape route for when the boss's HP gauge changes color, so we can dart out in case of any unknown patterns. Yes, we're fighting with only two parties, but we've absolutely got a chance, and I don't intend for us to lose a single member. So…to ensure that Shivata and Liten's countdown party is a success and to ensure that 2023 is a year of hope for all of us…let's pool our strength together and win this battle!"

For some reason, it turned into a bit of a pep talk at the end, and I was momentarily afraid that I'd overstepped my bounds.

"Hell yeah! Let's do this!!" Agil roared, pumping a fist, followed by a chorus of approval from the group.

I silently thanked the man and raised my fist in solidarity.

4:15 PM, December 31, 2022.

The hastily assembled floor boss raid opened the steel doors and set foot inside the labyrinth tower.

10

"SWIIIITCH!!"

Shivata and Liten gave the command in unison from behind their steel shields, blocking the small (though still over six-foot-tall) golem's three-part punch attack.

They used the force of the punches to leap backward, and Hafner charged between them, his greatsword raised. The thick blade glowed orange, and the system lurched the heavy warrior forward.

The overhead double-handed sword skill Cascade hit the small golem on the forehead, blasting away the remaining third of its HP. It fell apart along the seams of its limbs, and once it was a lifeless hunk of rock, shattered into little blue shards.

"That's quite some attack power," Nezha murmured in admiration.

I turned to him and whispered, "True, but he also hit it in the right spot. Did you notice how the golem had a symbol of some kind on its forehead?"

"Ah, right."

"That's the weak point of all golems, including the floor boss. Naturally, the boss is way taller, so normal attacks and most sword skills won't reach it…"

"I see. But this thing will," Nezha said, holding up the metal circle in his right hand.

"Yeah, the chakram can hit it. Just like with the minotaur king on the second floor, you wait for the right timing, and you'll be able to cancel the boss's special."

"Got it."

Meanwhile, A-Team finished its post-battle cleanup, and party leader Hafner gave the call to continue onward. I raised a hand in acknowledgment and gave the order to my team—B-Team—to follow.

The two parties had been taking turns fighting monsters, and for being assembled on the spot, the teamwork wasn't bad. While A-Team could have used the golden pattern of guard/switch/attack, I was more concerned about B-Team, which was stuck repeating attack/switch/attack. But between Agil's two-handed ax and Wolfgang's greatsword, they had enough power to knock back our opponents, giving Asuna and me the time to leap in and follow up.

What was most important, however, was the combination work of the two parties. At the larger chambers where we ran into mini-bosses, we tried having A-Team defend and debuff, while B-Team attacked from the sides and rear, but as I feared, there were a few times when B-Team got carried away and earned too much hate, drawing the boss's aggro away from A-Team. Since the hate statistic was hidden from players, we would just have to consciously hold B-Team back from attacking too much in the big fight ahead.

Until experiencing it for myself, I had no idea how difficult it was to be a raid leader. I understood a bit better Lind's feelings now, trying to lead his guild with ironclad rules and clear hierarchies. And on the other hand, I could also imagine Kibaou's desire to raise the feeling of guild solidarity and giving in to the temptation of the guild flag.

Once this mission was over I'd go back to my easy solo—er, duo—life, and never step into a leadership position again, I swore to myself as I walked down the dim hallway. Asuna prodded my arm to get my attention.

"Hmm…?"

"You know, I think it's getting more like it," she commented. I looked around and saw that the dungeon itself was indeed changing from its previous design.

The walls were scrawled with mysterious ancient letters and the massive pillars were now carved into stacks of angular golem heads, while the floor and ceiling were made of polished black granite. The increased interior detail was a sign that we were approaching the boss chamber.

I checked my window to see that it was after seven o'clock. Three hours had passed since we entered the dungeon, and considering the number of staircases we'd climbed, it was about time for us to reach the goal.

"Finally at the boss chamber, huh? I should have figured the labyrinth tower wasn't going to be easy to rush all the way through," Agil remarked, his hands on the back of his bald head.

I smirked at that. "Actually, the fifth- and sixth-floor towers have fewer rooms and simpler layouts. The tenth-floor labyrinth is insanely huge and complex, and even after three days in the beta, we never made it to the boss chamber."

"Ugggh…" groaned Agil's companion, Wolfgang. "So you guys just gave up on gettin' ahead right there?"

"We didn't give up, we ran out of time. I think I got the highest of anyone, but I was fighting one of those real bastard Snake Samurai when they announced the end of the beta test and teleported me back to the Town of Beginnings."

"Whoa, yer kiddin' about that Snake Samurai business, I hope. I hate snakes," the macho man grumbled, which drew a giggle from Asuna.

Wolfgang had long, scraggly brown hair down his back and an impressive beard of the same color, which gave him an appearance as lupine as his name. According to him, however, he got the name from a famous American steakhouse. If he raised enough money, he was going to open his own on the cow floor below, so it was no wonder that he got along with Agil the merchant.

"The meat from the giant snakes on the tenth floor is pretty good, so when you open your restaurant, you should put that on the menu."

"H-hell no! Steaks come from cows, and that's that! The only thing you'll find on my menu is perfectly prepared dry-aged beef!"

"Uh, you realize that if you age the beef, it's gonna lose all its durability and disappear, right?" Agil noted dryly. Argo cackled.

If he was limiting himself to beef, I was going to ask if he considered the tauruses in the second-floor labyrinth to be fair game, until a voice from A-Team, farther ahead, cut me off.

"Hey, look at that!"

I stretched up to see down the dark corridor and caught sight of something that was half what I expected and half not.

In the labyrinths before this point, these creepy corridors always had an eerie set of doors at the end leading to the boss chamber. Yet up ahead were not double doors, but a huge staircase as wide as the hallway. And above, there was a huge, gaping black hole through which the stairs rose. For now, there was no sign of any monsters in the corridor or on the staircase.

"Proceed with caution!" I warned, and Hafner responded in the affirmative. A-Team stayed up front, and we watched the sides and rear as we walked forward for half a minute.

A-Team stopped before the staircase, and when I caught up to them, I slipped through to stand at the head of the entire group.

"There are no gaps to the side," I noted.

At my left, Hafner said, "Meaning we'll just have to climb up. Our coordinates put us right about in the center of the tower."

"Hmmm…But will there be another hallway and then the door up there, or will it just be the boss chamber?"

"It wasn't like this in the beta?" Shivata asked from the rear. I turned around to speak.

"Nope. Before there was just another normal set of doors, then the chamber with the golem. But pretty much everything's been changed in one way or the other, so there might not be a grand meaning to the addition of this staircase…"

I looked ahead again, staring into the square of darkness at the top of the stairs, but I couldn't make anything out. No sooner had the thought of throwing a torch up there occurred to me than Argo passed me on the right, carrying a light.

"Guess we just gotta peer inside."

"R-right…Well, assuming that goes straight into the boss chamber up there, I'm going to go up alone to scout it first."

I turned back to give a formal command to the rest of the group, but Argo intervened, looking deadly serious.

"Hang on. Leave this to me."

"Huh…?"

"This staircase is worrisome. Could be a trap, where the stairs rise up from the floor to seal the exit. If it happens, I'm quick enough to slip out before it closes."

She kicked the stone step with the toe of her shoe. At that point, I noticed that even the side of the steps had those ancient letters carved into them, which made her suggestion seem all the more likely.

But I'd already forced Argo to do solo reconnaissance on the boss of the catacombs. Just because she came out fine that time didn't mean everything would go smoothly again.

"…Let's go together, then. I'm not backing down on this."

"Whaaat?"

"Don't give me that look! I may not be as fast as you, but I'm still a speed type. I'm capable of escaping, too, if the stairs start to move, you know."

"Sheesh! Fine, fine," Argo accepted, pouting. I gave the order for the others to watch our backs.

Asuna came forward and whispered, "Be careful." I reassured her that I would be fine and be back soon.

I put my foot on the very bottom step and began to climb the massive staircase carefully, after Argo. The darkness up ahead grew closer, bit by bit.

Eventually the stairs met the ceiling of the hallway and continued onward. It meant that the layer of rock separating the floor where the rest of the group waited and the floor above was extremely thick. The only source of light was Argo's lantern, and although it was brighter than a torch, the thick darkness rebuffed its prying light.

Once we had climbed over fifteen feet from the hole's entrance, I noticed a shift in the temperature. A heavy chill was washing over me from above. That was the air of a boss chamber.

"Argo," I called. The informant nodded, still looking ahead. Three, four, five steps later, the material under our feet changed.

The hobnails on the soles of my boots hit a hard, smooth surface, producing a sharp ringing. Immediately, there was an eerie *vmmm* vibration, and a number of lights sprang into being in the distance.

The pale lights, which looked like LED bulbs, cast away the darkness. When I saw what the light revealed, I gasped.

It was vast.

The circular chamber had to be a hundred feet across and fifty feet tall. That meant the entire top portion of the labyrinth tower was taken up by this one boss chamber. The curved walls had to be the very walls of the tower itself, and the ceiling would be the bottom of the sixth floor above.

But that left one question.

"...Wait...there's no staircase going up," I muttered, and Argo nodded as she put away the lantern. She cast a thorough glance around the chamber and said nervously, "There's no sign of a boss, either..."

It was my turn to nod. Until this point, the sequence was always: enter chamber, lights go on, floor boss appears. But even though we had moved from the staircase out onto the floor, there was no polygon block phasing into existence.

The floor and ceiling were flat and smooth, gleaming like black crystal, with fine lines crisscrossing here and there like electric circuits. I crouched down to touch one of the grooves, but nothing happened.

"You don't think...the ALS already beat it, do you...?"

"Not a chance. When we left Mananarena, we confirmed they were still in town. They've prob'ly left by now, but we got a good three-hour lead on 'em," Argo pointed out, inching forward.

"W-wait..."

"I don't think the boss'll pop unless we move a bit farther...You wait next to the stairs, Kii-boy," she said, proceeding cautiously.

I peered ahead of her, where thirty feet away there was a spot where the lines on the floor came together in a complex concentric pattern. It looked likely to do something, but that only made me more nervous. Argo knew it, too, though. I just had to stand here and watch her.

The information broker glided slowly, smoothly over the black surface, lit by the pale bulbs and, after a deep breath, stepped into the circle.

One...two...three...

Between the fourth and fifth second, a number of things happened at once.

The lines on the floor glowed, and an instantaneous, fierce vibration rumbled the entire room. I shouted Argo's name, but she was already preparing to leap away from the spot.

If she attempted the same thing a hundred times, she would have succeeded at evading ninety-nine of those times.

But in Aincrad, all outcomes were the result of system calculations that only *appeared* to be random. If the system decided it would be so, the player's will could not override that outcome.

The momentary vibration threw Argo off-balance, and she toppled into the circle.

The next moment, five square pillars burst up out of the ground in a pattern around her.

There were three long pillars. One shorter pillar. And one shorter still. The pattern...the layout.

They weren't just pillars. They were fingers. It was a giant hand.

"*Argooo!!*" I screamed, racing forward. She tried to stand up to escape the fingers, but a tumble in this world wasn't just a lack of balance, but a system-recognized negative status. She would be under a brief stun effect after falling and couldn't move until it wore off.

The black fingers, covered in glowing blue lines, started to close around the girl. I crouched, ready to pounce between them and rescue her...

"Stay back, Kii-boy!!"

It was a sharp command the likes of which I'd never heard from her. Argo's right hand flashed from her spot sprawled on the floor. Something flew by and grazed my left cheek—the pick she always had equipped at her side. My avatar's legs disobeyed my command and froze for just a brief instant.

With a deep, explosive rumble, the black hand trapping Argo began to stretch upward from the floor.

Up in the air, the five fingers clenched shut, tightly.

Through the cracks in the pitch-black fist, I heard a faint bursting sound and witnessed a glittering cloud of blue particles.

If I hadn't tasted that same fear in the catacombs two days earlier, I might have been truly too late this time.

When I had seen the one cloaked man holding the Chivalric Rapier +5, I lost all my cool. Just the image of her being PKed took over my mind altogether. I simply didn't think to check her HP bar in my party readout, but even after I did, I nearly convinced myself that it was just a delayed reaction from the game system. To my good fortune, her shout drew monsters that forced Morte and his friend to flee—but if I'd maintained my wits, I could have come up with a smarter plan.

I couldn't make the same mistake this time.

I tore my gaze away from the floating lights in the air and checked the bottommost of the six HP bars on the upper left corner of my vision. It had taken about 10 percent damage, but the bar was still intact. The crushing effect I saw was not Argo herself, but her equipment.

It was too early to be relieved, though. Argo's HP was slowly but surely dropping. She needed to be freed from the huge fist as soon as possible.

"Rrrah!"

I drew the Sword of Eventide from over my shoulder and slammed it against the black arm stretching up thirty feet from the floor. The collision produced an earsplitting blast, a shower of sparks, and a nasty vibration running from my wrist to my shoulder. A red damage line ran down the smoky quartz surface, but promptly vanished. The fist above did not open.

I held my sword to my left side to initiate a sword skill, trying to contain my rising panic. The light blue glow flashed back and forth at high speed before my eyes, creating a larger impact than the last.

The two-part Horizontal Arc got a clear reaction from the fist this time. A bellow like thunder erupted above, the arm pulled down toward the floor, and the fist opened.

A small shadow darted forth from the palm hovering twenty-five feet above, hurtling into a spin and landing next to me. It did a backflip away from the scene, and I took distance myself from the massive arm.

As the arm sank down into the floor with a smaller rumble than when it appeared, I heard Argo comment blithely, "Whew! That startled me."

"That's what *I'm* saying," I quipped, but in truth I was relieved. Argo ended up suffering only 15 percent damage, but her trademark hooded cloak was gone, and the leather armor below was in terrible condition. The bursting effect I'd seen was from the cloak.

"I think we should go back—"

"*Below*," I was going to say, but Argo cut me off.

"Kii-boy, down there!"

"…?!"

The light circuits running along the floor were undergoing a dizzying transformation. The blue lines were gathering around my feet, forming a number of concentric circles…

"Nwaah!"

Argo and I jumped away, immediately before the enormous

black arm burst from the floor again, clenching its fist audibly in the air.

It was a close call, but at least we'd identified one of its patterns. As long as we paid close attention to the lines, we wouldn't get snagged like that...

"Below, below!!" Argo shouted again.

"...?!"

I looked down to see that the concentric circles were forming again, despite the arm already being in place elsewhere.

"Mwah—!"

Another jump. A second arm erupted, just barely grazing the toe of my boot, and clenched another fistful of air.

"What? There are two?!"

"Most people have two arms, Kii-boy," Argo remarked rather calmly, given that she nearly died less than a minute earlier. "Look at how the thumb is in a different spot. That's a right and left hand."

"Oh...yeah, now that you mention it..."

Indeed, the way the two arms were placed, they looked like a giant stretching up through the floor.

That meant the grabbing attacks were done with for now. The down staircase was a good distance away across the chamber, and I started to head for it when I got a bad premonition and looked up. Those blue lines had been forming on the ceiling earlier, just as they had on the floor...

"I knew it!!" I shouted, grabbing Argo by the arm. The danger circles were forming directly overhead, like a targeting reticle.

This time it was not an arm that burst forth through the stone, but an enormous foot. Just behind me, a bare black foot, size 200, stomped onto the floor. The shock wave of the impact nearly took me off my feet, but I just managed to stay upright.

"Kii-boy, if there are two arms, that means..."

"I know!!"

I kept running, watching the ceiling. Sure enough, the lines wound together, forming another target.

"Here it comes!!" I shouted, but the blast drowned it out. The second foot stomped down harder than even General Baran, sub-boss of the second floor, sending more ripples through the floor. This time we were ready for it and leaped over the shock wave safely, then hit the brakes as we turned around.

Near the center of the hundred-foot-wide chamber, the two arms and legs stood like creepy towers. We had evaded the clutch-clutch-stomp-stomp combination, but since we ran toward the wall, we were now fifty feet from the stairs. It was hardly distant if within a safer environment, but in this battle, it was an endless expanse.

For the moment, the lines on the floor and ceiling and the giant limbs were still, so we could either try to sprint for the stairs now or watch carefully for a third arm or leg, or something else entirely.

"Don't move, Kii-boy."

"Huh?"

I started to turn toward her, but another "Don't move!" command froze me. I held my breath, wondering what she was talking about, given that the lines weren't moving.

"Look down very slowly, without moving your feet."

"O-okay," I obeyed, looking down at my feet with the bare minimum of facial and eye movement. There was black floor, blue lines, and my leather boots. "I'm looking...And?"

"Look closer. See how your feet and my feet are just barely not touching the blue lines?"

She was right. All four of our feet were touching nothing but flat floor, without intersecting any of the lines. But at its narrowest, there was less than an inch gap between our shoes and the lines, so any move would cause us to step on them.

"...So stepping on the lines causes those target circles to appear and summon the giant hands and feet?" I asked.

"That's what I think."

"...And if we move without stepping on the lines, we can get to the stairs without being attacked?"

"That's what I think."

Still, it was easier said than done. It would be one thing if the lines were in a lattice pattern, but they flowed and twisted in random arrays, and the spaces were only big enough to hold a single person at their widest, while barely an inch apart at their narrowest. Even carefully tiptoeing along, it would be extremely difficult to return to the staircase without stepping on a single line.

In that case, maybe it would be best to just make a break for it and expect to be attacked...but then again, that kind of desperate thinking is what gets you in trouble...

The floor trembled again. I looked forward in panic, but it wasn't an attack. The four limbs were retracting back into their respective surfaces. Apparently, if none of the lines were broken for long enough, the trap would reset.

Well, we'd just have to sneak our way back to the stairs, I decided, and turned to suggest this to Argo—but the next words to be spoken didn't come from me or her.

"Hey, you all right?!"

It was Hafner, who led the other nine up the stairs into the chamber. Twenty feet pounded the lines, causing four target circles to appear simultaneously on the floor and ceiling.

"Weird, the boss hasn't shown up yet?" Shivata squawked.

I drowned him out by screaming, *"Evade! Evade!!"*

If I'd had time to be accurate, I would have said that only those who saw the circles of blue light under their feet needed to evade, but it was all too sudden.

Point-three seconds after that, the raid members showed admirable reflexes in leaping back. But as the ten members had been bunched close together, Shivata and Lowbacca collided and fell in the process. And due to some cruel law of the universe, Lowbacca was one of the four who had stepped on the lines first; a target circle appeared like a menacing eyeball beneath the two where they fell.

Go-go-go-gong! Two enormous arms thrust out of the ground, and two enormous legs fell from the ceiling.

The right hand clenched empty air. The legs slammed fiercely against the stone floor.

And the left hand closed on Shivata and Lowbacca, lifting them high into the air.

"Nwaah?!"

"Whoa!"

Their surprised shouts were cut off by the shutting of the hand's fingers. These were two full-grown men, so unlike with tiny Argo, their limbs were sticking out, still in view—but there wasn't enough room to escape.

Because they were in the raid but not my party, their HP bars were visible in an abbreviated form. Still, the sight of the little horizontal bars bleeding downward only accelerated my haste.

Their damage wasn't as rapid as Argo's, thanks to their high defense and HP, but the real trouble was the armor-breaking effect of the grabbing attack. Shivata was the indispensable tank of A-Team, with his extensive experience as a heavy shield user. If he lost his armor, our battle plan would fall apart.

I just need an item that can freeze time for a minute—even thirty seconds! I wished frantically.

Given that we could stop the limb attacks by not stepping on lines, it was possible for this boss fight to go easier than usual, if we executed it properly. It would help us pause the battle, giving us a moment to drink recovery potions.

But I didn't have time to share that info with the others yet. I wanted to order them to rush back to the stairs, but they weren't going to run away with Shivata and Lowbacca trapped like that. Liten and Hafner already had their weapons out, preparing to battle the towering arm. Meanwhile, the arm and legs that missed in their attacks were returning to the floor and ceiling.

The instinct to fight wasn't wrong, but normal attacks would not undo the squeezing trap. You needed a sword skill above a certain level of power, I suspected, but with multiple panicked fighters using huge attacks in such a narrow space, it might lead to a collateral damage disaster. But who to command and how?

As my brain ran in overdrive, something hit my eyes like a meteorite. I had crossed glances with a pair of hazel-brown orbs.

Asuna. The only person standing still amid the chaos, waiting for me to say something.

I delivered the shortest order I could to my partner, fifty feet away.

"Parallel on the arm!!"

She nodded without missing a beat and held up her Chivalric Rapier, already drawn. Her sword skill Parallel Sting started with a forceful step forward. It carried her past Liten and Hafner, hitting the black stone arm with two lightning-fast thrusts.

The attack emitted bursts of light, and the same roaring sound as before issued from the ceiling. The fist opened, liberating Shivata and Lowbacca. They fell from thirty feet above, and Liten and Hafner did their best to catch them.

All four of them did lose HP, but the biggest news was that they'd escaped without losing any armor. That was a relief, but the tension wasn't over. The other limbs had already withdrawn, and new target circles were forming beneath Nezha's feet and over Okotan's and Naijan's heads, closer to the staircase.

"We can't escape now!" Argo shouted by my side.

I suspected she was right. The lines on the floor were spaced farthest apart toward the wall and bunched up closer as you approached the stairs. It was impossible now for all of us to get to the staircase without stepping on any.

"Everyone, run to the closest wall!!" I shouted at maximum volume, and within a second, everyone was sprinting. The next moment, a hand burst out of the circle next to the stairs, followed by two pounding feet. I sucked in a deep breath for another command.

"Once you're at the wall, stop and make sure you're not stepping on any lines!!"

The rest of the group looked down as they ran. The problem was that the lines were currently reconfiguring, making evasion impossible. Eventually the movement slowed until it was possible to track with the eyes, then slowed more...

"Now!! Avoid the lines and stop!!" I shouted for the third time. Within a small window, everyone else came to a halt.

I held my breath, looking back and forth between the floor and ceiling. No target circles yet. None yet, none yet...

"Ah..." came a quiet voice from nearby.

Nezha, who had been running in my direction, was standing on one foot, waving his arms in an attempt to regain balance. There was a fairly large gap near him, yet for some reason, he was hesitating to put his raised foot down there.

In an instant, I understood why.

He had been assigned a minor FNC (full-dive nonconformity) status by the NerveGear, meaning that he had difficulty with depth perception in this virtual world. That was why he'd given up on close-range combat to become a blacksmith. He didn't have trouble with walking or running, but the finer skill in judging the distance between his feet and the lines was a bit beyond his grasp.

"Hang on a bit longer!" I called, careful not to step on any lines myself as I approached him. When the chakram thrower leaned over and nearly fell onto the floor, I grabbed his outstretched hand and held him up.

"You're okay, just let your foot down there...Right below, that's it. Good job."

"S-sorry..."

Nezha's balance was returned. At long last, I could let out a heavy breath of relief.

We had successfully managed to get all twelve people to avoid stepping on the lines, giving us a much-needed pause. We couldn't let this moment go to waste.

I wasn't going to ask pointless questions about why they'd come up. The scouts had lost HP, and there were huge booming sounds coming from above—of course, they charged up the stairs.

"Everyone who suffered damage, drink a pot while you listen! Those arms and legs belong to the floor boss!" I announced. I could see Hafner's eyes bulge as he tilted a bottle to his lips. "You see those blue lines on the floor? Step on them, and the lines on the floor and ceiling start moving around randomly, creating target circles either below or above the person who stepped on it! When the lines stop moving, the arms come up from the floor to grab you, and the feet come down from the ceiling to stomp you!"

"...So you're saying that as long as we keep straddling the lines, the arms and legs won't attack us?!" Agil shouted from the other side of the chamber, quickly catching on. I couldn't see his expression a hundred feet away, but the echoes from the enclosed chamber were audible at least.

"That's right! At max, it can attack with two arms and two legs at once! If the arm grabs you, it'll lift you up about thirty feet and do simultaneous damage to your HP and armor durability! But if you hit it with a sword skill about equal to a two-hit attack from a one-handed sword, it'll let go of its prey!"

Once I made sure everyone had heard that, I continued, "I don't know how powerful the legs are because we didn't get stomped yet, but I'm guessing their damage is worse than the arms! And like with General Baran, they create outward shock waves when they stomp, so you might get tripped up if you don't avoid them!"

Again, the other ten acknowledged understanding. I consulted my memory of the last few minutes for anything else to say, but I couldn't think of anything.

"Well, that's all!!"

A stunned silence fell over the chamber.

A few seconds later, Asuna spoke up from about twenty-five feet away. "So if we stay just like this, the boss won't attack, but we can't hit it, either?"

"I...I think so. The silver lining is that if we had a full raid party, there's no way we could get all those people to avoid stepping on lines, but with our smaller number..."

I considered whether we should intentionally step on the lines so we could begin attacking, or if we should attempt to get back to the stairs to go down.

But just at that moment, as if the game system itself refused to allow such a relaxed moment to pass in the boss chamber, the lines in the center of the ceiling, directly over the stairs, began to move on their own. We were all frozen in place, so we could do nothing but watch in horror.

Gong, go-gong! The ceiling began to jut down in a complex shape.

The black surfaces started connecting, lining up along the glowing blue boundaries, forming a symmetrical object. It was a jutting forehead, sunken eye sockets, a square nose, and a horizontal mouth.

The rough, blocky "face," like something from the early days of 3-D game engines, was about ten feet tall from the forehead to the chin. The black sockets suddenly lit up with pale circles of light, and an eerie, complex symbol glowed in the center of the forehead.

As twelve pairs of eyes watched in silence, six HP bars appeared one after the other over the giant head. The first bar looked slightly shorter because of the sword skills we'd used on the arm, but the damage was paltry.

At last, the proper name of the fifth-floor boss appeared in a ghostly white font:

Fuscus the Vacant Colossus.

"The name...is totally different from the beta..." I whispered, aghast.

As if in response, the two pupil-less eyes moved, and the angular mouth opened wide. The blue symbol on the forehead turned an ominous red.

That was bad news, but I didn't have time to issue a defensive command. It wouldn't have helped, anyway.

The cave-like mouth let out a bellow loud enough to shake the entire labyrinth tower, and every member of the raid wobbled to some degree. Fortunately, no one stepped on any lines, but that was only a temporary relief. The moment the boss had bellowed, a defense-lowering debuff icon appeared under all our HP bars, and the previously still, blue lines burst into movement again.

The unavoidable defense-lowering debuff was bad, but it also broke me out of my shocked paralysis. I roared my orders to the group:

"Spread out and watch the lines carefully! Dodge them whenever possible, and if you step on one, check the floor and ceiling for the circles and get outta the way if you see any! If you can, attack the limbs when they appear!!"

I heard fierce, bold responses from around the chamber. At a much quieter volume, I told the nearby Nezha, "The gaps are bigger along the wall, so it's easier to avoid the lines! When they stop moving, aim your chakram at that symbol on the giant's forehead!"

"G-got it!" he responded, and ran to the wall nearby. The dizzying speed of the lines was slowing now. Next, I gave orders to Argo and Asuna.

"I'm going to trigger a line on purpose—get ready to use sword skills!"

"You betcha!"

"All right!"

I watched the lines on the floor closely. We'd gone to the trouble of grouping up tanks in A-Team and attackers in B-Team, but if the boss continued this irregular attack pattern, sticking to formation would only work against us. We'd just have to individually avoid the lines and find chances to counterattack on our own.

The countless lines sliding over the black floor slowed down… slowed down.

"…Here we go!" I shouted, stepping intentionally on one with my right foot. The lines reacted like a living creature, forming a target circle around my foot. Once it fixed into place, I leaped out of the way.

A black arm passed right before my eyes, tearing through the air. Asuna, Argo and I closed in from three directions.

I raised my new sword to deliver the Vertical Arc two-part skill, ensuring I wouldn't hit either of my companions. Asuna did another Parallel Sting, and Argo executed a three-part attack with the claw on her right hand.

Enveloped by a tricolor blast of light, the giant black arm flinched in pain. The face up on the ceiling roared in anger, and I noticed that the first HP bar was visibly lower than before.

The injured arm sank into the floor, and the lines repeated their dizzying dance. While I waited to try the same strategy again, I checked on the "defense down" icon from earlier, but it wasn't blinking yet. The effect was frustratingly long-lived.

I sensed movement on the ceiling and looked up to see the boss's mouth opening wide. The symbol on its forehead was glowing red. It was going to roar again—and would certainly cause a different debuff this time. I tensed, realizing it was point-less anyway.

But just before the boss could bellow, a little silver light shot across the room.

It was Nezha's chakram, whirling softly as it flew. It struck the boss's forehead with pinpoint accuracy, and the symbol returned from red to blue. The giant face shrank back, shutting its eyes and mouth and retracting into the ceiling a bit. Meanwhile, the rotating chakram made a hard turn back toward the direction from which it had been thrown.

So far, everything about the boss had been changed from the beta—except for the weak point on its forehead. Just being able to cancel out the debuff attack was huge on its own. I resumed watching the lines on the floor and held out a thumbs-up in Nezha's direction.

The lines stopped. This time the target circle appeared on the ceiling, but the idea was the same. I avoided the golem leg plung-ing down from above, and the three of us hit it with sword skills at the same time.

As the foot rose up into the ceiling again, I heard Hafner's voice from across the chamber calling out, "Affirmative! We'll try attacking next!"

Agil and Okotan chimed in:

"We will, too!"

"And us over here!"

I scanned the room and took note of the different groups: Hafner, Shivata, and Liten were on the north side of the stairs; Agil and Wolfgang were on the east side; and Okoton, Lowbacca, and Naijan to the south.

Heartened by the quick reactions of my fellow elites, I shouted as loud as I could: "I'll leave it to you!! Give it hell!!"

But even then, I was resigned to a grab or a stomp or two as they got used to the process.

Step on the line when it stopped, evade the onrushing limb, then hit it with sword skills. When the boss started its debuff roar, Nezha would cancel it with the chakram. Our hastily assembled raid party carried out the pattern admirably and was executing it safely by the third attempt. With both arms and legs being hit by simultaneous sword skills, the damage inflicted was hefty, and it took us less than ten minutes to wipe out the first HP bar, then the second, then the third.

Our plan prior to the battle was to pull back when the boss switched to a new HP bar, in case the attack patterns changed, but even into the fourth bar, more than halfway through, there was no alteration. It was unlikely to stay that way until the end, but we could probably get through one more before the shift.

Just as I was executing another Vertical Arc (having lost count of how many times I'd done it already) I heard Nezha shout with panic.

"Kirito! The wall!!"

I spun around. The blue lines from the floor and ceiling were stretching out onto the previously flat, plain walls. The two sides moved toward each other like some kind of prehistoric creature, filling in the blank space.

Like the bars of a cell.

"Retreat down the stairs! A-Team first, then B-Team!" I ordered spontaneously. If we left the boss chamber and it lost its aggro state, all the HP we'd worked to reduce would heal very quickly, but it was dangerous to go too deep when you didn't know what was ahead. We only needed one person to see the new attack patterns for himself, and I would serve that role.

"But—!" Hafner protested, and Shivata tugged silently on his cloak. The heavy warrior gave in reluctantly and ran for the stairs in the center of the room.

SAO was a cruel, cold game of death, but there were certain ways in which it maintained a minimum of fair play.

One was that there was always an escape route from a boss chamber. In most of the MMOs I'd played before this, the arena was inescapable once the boss fight started, but *SAO* was different. The water battle against the hippocampus on the fourth floor did have closing doors while the submerging attack was active, but it was still easily openable from outside.

So I believed that the fifth floor would naturally hold true to that pattern.

"Kirito!" Asuna shrieked, pointing to the ceiling.

I looked up to see that the giant face, which had been stuck to the ceiling since it appeared, was now gone. The three HP bars were still there, so we hadn't defeated it yet; the lines on the floor, ceiling, and now walls were still moving restlessly.

So where did the face go?

I looked all over the vast ceiling, feeling a sense of eerie foreboding stealing over me.

Then I heard Liten's helmet-filtered metallic voice cry out, "No, Shiba!!"

My eyes were sucked right toward the direction of the stairs.

In the center of the room, where the staircase had been just seconds before, the boss's face was bulging from the ground, and sunk up to his waist inside of the gigantic mouth was Shivata.

But why—why would it be there? Where did the staircase go?!

I was frozen in place, my breath held, when Hafner turned to me in the process of pulling Shivata from the boss's mouth.

"The stairs…turned into its mouth!!" he shouted. It took a brief moment for understanding to pierce my brain.

The boss's face disappeared from the ceiling and appeared in the floor. That was fine. But if the down staircase, our only means out of the chamber, turned into the boss's mouth, then nobody could escape the chamber.

No—more important now was rescuing Shivata. His heavy armor was bleeding red damage effects from the boss's black teeth, each one as big around as Mananarena's massive roll cakes. He hadn't lost any HP yet, but it was easy to imagine that if his armor broke, he'd suffer fatal damage on the spot.

"Dammit, not again!" Shivata hissed as he tried to pry open the boss's mouth—he'd already suffered the clutching attack earlier. Liten was helping him, but the enormous jaw was not opening in the least. On the other side of the face, Agil was repeatedly slamming his double-handed ax against the weak point on its forehead, but unlike when a single chakram strike could knock it back on the ceiling, it was easily repelling the heavy blade now.

Perhaps, like with the arms and legs, sword skills were necessary to affect it, but given that Shivata was trapped in its mouth now, he was hesitant to attempt them.

I wanted to rush over and help, but the lines were still moving on the floor. Hafner and Liten were too busy with Shivata to bother avoiding the lines, so if necessary, me, Asuna, and Argo would need to stomp on them to draw the limb attacks away.

"Damn...what's the deal with this boss and all the appearing and disappearing?!" I growled under my breath.

Nearby, Asuna rasped, "So that's what they meant by Vacant Colossus..."

She had figured something out about the boss's name. I glanced over at her, and she continued, "Vacant meaning empty, and colossus meaning giant statue...I think it's referring to the entire chamber. This room *is* the boss of the fifth floor."

"...!!"

I was speechless. I looked out at the entire room, the floor, ceiling, and walls writhing with organic glowing lines. If Asuna was correct, the twelve of us were trapped inside the empty interior of Fuscus the Colossus. If the whole space was part of the boss's body, then of course it could produce arms and legs wherever it wanted or change the stairs into a mouth.

"I don't care if it's a magical golem, this is crazy!" I wailed.

Meanwhile, Shivata screamed, "It's no good! I can't get loose!"

Hafner and Liten tried to offer encouragement, but there was fear in their voices as well.

"Don't give up, Shivata!!"

"We're going to save you now, Shiba!!"

"It's no use…my armor's going to break! Licchan, let go of its mouth!" Shivata cried, a remarkable act of willpower. But Liten only shook her head.

"No!! I'm…I'm going to save you!!"

That was right. We couldn't give up now. Shivata was nearly at full HP still, so even if he got hit by some sword skill damage, it wouldn't kill him outright.

My mind was made up. "Agil! Attack the forehead sigil with a sword skill!" I ordered.

But the burly fellow's bald head shook back and forth.

"I can't…there's no sigil anymore!!"

"Wha…?"

My mind was shocked into a blank state yet again, until the metal screech of Shivata's armor being damaged broke through it.

If he died here, the other members would be petrified, and we'd be reduced to running around from Fuscus's unfair attacks helplessly. And since the stairs were gone, there was no escape anymore. The entire raid party could be wiped out.

Is this it?

My unsteady eyes traveled over to lock on to the profile of Asuna's pale, frightened face.

The same face I'd been looking at on the spiral staircase up to this floor, when I promised that I would protect her until she didn't need me anymore.

Perhaps I never had the right to make such a promise in the first place. From the moment I abandoned my only friend in this game of death, right at its start, my path had been set in stone. I was meant to wander its wastes alone, without a goal.

Was this my punishment, meted out by a digital god? My just desserts for not only seeking a partner to protect, but also leading a group into battle against a boss...?

At my feet, the blue lines that served as Fuscus's nerves slowed their movement.

In the distance, Shivata's armor cracked, spilling bright red damage effects.

The Sword of Eventide suddenly went heavy in my right hand.

Right at the moment of despair, when every player present might have thought all was lost—

"I won't let you...kill Shibaaaaaaa!!" Liten roared ferociously, and launched into a totally unexpected plan.

The steel-covered heavy warrior jumped onto Fuscus's square jaw and thrust herself without hesitation into the mouth with Shivata inside. His Iron Mail burst into a cloud of little blue shards. The lines of teeth plunged cruelly toward the swordsman's torso, but when they hit Liten's steel plate, they crunched, sending up sparks and stopping still again.

"Wha—! Licchan, why would you do that?!" Shivata demanded, grabbing his partner's shoulder.

As she pushed against the golem's mouth with both hands, she said, "B-because I'm a tank! It's my job to protect others!!"

Fifty feet away, those words struck my numbed brain like a hammer.

Aside from Argo and Nezha, Liten was the last member to join the raid party, and she was fulfilling her role more bravely and admirably than anyone. I wasn't even directly exposed to danger, and I was ready to give up.

Liten's job was to protect.

My job now was to think.

Think. Think until every last brain cell burns into ash.

Fuscus's weak point...Where did the forehead symbol go? It couldn't have just vanished. If he was a golem, then there had to be a symbol or letter carved somewhere on his body, as the Hebrew legend suggested.

Fuscus's face vanished from the ceiling and appeared in the floor. That meant that most likely, the symbol had moved from its forehead to some other location. Somewhere on the floor, walls, or ceiling? No, there was a place more likely than those.

I squeezed my weapon's handle and shouted toward the group at the center of the chamber, "Do whatever you can to avoid the lines, guys! If you can't help it, then climb up on the boss's face!"

They looked toward me in surprise, then nodded. Hafner, Naijan, and Okotan, all heavily armored, clambered onto the boss's cheeks and forehead, while Agil, Wolfgang, and Lowbacca spread apart to focus on the floor.

Next, I issued commands to my companions nearby.

"Asuna, Argo, Nezha! Step on the lines to bring out the arms and legs! That symbol has to be on one of them! If you find it, we'll all attack!"

"Got it!"

"You bet!"

"I'll try!"

All three of them crouched in preparation. As the lines slowed down, they seemed to react briefly as they crossed beneath each foot. There was no need to avoid them this time, but the evasion would be easier if the target circle appeared in front. I rebalanced my feet and, the instant the lines stopped, used my left leg to step on the one directly in front of me.

Immediately the blue lines swirled into a concentric pattern beneath my boot. I leaped back.

It was Fuscus's left arm that shot up toward me, his right arm at Argo, his left leg at Asuna, and his right leg at Nezha, all at about the same moment.

I swung around the arm, searching frantically, but there was no symbol. I didn't hear any of the others shout about it. If I was wrong about this, we were going to lose both Shivata and Liten.

It had to be there. It had to…it had to!

"I found iiiiit!"

The panicked, lilting scream came from Nezha, twenty feet away near the wall. I spun to see the chakram user pointing at the back of the left leg's blocky knee. But he had been so focused on looking for the symbol that he wasn't able to evade the shock wave after the stomp—he had toppled to the floor and couldn't get up.

The attack finished, the leg began rumbling back up toward the ceiling. The back of the knee was twelve feet off the ground— about as high as I could reach, but I had no other choice.

"You're not getting away!" I shouted, racing toward it. I held out my sword as I ran, preparing Sonic Leap, the longest-distance jumping sword skill at my disposal…

"Duck, Kii-boy!!" came a shout from right behind me, and I instinctually crouched.

The next moment, something slammed onto my right shoulder. I just barely managed to stay on my feet, looking up to see the leaping silhouette that had just used me as a launching pad. Even with every last point put into agility, her air was nothing short of stunning.

When Argo the Rat hit the peak of her jump, the claw on her right hand glowed purple. The system acceleration sped her up, tiny body flipping as it hurtled forward like a cannonball. If I recalled correctly, that was the claw-type charging skill, Acute Vault.

At odds with Argo's epithet, she shot forward with carnivorous, feline ferocity, digging deep into the back of the left knee. When three diagonal damage lines covered the blue symbol, I heard a deep roar like subwoofer feedback from the rear.

I turned around, boot soles sliding, to see Fuscus's face protruding from the floor, mouth agape in a howl. Shivata and Liten popped right out of the mouth, pushed by the sheer pressure of the sound, and fell to the ground together.

Liten's plate armor had ugly-looking damage spots on it, but hadn't broken entirely. As long as it didn't fall apart, it could be repaired.

Fuscus's face sank into the ground, mouth still wide, and disappeared. Like before, the descending stairs were left behind.

After a brief pause, the players present raised a cheer in unison. Hafner leaped onto Shivata with joy and hauled him up onto his feet, while Okotan extended a hand to pull Liten up.

I was relieved that we had at least avoided the worst-case scenario, but the fight was still far from over. I looked around cautiously and spotted Fuscus's face in the center of the ceiling. Its circular lighted eyes blinked, while its mouth opened into a diamond and boomed with an eerie *vwo, vwo, vwo* laugh. The symbol was back on its forehead, but there was no telling when it would vanish again.

"Guys! It's too early to celebrate!" I shouted, brandishing my sword. "Let's keep fighting now that we know the change in its pattern! Shivata, I want you to go down the stairs and recover HP!"

Without his Iron Mail, it was too dangerous for Shivata to continue fighting, I thought—but the veteran front-runner already had his equipment mannequin open. He shouted, "Sorry, but I'm gonna ignore that order! I'm not walking down those steps until we beat this boss!!"

"But your armor—!"

"I have a replacement set! I can still fight!"

Just as he said, his shirt was promptly covered by a fresh set of heavy armor. It looked a bit weaker than the Iron Mail he'd just lost, but there was enough defense there to do the job.

"…All right! Just don't push it!" I called out. Shivata gave me a thumbs-up, potion in his mouth. Up on the ceiling, Fuscus mocked our newfound determination again. The glowing lines resumed moving.

From that point on, we managed not to stumble into any major injuries, though we didn't exactly break it down into perfectly stable patterns. The big trouble was still when the boss's face moved to the floor; nobody got gobbled up like that again, but because the position of the symbol shifted around to different limbs, there were a few times we failed to prevent the debuff voice attack in time. In addition to lowered defense, the debuffs caused a variety of random effects like reduced vision, reduced hearing, reduced balance, and slipping damage, and those suffering sensory effects couldn't always avoid the grabbing and stomping attacks.

But with admirable coordination, our impromptu raid managed to free the trapped members or carry the stomped ones to the wall for healing. After nearly thirty minutes, we had taken down the fourth and fifth HP bars, and at 8:05 PM, about an hour after the battle started, we reached the sixth and final bar.

"*Vwohhhhh!!*"

The face in the ceiling roared at maximum volume and the eye rings turned a deep red. "It's gonna change patterns again! If you're short on potions, say the word!" I shouted.

"I'm in a bit of trouble!" "Me, too!" shouted Hafner and Wolfgang, so I pulled two small bags containing six potions each out of my inventory and handed them over. Meanwhile, the blue lines crisscrossing the entire chamber were moving in an entirely new pattern.

The floor lines shrank around the staircase in the center, then returned toward the outer walls. As they reached the walls, they climbed up vertically, gathering around the face in the middle of the ceiling.

The lines that had harassed us all battle long disappeared, leaving only blank black floor behind. All twelve of us tensed nervously.

The blue light writhed wildly around Fuscus's face like a mane, and he dipped downward. The lines gathered into four thick bundles, target circles forming at the end of each one. The players stuck beneath them darted away, but the arms and legs that appeared were slower than before. This time, they continued growing, producing elbows and knees, eventually shoulders and hips, then a blocky torso…

"*Vwooooaaaa!!*"

Fuscus the Vacant Colossus, boss of the fifth floor, separated from the ceiling as a proper humanoid golem at last, roaring even louder than before.

"Retreaaat!!"

I didn't even need to give the order. Everyone was sprinting to the south side of the chamber. A moment later, Fuscus landed on the floor with a deafening crash.

The blue lines covered the surface of the thirty-foot-plus giant's body. Starting from the face, they quickly turned from blue to an angry bloodred. In seconds, it was red all the way down to the tips of its feet. Fuscus roared for a third time and raised its arms high, the ends bulging like hammers.

Seeing that my companions had been bowled back by the sight, I called out orders instinctively.

"Now that the boss is human-shaped, we can use our original strategy! A-Team blocks, B-Team attacks! Prioritize hate management!'

"G-got it!" said Hafner, leader of A-Team, and called for his party members. Asuna, Agil's group, and I fanned out on either side so that the heavy fighters were in front of the boss, and the lighter troops were to the sides, weapons bristling.

"Let's whittle down that last bar!!" I called.

"*Yeah!!*" came the responses in a fierce wave. The boss responded by stepping forward with a massive, heavy foot.

Shivata and Liten, main tanks of A-Team, came forward, holding their shields up on the left side. With perfectly synchronized motions, they raised their right hands and thrust their left hands forward. The shields glowed silver and rang like temple bells. It was Threatening Roar, a taunting skill that required high Shield skill proficiency.

Depending on the boss's type, it sometimes had no effect, but fortunately Fuscus was susceptible; he roared and moved faster. Shivata and Liten stood bravely against the enormous golem, which was even bigger than Asterios the Taurus King of the second floor.

"*Vwoagh!!*" our opponent bellowed, raising his right fist to nearly scrape the ceiling and slammed it down onto the pair. They stood fast against the blow with their shields.

Even tanks had to perform upkeep on their shields, so the ideal defense was a sidestep move, but they wanted to see if blocking was a viable strategy while they still had the leeway to try. As I watched with equal parts admiration and terror, Shivata's heater shield and Liten's round shield collided with the giant boulder fist, generating a huge blast and a flash of light.

Sure enough, they were pushed about six feet back, but stayed on their feet without suffering damage. Since that was just a normal attack, they certainly wouldn't be able to block a special attack with unique effects. But just knowing something could be blocked was a mental boost. Fuscus's right arm was briefly immobilized after the attack, and Hafner tore into it with Cataract, a two-part greatsword skill that knocked down about 3 percent of the last HP bar.

"All right…let's attack!" I ordered Asuna, leaping into motion. I struck the golem's tree trunk–sized left calf with a Vertical Arc. When the pause ended, I yelled, "Switch!" and pulled back. Asuna jumped into my spot, dancing into a high-low Diagonal Sting.

At the right leg, Agil and Wolfgang were swinging their two-handed weapons with abandon, tearing out solid damage. Fuscus faltered with the damage to its legs, roaring. For a moment I was afraid we'd pushed too hard, but thankfully, the golem kept its sights on our tanks.

In the distance along the wall, Nezha was preparing to launch his chakram at the weak point, while Argo darted nimbly across the chamber, leaving healing potions on the floor around A-Team.

"It's finally looking more like a boss fight!" Asuna murmured as she darted back past me.

"Yeah…but it's not going to just end without a struggle. Stay focused!"

"Of course!" she replied, a grin tugging at the corners of her mouth. There was nothing of the old newbie Asuna from the first two floors left in her. There were many pieces of knowledge left to teach her, but perhaps the moment that she "didn't need me anymore" was going to come sooner than I expected. The sudden realization caused the breath to catch in my throat.

But that was what I wanted, of course. Only when she left my side and joined a major guild would her ability truly blossom. It was all for the sake of beating this deadly game…Asuna was fighting to get herself back to reality, too.

I clenched the grip of my sword and returned the smile to my partner for now.

"Okay…next time we'll attack a different spot and find its weak point."

"Sounds good. Maybe it's an Achilles tendon or a pinkie finger," she suggested confidently, whipping her silver rapier back and forth.

As I suspected, Fuscus's attacks expanded to include simple punching attacks, a foot-stomping combo, that aggravating debuff voice, heat lasers from the eyes, and a frenzy mode for his final stage.

I considered a brief retreat every time the pattern changed, but the six members of A-Team, particularly Shivata and Liten, were standing strong through the occasional potion rotation.

When the last HP bar went red, all six of them withstood the golem's furious double-fisted whirlwind attack. Shivata turned to me and yelled, "Kirito! You can have the LA, just make it look good!!"

At that, I had no choice but to put on a show. "All right! I'll take it, then!!"

I rested the dark-elf Sword of Eventide against my right shoulder and ran with all my might.

It hadn't been powered up yet, but the sword had a magic boost of +7 to AGI, a remarkable effect for just the fifth floor. I made full use of my speed boost, sprinting at full blast as I drifted toward the wall. When I got there, I leaped onto the curving surface and kept running, practically parallel with the ground, passing over A-Team on defense, and when I couldn't climb any farther, I jumped as hard as I could.

Fuscus's enormous face was directly in front of me. The red ring eyes shrank, trying to focus on the small leaping human approaching them.

"*Vwoaaaaaaaah!!*"

I did my best to cut through the golem's bellow with a shout of my own.

"This is…the eeeeeeend!!"

I held the blade at my left side and activated Horizontal Square, a four-part skill that no other player had yet learned.

The longsword whirred like a coaxial helicopter rotor, striking Fuscus's red forehead symbol with one, two, three, four glowing lines.

The sigil split off of the surface and vanished into a little glow of light.

The ringed eyes began to blink irregularly.

The red lines covering its body flashed brighter. Something like flame erupted outward from the lines—and Fuscus the Vacant Colossus, boss of the fifth floor, exploded.

The Last Attack bonus readout appeared as I landed on the ground again and fell to one knee.

The boss's death effect was more impressive than any of the previous ones, but even after it faded away at last, no one spoke.

Amid the silence, I noticed a change in the texture of the floor. That smooth, crystalline reflection was gone, replaced by the same rough, dark-blue stone that the tower was built from. I reached out, still kneeling, and touched the craggy surface. The entire floor suddenly began to rumble.

At first I was afraid that, like on the second floor, there was another boss to deal with. This time, a new object descended from the ceiling, and to my great relief, it was not an arm, leg, or face, but a spiral stone staircase.

"…It's over…"

I wasn't watching, but I guessed the voice belonged to Shivata or Hafner. Like the breaking of floodgates, that comment let loose a storm of cheers from our little raid party.

I wanted to join them more than anything, but an onrush of fatigue threatened to knock me out; it was all I could do to steady myself by jabbing the sword into the floor. As I struggled to use that prop to get to my feet, a pale hand appeared in front of my face.

"Good job, Kirito."

I clasped it and pulled myself up to a shaky standing position. My partner was grinning next to me, her rapier already put away. We celebrated with a light fist bump.

Behind us, an even louder cheer arose, so I turned to see Shivata lifting Liten up into the air. He was spinning her around, holding her under the arms, as though that full plate armor weighed nothing at all.

"...Looks like they could be the talk of Aincrad by tomorrow," I muttered, but Asuna shook her head.

"Nobody here is going to spread irresponsible rumors. I don't think even Argo would sell info on them."

Argo herself was standing not far away, and she managed a brave, "N-nah, never!" Nezha joined in the laughter, and the four of us all shook hands.

"You were an excellent leader, Kirito. Why don't you try recruiting members to start your own guild?" Nezha suggested innocently. I shook my head in vigorous terror.

"D-don't even joke about that. Besides, there's no use inviting you, remember?"

"That's not true. I'm sure the entire Braves team would love to join your guild, Kirito."

"Nope, no way. Then Hafner would kick my ass and accuse me of having planned that all along," I protested quietly, glancing over to see that he and Okotan were still enraptured in the glow of victory. I had reluctantly taken on the role of raid leader to *prevent* a disastrous split between the DKB and ALS, not to lay the sparks of fresh conflict.

In any case, we had beaten the boss without losing a single person, so disaster was averted for now. The only issue was the item in question, I thought with a weary heart...

At that very instant, my body was shot through with an unpleasant shiver, as though a needle of ice had pierced my spine.

I was so involved with the strategy of the boss that I'd forgotten the most important part until this very moment.

The most basic of *SAO* rules.

When any monster—including bosses—dropped an item, it would appear directly in the player's inventory...and even other party members would not know about it.

Meaning that when the group's celebration ended and we got to the post-battle phase, I would ask about who got the guild flag, the ultimate purpose of our entire plan. And if no one raised their hand, it meant that either there was no flag dropped by the fifth-floor boss in the official release of *SAO* or whoever actually got the flag wasn't telling anyone—and I would have to discern between the two.

Technically, it was possible for all of us to set our menus to visible so that everyone's gains could be examined. But the contents of one's inventory was the most crucial of personal information in *SAO*, and even bossy guild leaders like Lind and Kibaou would not dare conduct forced inspections of their members' items.

I briefly considered sorting the item lists to have the newest items at the top, but I discarded that one as well. The sort feature worked only on the main inventory window, like a root folder in a file-based OS. It didn't work on the subfolders—if the flag had been moved to a container or sack within the inventory, it wouldn't show. I'd have to inspect all those containers, and if it was within a multilayered sub-storage, like a sack inside a box inside a sack inside a box, not only would the process take forever, but it would be easy to miss.

I should have noticed the issue before we started the fight and talked it over. If we had established a protocol wherein nobody opened their window after the boss was defeated, and we then checked just our main inventory screens one by one, nobody would even attempt to hide the item.

So what should be done? Did I raise the issue now and get permission to check everyone's stuff? Or did I put my hopes on the probability that someone would materialize the flag and drop it out in the open, preventing my fears from coming true in the first place?

"What's wrong, Kirito? Does your tummy hurt?" Asuna asked, noticing my unnatural state.

"*What am I, a little kid?*" I wanted to snap, but I wasn't in the mood for jokes. I looked at Asuna, Argo, and Nezha in turn and asked, "Um…did the guild flag drop for any of you?"

All three of them shook their heads. Asuna gave me a questioning look, so I shook mine in return. "Nope, nothing for me…"

"Ahh. So it must be someone over there."

It was then that Asuna and Argo realized my concern. The two girls grimaced and muttered, "Oh, right…" and "Dang, how careless I was…" That got Nezha's attention.

But the chakram thrower only grinned and said quietly, "It'll be fine. We all worked as one to win this fight. I'm sure they'll come forth."

"…Yeah, I'm sure…" I replied, then turned and steeled myself.

The spiral staircase touched the floor about ten feet away from the descending stairs. It met the stone seamlessly, as though it had always been in that exact spot.

As I approached, Shivata lowered Liten at last and turned to me, beaming. "Hey, we did it!" he cheered, raising his hand. I tried to put on the most natural smile I could summon as I slapped his palm.

The sound brought the other members over, and I addressed the entire group.

"First, congratulations, everyone…and thank you. We managed to beat the boss, and it was thanks to your incredible effort. Lots of stuff didn't go according to plan—I mean, our reconnaissance run ended up being the final attempt—but you all did admirably against undoubtedly the toughest boss yet."

I paused, and Hafner, hands on hips, filled the silence—but not with what I expected.

"Given my position, I probably shouldn't be saying this, but... maybe we were able to defeat a gimmicky boss like this without casualties *because* we only had a dozen members. If it was a full raid of forty-eight, I feel like it'd be impossible for every last one to avoid those floor lines."

As if noticing what he was just saying, he then looked at the ALS's halberdier. "Uh...Oko, do you think the ALS was planning to attempt the boss with just their core members because they knew how to tackle it properly?"

Okotan lifted his hands in a shrug and said, "Nope, I think that was a total coincidence. Plus—and this is totally off the record—I don't think the ALS's three main parties could have done this without losing anyone. We don't give members any orders based on build, so we don't have any pure tanks in that group. It's too tough a role for too little experience gain. Scouting Liten was a big step toward fixing our tank situation...I knew she would be a bearer—I mean, a bear for us."

"I am not a bear, Oko!" the maiden in love protested from inside her damaged plate armor. Okotan smiled in mild panic at the unintended insult, but Shivata, Hafner, and Agil's team roared with laughter.

With the conversation at a lull, Shivata opened his window and looked at it, then at me. "It's already eight thirty. The ALS could be showing up any moment now. Have you thought about how we're going to return, Kirito?"

I was taken aback; I'd been occupied with a different question.

"Uh...yeah, right. We might run into the ALS if we go back down the tower, so I think we should go up to the town of the sixth floor and teleport back to Karluin through the gate. We went to the trouble of beating the boss; you all want to see the next floor, right?"

"You bet I do! I'm so excited!" Hafner bubbled. The group laughed again, but I cut them off by raising my hand.

"Like Shivata just said, we don't have much time. I'd like to rush up to the next floor, but before that, there's something very important to take care of."

The group grew serious again with my expression and tone of voice. I motioned Asuna forward, then looked at each of the raid members in turn: Hafner, Shivata, Liten, Okotan, Agil, Wolfgang, Lowbacca, Naijan, Asuna, Argo, and Nezha.

"The purpose of this fight was to get the guild flag from Fuscus. I want whoever got the flag to speak up now."

"Oh, right, that was the point. I totally forgot," said Agil. He rubbed his head and held his empty hands out, indicating that it wasn't him. His companions shrugged or shook their heads, and the pairs of ALS and DKB members gave similar reactions. Of course, neither Asuna, Argo, nor Nezha spoke up, either.

After five seconds of silence, Wolfgang said hesitantly, "It's not...you, Kirito?"

"Nope...didn't drop for me."

"So that means the fifth-floor boss in the official game didn't have this flag after all?" the wolfman asked in surprise, stroking his beard. Meanwhile, the even hairier Lowbacca raised his arms over his head in disbelief.

"Well, what a bunch of nonsense over nothing! What was all that hard work even...for...?"

His words slowed and faded out as he came to a realization. At the same time, the expressions wore off of everyone else's faces.

The possibility that someone had the guild flag and wasn't announcing it to the group mercilessly shredded the post-victory glow hanging in the air.

The companions who had fought the boss with one heart and one mind now looked at one another in suspicion. It was stoking all my worst fears.

It would be so easy to simply declare, "The fifth-floor boss did not drop any flags," and head upward.

But that only put off the problem at hand. In fact, I would be abandoning my duty.

Because I already had a suspicion about who had earned the guild flag and was hiding it from the group.

Of course, I couldn't present undeniable evidence, but if I framed the discussion just right, I might be able to put pressure on the guilty party. Still, if they insisted innocence, I could not force an inspection of their inventory or threaten with my naked blade. I had to produce a willing confession, not create a stalemate.

But how could I fashion that outcome?

I'd never attempted to understand the minds of others before this; I only pushed them further away from me. Even with my family in the real world, the people whose faces I saw every day, I often found myself wondering what they were thinking, what kind of people they truly were. The feeling of not knowing who another person really was drained the feeling from my real life, and at times filled me with an inexpressible emptiness.

I found my escape from real life in online games starting in elementary school because the idea of communication through an avatar seemed very natural to me. The 3-D avatar and the real human manipulating it were in separate realms, completely isolated from each other. That way I didn't have to worry about who anyone else was.

That was why *Sword Art Online*, the world's first VRM-MORPG, appealed to me so much. My application to the beta test and eventual imprisonment in this virtual world were essentially inevitable.

But from the day the log-out button disappeared and my avatar turned into my own body, I tried to distance myself from people again. I abandoned Klein, my very first friend, and was nearly killed by Kopel, my very first collaborator—but the root of the problem was with me, for being afraid of getting close to others.

Once this world became my second reality, I tried to have zero connection to anyone else, just like before. The player was always a player; even with my life on the line, I would continue to role-play under a fictional name. Maintaining that mind-set allowed me to engage in a minimum of communication with other people.

I might be able to pressure whoever was hiding the guild flag with logic, but I could not convince them in the truest sense of the word...

I let out my breath, started to lower my head.

But my attention was drawn by a small but bright light in the right corner of my vision.

The source of the light was a pair of hazel-brown eyes, staring straight at me. Not pleading, not urging—just watching, silently.

Asuna.

Since the start of this game, I had undoubtedly spent more time with her than anyone else, yet she remained an enigma to me. I wasn't honestly sure why she kept working with me. There were so few times I felt I truly understood exactly what she was thinking, I could count them on my fingers.

But for whatever reason, I had never felt that sensation—that suspicious *"Who are you really?"* question—about her, not even once. She always existed in a neutral state at my side, angry, sulking, laughing.

She wasn't acting out a temporary disguise of herself here. Whether her body was a digital avatar or not, she was herself. Asuna could be more natural with herself than anyone, not because she was a newcomer to MMOs, but because she possessed a firm sense of self.

When I first found her in the labyrinth tower, she was empty eyed and nearly suicidal in her abandon. Now she had found a reason to fight, gained knowledge and skill, and had worked her way to being one of the very best players in the game.

Could I change like that, too?

I returned her glance and resumed facing the group.

My upright stance bent at the waist, and my head lowered into a deep bow.

The vast chamber echoed with startled murmurs. I searched for the right words—not as a speech, but my own true thoughts.

"First, I need to apologize to you all. I should have started discussing how to handle the guild flag first, before we started the fight. We needed to know what to do if the flag dropped and how to confirm if it didn't. It was my mistake that we didn't do that until now. And that has caused mistrust among the group..."

I straightened up at last, looking right at the faces of the other eleven.

"But I don't want the ALS and DKB to fight over the flag...I want both guilds to work together and help us expand our frontier in the game. That's why I summoned you all here to take part in this boss raid. It was what I believed before the fight, and it's still what I believe, now that we've won."

I paused, and silently called upon the late knight.

Diavel, what would you have done here? I can't be your successor. I don't have the nobility, the leadership that you represented. But the desperate way you went after the Last Attack, the honesty with which you asked your former rival to carry things on—I admire those qualities.

Yes, I had to do everything I could before giving up was an option, just like Diavel did against the first boss. Just like the Legend Braves did against the second boss.

I drew my right foot back to an even position with the left. Straightened my spine, all my fingers, and held my hands at my sides.

From my position standing at attention, I looked directly at a single player, then bent at the waist, lowering my head as far as I could, until I saw nothing but the blocky stone floor.

"...There is no longer any way to determine who got the guild flag using system tools. So I'm begging you. I don't want you to give it to me...I want you to let the group determine its use. For the sake of the frontline team...For the sake of all those players waiting on the lower floors...And for the day when someone finally beats this game."

Silence filled the chamber.

The murmurs were gone, as were the clearing of throats, the rustling of equipment, and even breathing.

The silence was so complete that it almost seemed as if the auditory input had been cut off somehow.

A clanking metal footstep broke that illusion.

The footsteps, somewhere between the dull thud of heavy armor and the light pad of leather armor, approached with purpose and stopped right in front of me. From above my bowed head came a calm voice.

"Please straighten up, Kirito."

"..."

I slowly looked up to see the oldest member of the raid...the head scout of the ALS, Okotan.

I took his outstretched hand and straightened my back. This time, it was his turn to stiffen formally and bow.

"Kirito, my companions, I am very sorry. I was the one who failed to announce that I had earned the guild flag."

No sooner had his confession and apology ended than a muffled voice came from the back. "Oko...! But why—?!"

The figure stepped forward, raising the visor of the armet helm to continue in a sweet, clear voice, "Remember what you said? That the entire frontline group needed to stick together, that our two guilds shouldn't be fighting...Why would you do this?!"

When the tear-streaked plea was over, Okotan turned and bowed again to his guildmate. "I'm sorry, Liten. I'm afraid I've betrayed your trust."

He turned back to me and opened his window. After a few taps at his inventory—it seemed to have been hidden in a subfolder, as I suspected—he materialized an item.

With a spray of little dots of light, a ten-foot-long spear appeared, even longer than the halberd slung over the man's back. In fact, while the end was pointed, it was not a spear. A pure white triangular banner was attached to the upper end, wrapped gently around the mirrored silver handle.

"Ohhh," someone murmured with awe.

I had never seen it before, either, but it was clear at a glance that this was a very special item. Fine detail adorned the tip and the

butt of the slender shaft. The border of the banner and the lus-
trous material were elegant and filigreed. The sheer presence of
the item cast it in a different light altogether from the other items
of the lowest floors of Aincrad.

Okotan hefted up the guild flag, witnessed in person at last,
and asked gently, "Kirito, you looked directly at me. Could you
tell me how you knew I was the one?"

"Ah...yes." I took my eyes off the flag and looked the halberdier
in the face. "Okotan...were you a heavy FPS player before you
joined this game?"

He was taken aback by the way I turned the tables back on
him, then nodded. "Yes...for a while, I played shooters more than
MMOs."

My suspicions confirmed, I started to explain the detail in his
words that stuck in the back of my mind.

"Well, I only tried them a bit...but you know that type of team
battle in shooters called CTF: capture the flag. The one where two
teams fight over a single flag."

"Right," said Shivata, who clearly had no idea where I was going
with this. I pressed on.

"In that mode, the player who has the flag in his possession is
called the flag carrier or flag bearer—bearer for short. And earlier, you said, 'Liten would be a bearer—no, a bear for us.' You
changed the word on the fly, but I figured you wouldn't have
thought to use that word at all unless the flag had dropped into
your inventory and was already on your mind."

When I said it aloud, it sounded less like a reasoned, educated
guess and more like a nonsensical accusation, but Okotan only
nodded his head slowly.

"Ah, I see...I suppose that's what I get for attempting something I'm not used to." He looked down at the beautiful flagpole
in his hands and smirked bitterly. "Maybe I'm not in a position
to say this, but...Kirito, Liten, everyone...I want you to believe
me. I did not participate in this raid for the purpose of stealing
the guild flag for myself. I have no connection to the inner circle

of the ALS. At first, I wanted nothing more than to protect the relationship of the two guilds…That was my only desire. But…"

Okotan's finely whiskered mouth twisted, and his eyes clenched shut. His hoarse voice echoed through the stone chamber.

"When this flag…the Flag of Valor, dropped into my inventory, and I realized nobody had noticed and that I could hide it if I wanted—the thought entered my mind. The thought that I could use this as a bargaining chip to have the two guilds united into one…"

Hafner's armor clattered faintly, but he bit his lip and maintained silence. Shivata and Liten looked at each other but also said nothing.

When Okotan opened his eyes again, the self-mocking smile returned, and he shook his head. "But that would never happen. If the guild flag appeared in the hands of an ALS member, then the rest of you would know that I had kept it. How could we have a good-faith negotiation like that? It was a stupid dream. Once again, I apologize to all of you for my foolish actions."

Still holding the flag, Okotan bowed deeply again. Hafner clanked forward a step, his fists clenched.

"Yes, that was a stupid thing you did! So stupid, in fact, that it could have led to open war between our guilds! But…your dream wasn't stupid at all!!"

Okotan's shoulders twitched. The DKB's subleader took another heavy step forward and, in a slightly quieter tone, continued, "I had a little dream of my own during that battle. If me, Shivata, you, and Liten could fight together so well, being in a party together for the first time, then maybe there was no use to all our bickering…Maybe we shouldn't split into two squabbling guilds, but form our ideal parties. And I'm not gonna give up on that dream. Maybe it won't lead to our guilds merging…but I'm not going to stop thinking about what-ifs. So…so I forgive you!!"

Hafner's sudden speech paused, and he surveyed the rest of the group. "If any of you still can't forgive Oko and want to see him penalized in some way, raise your hand now!"

Agil spread his hands wide and smirked. "C'mon, Haf, you know that when you put it that way, nobody's going to raise their hand."

The Bro Squad all nodded agreement, while Asuna, Argo, and Nezha smiled. Okotan's back trembled, his head still lowered toward the ground.

"...Thank...you."

His voice was halting and raspy, but with the echoing of the stone chamber's floor and walls, everyone heard it loud and clear.

11

"WELL, I WOUND UP WITH THE THING...SO WHAT DO I do now?"

Holding it in my hand, I looked up at the mirrored silver pole, which stood planted in the stone floor.

I was the only person remaining in the boss chamber of the fifth floor. I'd sent the rest of the team up the spiral stairs, reassuring them I'd follow in minutes.

The stone-built chamber was utterly silent now, without a trace of the ferocious battle with the golem just minutes earlier. With the tension gone, I was now heavy with fatigue. I hobbled over to the wall, using the flagpole as a cane, and sat down with a spoken "There we go."

The solitude was for me to think about a few things.

First, Hafner had taken a vote, and the unanimous opinion was that I should be forced— Er, *allowed* to keep the guild flag. I tapped the side of the heavy pole with my left thumb to bring up the property window.

At the top was the item name, FLAG OF VALOR.

It was categorized as a long spear, but according to the info from the beta, the attack power was extremely low. It was the magical effects that were truly extraordinary. That was the same as before, too—so long as it was planted in the ground during battle, any guild members within fifty feet of the flag would receive its benefits. This chamber was about a hundred feet across, so if the flag bearer stood right in the middle, the whole interior would be covered by the effect.

To register the flag to a guild, all it took was for a player with guild leader status to hit the REGISTER button at the bottom of the property window. The pure white banner would automatically change to the colors of the guild, and the flag could not be reregistered with a different guild. In other words, if Kibaou registered the flag and the ALS later merged with the DKB into a new guild, the flag would be useless to them. That could be circumvented by disbanding the DKB and having all its members join the ALS, but that would never happen.

In that sense, Okotan's idea to use the flag as a tool to merge the two guilds wasn't technically wrong, just realistically very unlikely. Hafner and Okotan had reached a sort of mutual understanding, but that was a miracle brought about by the success of our tremendous mission to defeat the worst boss yet with a tiny group. Once we started on the sixth floor, they would return to their guilds and resume status as rivals.

But surely today's events would not go to waste. They had been implanted deep into the memories of those involved and would someday bear flowers, I told myself.

I opened my window and placed the guild flag onto it. With a little *bling*, the massive flagpole vanished into the inventory window.

All I could do for now was stash it, but it took an act of will to put away an item with such incredible stats. It was imperative that I find an ideal use for it.

The clock on my window said it was past eight thirty. The ALS could come charging up the stairs at any moment.

The second thing on my mind was how to handle them.

I had the option to race up the spiral staircase and take the teleport gate on the sixth floor back down to Karluin. But if I did that, Kibaou's group would not know what happened.

They might go crazy looking for a way to summon the boss. That wasn't something I wanted on my conscience.

I supposed I had a responsibility to explain that I had jumped the gun on their plan to jump the gun. So I leaned back against the wall and shut my eyes, waiting for the ALS to arrive.

After a while, I heard the sound of footsteps.

It seemed rather early for them, but then I grew suspicious. There was only one set of steps, and it was coming from above, not from below.

When I opened my eyelids, I saw a fencer in a light purple cape descending the spiral staircase from the sixth floor.

"Asuna..." I willed the strength into my legs to stand. "What is it? Didn't you go to the city up there?"

She shrugged her caped shoulders as she stepped off the staircase and approached.

"I heard an interesting story as we were climbing the stairs, so I thought I'd tell you about it."

"Oh...? Wh-what kind of story?"

Asuna stopped next to me and turned around so she could lean back against the wall.

"It's about the source of Okotan's character name. What do you suppose it is?"

"Huh...? W-well, I'd be lying if I said I wasn't curious. He didn't seem like the kind of person who would be quick to anger, as the 'oko' would imply...Hmm. Does he like o-*kotatsu*, those low tables with the heater underneath?"

"Bzzzt!"

She crossed her index fingers in an X and grinned. "It's the name of a river that flows into Lake Shikotsu in Hokkaido. He grew up near there and had a soft spot for the place."

"Ohhh...Now that you mention it, Kotan sounds like an Ainu-ish name...But did you really come back here just to tell me that?"

"Of course not," she said, contradicting her earlier statement, but didn't elaborate.

It was a reminder to me that she was truly an enigma. But before I could come up with a reply, she suddenly asked, "You stayed behind to negotiate with the ALS squad, didn't you?"

I tilted my head at an awkward angle, neither a nod nor a shake. "Er, I wouldn't...say that...necessarily..."

"I wouldn't have anything to do up in town anyway. I'll join you," she declared.

"Uh..."

The ALS would be furious when they learned we had beaten them to the punch, of course, but it wouldn't turn dangerous...I thought. But that depended on how serious they were about getting the guild flag. Did they just want to ensure the DKB didn't get their hands on it—or were they determined to seize it at any cost?

Even if it was the latter, I couldn't believe they would turn their weapons on a fellow player outside of town. They were game clearers, not bandits. On top of that, I knew that Asuna would not listen to any orders to leave.

"...Thanks. Just don't provoke them, please..." I pleaded. Asuna murmured that she understood.

For the next five minutes, we waited along the wall, chatting about mindless subjects.

Eventually, the sound of many clanking footsteps approached from the descending staircase. Two, no, three—it had to be the ALS scout party.

The lightly armed fighters raced into the room in a triangle formation, looking around sharply. From my spot on the wall, I called out, "Hi, guys."

The men all looked in my direction, and their eyes and mouths went huge. The captain type lowered his sword and gasped. "B-Blackie?! What are you doing here?! Where's the floor boss...?"

"Sorry. Already beat him."

"..."

After a full five seconds of silence, the captain sighed and shook his head. One of the two in the rear mumbled, "Y'know, I just had a feeling..."

* * *

One minute later, the full, twenty-four-man ALS core group and the duo from the true pioneer group faced one another across the descending staircase.

Some of the men dressed in matching moss-green and dark metal gear whispered among one another in the back, but the spiky-haired guild leader Kibaou stood boldly in the center, his arms crossed, eyes and mouth shut tight, maintaining his silence.

Figuring it was a good opportunity to refresh my memory on the names and faces of the main ALS members, I turned to Asuna and whispered, "Do you know any of their names aside from Kibaou?"

"Umm…the one to the right of Kibaou with the trident is Hok-kai Ikura. The one with the scimitar on the left is Melonmask. And to the left of him with the short spear is…Schinkenspeck, I think…?"

"…Well, I'm glad they're not *all* named after food," I muttered, suddenly struck by a pang of hunger.

Asuna promptly added, "Schinkenspeck is a type of Austrian smoked ham. It's well spiced and quite delicious."

"…When we get back, we have to eat dinner…"

Before Asuna could reply to that suggestion, Kibaou's eyes flashed open, and arms still crossed, he shouted, "At any rate! It seems clear y'all beat the boss, so I will tell you congratulations! But if you don't explain a few things right here an' now, we won't be able to go traipsin' back to town!"

"Uh…yeah, I get it. I'll explain whatever I can," I said. Kibaou thrust out his hand, index finger upright.

"First! You ain't gonna tell me it was just you who beat the boss all on yer own. Where'd you get the muscle?!"

"I'm afraid I can't tell you that," I replied. Kibaou's eyebrow arched, but he withheld comment and straightened another finger.

"Second! It ain't a coincidence that ya beat the boss just before we showed up! How'd ya know we were gonna tackle the boss tonight?!"

"Sorry, can't tell you that, either."

His eyebrow twitched again. Half the members with him looked ready to explode with anger, while the other half shook their heads in disbelief or resignation. I heard one of them yell to take the questions seriously, but Kibaou silenced him with his hand and held up a third finger.

"Those were just the warm-up. But this one you can't back out of answerin'...The floor boss musta dropped an item called a guild flag. What happened to it?!"

"..."

Now it was my turn to fall silent.

Not because Kibaou had caught me in a trap, but because I knew it was necessary for me to be honest about it. There was a danger to doing that, however slight. In the worst-case scenario, the twenty-four players could draw their swords to PK me. If that happened, I needed Asuna to escape up the spiral stairs.

Simulating how that reaction would play out inside my head, I nodded.

"Yeah...it dropped."

The ALS members murmured, stunned. I held up the index and middle fingers of my right hand and swiped them straight down.

My menu appeared with a bell chime, and I used it to materialize the item I'd just placed inside it.

The murmuring increased when they saw the ten-foot-long silver flagpole appear in a shower of light. I gripped the pole around the middle, closed the window, and loudly stomped the butt of the Flag of Valor onto the stone floor of the boss chamber.

"This is the guild flag. As I'm guessing you already know, planting it on the ground like this provides four buffs to all guild members within fifty feet of the flag. It's an extremely helpful item against bosses, but once registered to a guild, it can never be changed."

My explanation was rather abbreviated, but even then, the ALS members were stunned into muttering for a third time. Some of them looked up at the pure white banner, clearly envisioning it dyed with the color and logo of the ALS.

But Kibaou had the presence of mind to hold steady. He snorted and got to the business at hand.

"Well, well, well. You got yer prize, just like a true beater. So, since you refuse to join any guild…whatcha gonna do with that thing?"

This was the centerpiece of the conversation.

I sucked in a deep breath, tensed my stomach, raised the guild flag—and slammed the butt against the ground with a *crack*.

"I am not opposed to leaving this flag in your care, Kibaou. However, I have two conditions."

"Let's hear 'em."

"While there are two, I need only one to be satisfied. The first is if a future boss drops the same item. In that case, I will offer this flag freely to the guild that does not receive it, so that the ALS has one and the DKB has one."

I heard cries of "When will that happen?" and "That's just wasting time until then!" from the back. But Kibaou only nodded, prompting me to continue with a glance. I took another deep breath and delivered my second condition.

"Or if the ALS and DKB join forces to form a new guild. In that case, I will give you this flag instantly and without further requirements."

Over three seconds of heavy silence passed.

It was torn to shreds by a cavalcade of bellowing voices.

"We…we can't do that!!"

"Merge with those elitist pricks?! You're joking!!"

"Go and suggest the same thing to them! They'll tell you you're crazy!!"

Two dozen angry men inched forward. At my side, Asuna grew noticeably stiffer. I continued to stand tall against the shouts, mentally measuring the distance to the staircase.

Just then, a high-pitched shriek cut through the rabble.

*   *   *

"I...I know the truth!! They're not planning to give us the flag from the start!! They're demanding the impossible from us so they can keep it and start their own guild!!"

That ugly, eardrum-piercing voice was familiar to me.

It was the voice that revealed I was a former beta tester in the first boss chamber.

The voice that suggested the Legend Braves' scam had caused a fatality in the second boss chamber.

The voice that claimed Asuna and I were trying to monopolize the Elf War campaign quest in the third boss chamber.

Breaking through the crowd was the dagger user, whose name was Joe, I recalled. He wore a leather mask with holes for his eyes and mouth, which made him look ridiculous but also hid his facial features.

Joe pointed a finger at me, bent like a claw, and shouted, "We don't gotta listen to their nonsense, Kiba! There's only two of 'em! There are plenty of ways we can take that flag back!!"

Wait.

I'd heard that screeching voice somewhere else, too. Not in a big group like this...but in town, or the wilderness, or a dungeon...

Just as my mind was about to seize on some kernel of understanding, a deep, threatening voice growled, "You mean by force, Joe?"

"Exactly!! We got four full parties here, and there's only two of 'em. It would be easy to..."

"You idiot!!" Kibaou thundered, grabbing Joe by the shirt. He lifted the smaller avatar and practically head-butted the leather mask. "Yeah, the info on the guild flag you brought us was accurate, but no matter how important it is, if we draw swords on another player, that makes us nothin' but a buncha thugs and criminals! Sit yer ass down and think about why the ALS exists again!"

He thrust Joe away and turned back toward us, lowering his head despite the grimace on his features.

"Sorry about forcin' you to hear that nonsense. As far as those conditions go…can I assume you'd tell the DKB the same things?"

"Uh…yes, of course."

"Then I'll let you hold the flag for now. Wouldn't hold out hope for that merger, though."

By Kibaou's standards, it seemed like a rather easy resignation, but I suspected that it was just a sign that he, too, thought of the flag like an unstable bomb.

While not all of them looked entirely satisfied, the other members had no choice but to fall silent at their leader's order. Joe glared at us briefly before returning to his position.

Kibaou crossed his arms again, puffed out his chest, and barked, "We're goin' back now! Nice work, y'all!" He started for the stairs leading down. I was in the process of putting the guild flag back into my inventory and looked up with a start at the spiky head.

"Actually, they should have activated the sixth-floor gate already, so if you want to return to Karluin, it might be faster that way."

"I see."

Kibaou spun around on his heel and headed for the spiral stairs instead. When he passed by me, I thought I saw his lips quietly form the word *thanks*, but that was probably my mind playing tricks on me.

It took a while for twenty-four sets of feet to disappear up the stairs. When silence arrived at last, I felt the tension within me finally snap, and I let out a long breath.

"Ahhh…Well, out of all the possible outcomes I considered, that was definitely one of the better ones. I still have to tell the DKB about this, but for now—nice work, Asuna. Let's take a little rest and then…"

"*Go back*," I was going to finish, but the words caught in my throat.

The fencer had been standing there and listening during the entire conversation with Kibaou, her presence regal and confident.

But now two tears trailed silently down her pale cheeks. They formed drops under her slender chin—glittering as they collected the light from the vast chamber—then fell, one and then the other.

"A…Asuna…?" I whispered, completely dumbfounded by why she would be crying.

There'd been some tension in the showdown with the ALS, but Kibaou had kept a cool head, so I'd never felt in danger for my life. The boss battle before that had been a much more terrifying ordeal. And Asuna had never raised a peep of concern during the long fight, so why cry now?

Eventually my mind ran out of steam and went blank. She looked straight at me, not bothering to hide her tears. Despite the situation, I couldn't stop myself from thinking that those wet hazel-brown eyes were the most beautiful thing I'd ever seen in the world.

Her pale lips parted, vibrating the virtual air.

"Why…why…"

She clenched her eyes shut, dripping large orbs of fluid, then raised her voice.

"Why do you have to be talked to like that…? After how hard you worked…After you risked your life to fight for the sake of the group, for the sake of everyone trapped in here…After you bowed to them and apologized…Why do you deserve this?"

It took some time for those words, spoken in a voice like a tiny silver thread pulled to its absolute tautest, to form meaning in my head.

Asuna was crying for my sake.

But that understanding did not tell me how I should have reacted. Her wet cheeks scrunched up.

"This is wrong. They make their guilds, pull all their friends in, do whatever they want, bicker with each other…and you ran yourself ragged for their sake, only to get accused like that…It's wrong. It's absolutely wrong," she protested, shaking her head. Asuna looked up at the ceiling and pursed her lips, helpless to stop the streaming tears.

Finally I succeeded in sucking in a breath. I took a step toward my partner and managed to put my thoughts into words.

"…That's what I chose to happen. I chose not to join a group. I'm not fighting because I want people to recognize me…or praise me. As long as I can protect myself and those around me, the rest doesn't matter to me."

I had kept that ugly bit of ego hidden from Asuna all this time. I didn't have a shred of dedication to others or self-sacrifice. The reason I avoided joining either of the two big guilds, and formed my own boss party, and nearly killed myself fighting, and apologized to the group afterward was for no other reason than my own survival.

"So…I don't have the right to be recognized or praised. You don't need to cry for…"

An impact against my right shoulder cut me off. Asuna was clenching her fist.

"I'm the one who decides who I should cry for!" she shouted, her face a mess. She used her other hand to rub at her eyes and attempted a smile. The hand still pressed against my shoulder opened up and grabbed the surface of my coat instead.

"In that case…I'll be the one to praise you, Kirito. I'll do whatever I can for you…whatever you say."

Later—much, much, much later—Asuna would confide to me, *"A part of me was worried about the possibility that you would say something really crazy,"* with a gentle, beaming smile.

But at this moment, I wasn't capable of saying anything crazy. The best I could do was offer her a very awkward smile.

"…Just you saying that is enough for me. I don't want you to do anything for me…"

"Then, sit down!" she ordered abruptly, pushing hard. I gave in to her force and lowered myself to one knee.

Suddenly, her hand left my shoulder. It circled behind my head and pulled me against the light steel plate covering her chest.

Her left hand slowly, gently, tenderly stroked my hair. She repeated the motion over and over and over.

The softness of her hand. The scent like spring sunshine. The warmth of her body touching mine.

As I soaked in these sensations, I eventually came to the realization that tears were brimming in my own eyes.

The exhaustion that had set in over the fifty-five-day battle that had taken me from the first floor through the fifth.

And the support, healing, and courage that the fencer's presence had brought me throughout that time.

These things kept me locked in place, submitting to Asuna's embrace for a long, long time. And throughout, the movement of her hand never, ever stopped.

12

"TENNN, NIIINE, EEEIGHT, SEEEVEN..."

Karluin, main city of the fifth floor, rocked with the voices of over a thousand players chanting in unison.

"Siiix, fiiive, fooour, threeee..."

There was no screen showing the numbers or an MC leading the crowd through a mic, but the countdown continued in perfect harmony regardless.

"Twooo, ooone..."

A number of flames leaped up from the teleport gate at the center of town, toward the bottom of the floor above.

As the crowd chanted "Zero," a huge circle of flowers bloomed in the dark sky.

The cheers of the players blended into the booming of the fireworks. Calls of "Happy New Year" and "Congratulations" echoed off the buildings, and several players celebrated the moment by firing colorful sword skills against walls here and there.

We were standing on the terrace of the ruined old castle on the east end of Karluin, which offered us a view of both the fireworks display and the celebration below. It was a hidden spot, so no one else would bother us. I was absorbed by the show of light and sound, but my partner nearby was not.

"Happy New Year, Kirito!" she bubbled, holding out a narrow glass with a smile.

"Happy New Year," I replied, clinking it with my own glass. We drank the Champagne—if you could call it that; at the most it was bubbling golden wine—and shared a smile, then looked back into the sky over town.

"I didn't realize they had fireworks…Where do they sell them, I wonder?" I murmured, squinting as I watched the colorful bursts. Asuna was on the fireworks team of the party-planning committee, so she had the answer.

"Liten told us there was a fishy item shop in a little corner of the Town of Beginnings. They spotted the fireworks there first, and that was what gave them the idea for the countdown party."

"Oooh…I wonder if those fireworks cause damage if they hit a monster…" I suggested, which earned me the first look of exasperation of the year from Asuna.

"I'm sorry to inform you that they are only usable in town."

"Oh, I didn't realize…"

"More importantly, it's almost over. Go on, watch those fireworks properly before they finish."

At her suggestion, I looked over the town, where the highest number of flames yet were rising from the ground. *Da-da-da-da-doom!* They exploded at the same time the colorful flashes appeared, filling the night sky and sparkling like rain before they vanished. Another cheer rose from the town, and when it died down at last, I turned to Asuna.

"So it's 2023…" I mumbled, trying to grapple with the concept that a new year had actually begun. "It's hard to believe we've been here for two months…"

"Yeah. When I was hiding in that inn room in the Town of Beginnings, each day was like an eternity, but once I started helping out, they started passing in a blink."

"Well, sure. When you start doing quests, raising skill levels, gathering ingredients, and so on, there aren't enough hours in the day to manage it all. Still…"

I paused, and Asuna looked at me expectantly. I turned to the sky, which was dark again, gazed at the massive lid of steel and rock, and shook my head.

"…Just thinking, 2023's going to be a very long year. We've got twelve whole months, after all."

"Well, of course we do!"

She jabbed my shoulder, and I made an exaggerated display of falling over.

In all honesty, I was wondering how long we could maintain our current pace of advancement.

It took one week to beat the third floor. Six days for the fourth. And this floor took only four days to finish. But the reason that kind of power playing worked was because we were maintaining a margin safely above the recommended level for each area. Since the monsters were comparatively weak, we could cruise through quests and raise our skill levels and gather ingredients without stressing about it.

But that would not last forever. It would get harder and harder to maintain the safety margin, until the point that we were spending every waking hour of the day farming monsters. And because we would need to fight tougher monsters for better experience gain, that would involve a heavy mental toll as well. By the time we got to the tenth floor, the spot where we ended the beta, the difficulty of beating each floor would be much worse than it was now.

But bringing that up now wouldn't change a single thing about it.

The point was, we'd survived to see a new year. No doubt the news that the fifth floor had been beaten on the very day of the countdown party would be a huge morale boost. It gave the DKB a nasty surprise, but tomorrow—er, later today—I would join Shivata and Hafner in properly explaining the situation of the guild flag to them.

For now, I was going to enjoy the biggest festival ever held in Aincrad. That would help create energy to fuel our conquest of the next floor.

I started to pour a fresh glass of Champagne for myself, then realized the bottle was running low. I turned to Asuna, who was nibbling on some cheese, and said, "I'm going down to get a fresh bottle and some food. Wait for me here."

"Thanks. Be careful."

I waved at her and went back into the castle.

The terrace was a special hidden spot, but the front courtyard of the castle was the main party area, where Agil was set up as a food vendor. He had an assortment of specialty foods from all five floors available, so I charged through the castle, thinking excitedly about which items would give Asuna the creeps.

I raced down the steps from the fourth floor of the castle to the third and headed through a secret door down a dusty passage. Past a long row of pillars, I made my way to the main stairway of the castle.

Just then, I felt a powerful chill at the nape of my neck. I instinctively leaped sideways, but a sharp object pressed against my back, through my coat.

Someone hiding in the shadows of the pillars had jabbed the point of a blade against my back.

This was not a prank from a familiar person. If this individual had been hiding for fun, even swept away by the celebratory mood as I was, I would have noticed. The mystery person had been concealed with the Hiding skill...one proficient enough that even my Search skill did not detect it.

I felt the person's face approach my frozen ear. It breathed softly and whispered,

"It's showtime."

It was a cold, deep voice, one I'd never heard before. It had more inflection than was necessary, yet there was not a hint of emotion in it.

"...Who are you?" I demanded in a rasping voice, measuring the timing it would take me to leap away. But the pressure of the point against my back increased only a bit.

"Whoopsie—stay still, now. Wouldn't want you to move and get stabbed by my knife."

The only person I could imagine doing such a thing to me was Morte, the duel PKer whom I already had a history with. But this voice and the way it spoke was utterly different from his.

I contained my breathing and whispered back, "We're in town. You can't threaten me with that thing here."

I was absolutely certain of that fact.

But the mugger at my back ruled that defense out.

"Come on, Blackie, get it right. Only the front courtyard of the castle is in town. The interior is a dungeon, remember?"

"Wha...?"

I fell silent, frantically searching through my memory.

There were indeed a number of quests set around this ruined castle, and the secret doors here and there made it like a dungeon. But there weren't any monsters—plus, there was no OUT-SIDE FIELD notice when I entered the castle.

But it was also true that Karluin was more vague than normal when it came to the boundary between the safe and unsafe areas. I couldn't deny the possibility that I was so carried away with the party atmosphere that I simply missed the message.

But even then...

"This isn't the real world. That's just one knife. Even an ultra-powerful boss drop wouldn't have enough power to wipe out my HP with one hit. And it would make you an orange player...You don't think I'd just stand there and take it, do you?"

"Oooh, very brave of you. Sure, it won't do much HP damage... but what if I told you this blade has level-five paralyzing venom and level-five damaging poison applied to it?"

"...!!"

The fierce point of the weapon poked me twice again, teasing now.

It was impossible. Even monsters were using only level-2 poison at this stage, and the poisons a player could make with the Mixing skill were only level 1, due to the materials available. But

that was all I knew from the beta…and I'd been shown time and time again that my memory did not *guarantee* anything in Aincrad anymore.

If his threat was true, then I would collapse on the spot for at least ten minutes if I was pricked, plenty of time for my HP to run out.

I sucked a tiny breath into my stiffening chest and expelled it in words.

"…What do you want?"

The voice chuckled just behind my ear. It was a theatrical laugh; quite joyful by the sound of it, yet clearly containing no true emotion within it.

"Isn't that obvious, bro? I want to have fun."

"Fun…?"

"That's right; I wanna have a good time. They built this incredible stage for us, you know? I want to throw a wrench into the works and really make it dramatic."

After that statement, I finally understood who the man standing behind me was.

I didn't know his name or face, of course. But I knew him.

"You're…Morte's boss. The one who taught the Legend Braves about the upgrade scam, and the one trying to making the ALS and DKB fight…The Man in the Black Poncho," I accused, voice rasping. He whistled in admiration.

"Ooh, I like that nickname…nice John Wayne Gacy vibe to it. So…shall we find somewhere else to go?"

"…Where do you intend to take me?"

"Underground, of course. Killers always go down in the basement, right?"

There was indeed an underground floor in this castle. It would all be over if I went there. No one would hear my screams. And the basement had monsters in it—that was unquestionably out of the safe haven. It would be suicidal to do as he said, but given that I couldn't rule out the level-5 poisons on his knife, I had no choice but to obey…

…No.

If he really had level-5 paralysis at his command, he didn't need to threaten and order me around. He could just poke me with it and carry me anywhere he wanted. It would be easy to drag my body into the basement.

The paralysis was a bluff.

And I guessed—no, I *knew*—we weren't out of town.

Morte and this man were PKers using provocation. The one tool someone used to provoke others was language. He was trying to convince me that I was already in a dangerous area to make me move to a place that actually was.

"…Got it," I said, and stepped forward.

The moment a tiny space opened between my back and the tip of the knife, I leaped back hard. The knife slammed into my back, of course, the sharp tip tearing through the leather coat and shirt, then—

—Filling the hallway with a purple flash. A shock hit my back. The Anti-Criminal Code kicked in, generating an automatic wall that pushed me and the knife apart.

"Shit!" the man swore. I held strong against the impact and pulled my sword free as I spun around.

"Raaaah!"

I unleashed the Slant sword skill. It wouldn't damage my opponent, of course, but my intention was to temporarily pause him with the knockback effect and hopefully alert Agil's group in the courtyard below with the flash and sound.

I caught sight of a black figure attempting to leap away.

It was quite tall. The thin body was shrouded in a black, hooded short coat that shone with a reflective finish—a poncho. I couldn't see the face under the hood, but there were black curls at the base of his neck.

My system-accelerated blade bore down on his breast. If I could force him to fall over, I could keep him in a pseudo-stunned state by continually hitting him with sword skills.

But the man's airborne body retreated with impossible speed for a jump, and my sword hit only empty air.

"Not done yet—!"

I drew back my blade for the charging skill Rage Spike, hoping to time it for when he landed. The poncho man had to have a very high Acrobatics skill, but even he couldn't jump back faster than a charging skill.

The moment I lurched forward on my left foot and broke out of the post-skill delay, my sword began to glow brightly.

But once again, the man in the poncho betrayed my expectations.

Right before he landed, he tossed a small sphere onto the ground. It exploded on impact, throwing up a thick black smoke that filled the hallway.

A smoke screen?!

I had never seen that item in *SAO*, either now or in the beta, but I executed the sword skill anyway, in the direction I expected my adversary to be.

The special metallic sound unique to charging skills rang out, and the sharp tip of the Sword of Eventide ripped through the smoke. I felt it graze something, and there was a small flash of that purple system effect again.

That was all. When I landed, I slipped out of the smoke and quickly scanned my surroundings.

But the man in the black poncho was nowhere to be seen. I tried to make full use of my Search skill, concentrating hard on my vision and hearing, but I caught neither moving shadow nor footstep.

"*...Until we meet again, Blackie.*"

I turned around in the direction I thought I heard the message come from, but the clearing smoke sitting in the dim hallway just mocked my solitude. I ground my teeth together, realizing I hadn't even caught sight of his face—but then I spotted something.

A midsized knife, lying on the ground on the side of the hall.

I walked over to pick it up. It was all black with a simple design, but even in my level-19 hands—I'd gained a level in the boss fight—it felt quite heavy.

I tossed the nonpoisoned weapon into my inventory, then realized I shouldn't be hanging around. The man might not have been acting alone. Morte, the other cloaked man in the catacombs, or even more companions could be lurking around any corner.

"...Asuna," I muttered, and turned around to sprint at full speed.

What if they used the same methods to lure Asuna out into the open?

In terms of power, she was in no way inferior to Morte, but she didn't know much about PvP combat yet. She asked for instruction when we first got to this floor but had backed down at the last moment. She wouldn't be able to handle these tricksters and their unpredictable ways.

I raced back up the hallway, used a switch in the little dead-end room to open a secret door, then took the stairs up to the fourth floor, three steps at a time. All that was left was to spring down the hall and make a hard turn onto the terrace.

"Asuna!!" I bellowed. The fencer turned away from her view of the bustling town and looked back at me in surprise.

"Wh...what's the matter, Kirito?"

"..."

In the moment, I had no answer. I just stood in the doorway to the terrace for a while before walking over to her.

"H-hey, what are you—"

I held out my arms, circled them around her slender body, and pulled her close.

Only when I felt the warmth and pressure of her avatar, her body, did I exhale with relief. In the morning, I would give her a proper dueling lesson this time. For now, I just held her close to me.

After a while, she moved her hands and patted my back, like I was a child.

Her gentle whisper sounded in my ear.

"Will you let go now? I'm going to hit you with a sword skill."

"Ah…uhmm…this area might be outside of town…?"

"Of—course—it's—in—town!!"

Her left hook slammed into my gut, resulting in a heavy shock wave and a shower of purple sparks.

(End)

AFTERWORD

Thank you for reading the fourth volume of *Sword Art Online Progressive*, "Scherzo of Deep Night."

Since I started the *SAOP* series by calling the first-floor story "Aria of a Starless Night," I have named the various subtitles after the names of musical pieces. The "Scherzo" of the fifth floor means "joke" or "jest," and refers to a piece of music that is fast and playful. There is a very famous scherzo called "The Sorcerer's Apprentice." You might have heard it in the Disney animated film *Fantasia*, but I personally feel that this song is well suited to the PK gang Laughing Coffin...The "Deep Night" descriptor was an attempt to represent the general mood of the fifth floor, but looking at it now, it comes across as rather juvenile (*laughs*).

Anyways. In each volume of *SAOP*, I try to operate on a general theme. The theme of Volume 4 would be "the squirming of Laughing Coffin," while the hidden theme would be "Kirito and Asuna's relationship." I intended to depict the plotting of Laughing Coffin (their name has not yet appeared in the story, of course), who will emerge from obscurity to lead a long, long fight against Kirito—while on the other hand, attempting to show the current relationship status of Asuna and Kirito, who have been temporary partners up through the fifth floor now. That was how the first half of this volume ended up being from Asuna's viewpoint. As a matter of fact, I have a difficult time writing Kirito from the eyes of other characters (he tends to end up looking cooler than necessary), but I feel like Asuna provides the most natural view of him. Of course, he does inevitably end up preening here and there.

In Kirito's half of the story, I really delved into the boss fight for the first time since the second floor. I tried depicting not just a bunch of attack patterns, but the boss chamber's tricks itself, and just coming up with the ideas really took it out of me (*laughs*). The designers who come up with real bosses in MMOs and the programmers who implement them into the game are something else, I tell you…Instead, you got the fifth-floor boss from the mind of an amateur; I hope you enjoyed it anyway.

To my poor editor Mr. Miki and illustrator abec, who suffered through the most exquisitely terrible scheduling in Kawahara history, my deepest apologies! Mr. Miki's own book comes out in Japan on December 10, the same day as this volume, and abec's *SAO* art book will be released in January 2016! Please check them out if you get the chance!!

Reki Kawahara—November 2015